Aphrodite's Workshop

for Reluctant Lovers

MARIKA COBBOLD was born in Sweden and is the author of five previous novels: *Guppies for Tea*, selected for the WH Smith First Novels Promotion and shortlisted for the *Sunday Express* Book of the Year Award; *The Purveyor of Enchantment*; *A Rival Creation*; *Frozen Music* and *Shooting Butterflies*. She lives in London.

Aphrodite's Workshop
for Reluctant Lovers

MARIKA COBBOLD

BLOOMSBURY
LONDON · BERLIN · NEW YORK

First published in Great Britain 2009
This paperback edition published 2010

Copyright © 2008 by Marika Cobbold

Bloomsbury Publishing Plc
36 Soho Square
London W1D 3QY

www.bloomsbury.com

Bloomsbury Publishing, London, New York and Berlin

A CIP catalogue record is available from the British Library

ISBN 978 1 4088 0073 7
10 9 8 7 6 5 4 3 2

Typeset by Hewer Text UK Ltd, Edinburgh
Printed in Great Britain by Clays Ltd, St Ives plc

FSC
Mixed Sources
Product group from well-managed
forests and other controlled sources

Cert no. SGS-COC-2061
www.fsc.org
© 1996 Forest Stewardship Council

To my daughter, Harriet,

who asked the questions

Prologue

LIFE WAS GETTING TOUGH for Mother, otherwise known as Aphrodite, goddess of love. It was commonly thought that she was failing in her work and that love was being brought into disrepute. The inhabitants of Great Britain were of particular concern. The statistics were appalling, with one in three marriages ending in divorce and a growing number of children being brought up in single-parent families.

So Mother was freaking, blaming me, Eros, who quite frankly had enough to deal with, being just a kid and going through a difficult phase, not just because of the confusion over who my father was, but also because of the rumours going around that I didn't actually exist, being instead a phenomenon, an idea, not a person at all.

So what I'm saying is that if Rebecca Finch was *planning* to make things worse she could not have picked a better time.

PART ONE

Rebecca

I WAS TRAVELLING ON the 17.43 Eurostar from Paris when it occurred to me that my mother's unshakeable belief in enduring love might be due to my father having had the good sense to die young. This revelation, like most revelations, only seemed sudden; in fact it had been long in coming, growing steadily, nurtured by a trickle of circumstances just below the level of consciousness.

I had been watching the woman across the aisle, surreptitiously, I hoped. Everyone had their own special interests, the things that captured their imagination and held it; Tim, my ex-husband, for example, was fascinated by boats, boats and barometers. For my mother it was memories and dreams of what might have been. Amongst my friends, Bridget could gaze for hours at the stalls of a food market whereas Matilda had never got over a childhood fascination with clouds. As for my partner, Dominic, he enjoyed Victorian and Edwardian watercolours and leggy blondes. For me it was people. If you tried to explain to me how telephones worked or how emails travelled wire-less from computer to computer I would listen politely but my heart would not be in it. But tell me about the beautiful woman next door and why she always stands waiting for the postman on a Wednesday and you have my full attention.

The woman across the aisle looked to be in her late thirties. She was blonde, a little plump. She was wearing a black gaberdine skirt-suit and flesh-coloured tights and her shoes were mid-heeled courts. She wore a fine gold chain with a small plain cross around her neck and an ornate silver band on her right ring-finger. Her hair was surprising, falling in silky waves down to her shoulders. She was engrossed by the novel she was reading; I could tell from her changing expressions and the way she turned the pages with fingers that could barely wait for the eyes to catch up.

The trip to Paris had been Dominic's idea, his surprise for me. I had found the folder in the fridge, on top of the carton of eggs. Dominic had been waiting for me to come down for breakfast and as I filled the kettle and got out my breakfast cup I could sense his impatience. When finally I had opened the fridge he had made a show of reading the paper but I knew he was watching me over the top of the pages. I picked up the folder, cold and damp from the fridge, and opened it. One ticket for Ms Rebecca Finch and one for Mr Dominic Townsend. I hadn't turned around straight away, needing a few seconds to change my expression from panic to pleasure. I didn't have time to go away. I didn't need a holiday: we had had one, three, no maybe it was four, no actually, six months earlier; anyway, not a very long ago. What I needed were days of uninterrupted solitude with no other demands on my time and energies than that of work. Facing the open fridge, inhaling the chill air that smelt of ambitious French cheeses, I attempted an expression of joyful surprise. I noticed the little heart pierced by an arrow, his sign to me, on the ticket folder and I felt a mean-spirited and ungrateful woman.

I spun round and widened my smile.

'Wow,' I said. 'Wow wow wow, a trip to Paris. And we leave tomorrow. Goodness!'

He frowned up at me from his chair.

'I thought you'd be thrilled.'

'Oh I am, I am.'

I rushed over to him and hugged his shoulders, resting my chin on his dark head. Dominic was at his best in Paris. I suddenly longed for the way we used to be: long Sunday lunches when we hardly ate a thing as we were too busy talking and listening, never letting go of the other's hand as we strolled, going to sleep in each other's arms and waking up smiling.

He took my hand, pulling it to his lips.

'I should hope you are. You are a very lucky woman. Anyway, do you know how long it's been since we were last in Paris? I've booked us into this little *pension* Amanda was telling me about. I know you like that other place but it'll be good for you to get out of your comfort zone.'

And I really had enjoyed the trip, barely thinking about work but just walking, reading in cafés, and watching, of course. It had been three such very peaceful days. There had been no time to keep, no itinerary. If I wanted to sit and read for an hour over breakfast I could. If I wanted to slip into a cinema instead of going to a museum, I could do that too. As I rested my head against the seat-back, fast-forwarded through the landscape, I thought Dominic was right, a few days away was exactly what I had needed.

The trip had not begun so promisingly, however.

'Have you got the keys?' Dominic had asked as we were about to leave the house. 'Oh please don't give me that vague look.'

I had narrowed my eyes in an obvious attempt to concentrate.

'In the dish?' I said.

'If they had been in the dish I wouldn't have had to ask you for them.'

I nodded.

'Of course.'

'So *where are they*?'

'The keys?' I searched my mind for clues but all I saw was Dominic like a giant bottle filling up with ire. When had I last had the keys? When I had come home from somewhere, of course. And when had that been? My brow cleared and I smiled with relief. 'The day before yesterday!'

'What are you talking about?'

'That's when I last went out so that's when I had the keys last.'

The bottle overflowed.

'I can't do this! You know I get stressed when I travel. Do you wind me up deliberately? And what do you mean you went out the day before yesterday? Haven't you been out since?'

'I was getting on so well with work I didn't want the disruption.'

'You mean you haven't even been out for a walk around the block? That's disgusting.'

Then I remembered. I had packed the keys in my sponge bag last night so that I wouldn't forget them. I squatted down in the hallway and opened my suitcase, hauling out the white-and-blue-striped bag and lifting out the silver-heart key ring.

'There they are.' I grinned at him. 'I knew I hadn't lost them.'

'For fuck's sake!' He had snatched them from me and put them in his pocket.

On the Eurostar platform he had given me one of his rueful smiles.

'I'm sorry I yelled at you.'

I had tried hard not to resent his apology but I didn't altogether succeed. When we first met I had found his facility for apologising endearing, generous even. For my ex-husband, the word *sorry* seemed to come equipped with two hooks, one for each side of his gullet, preventing it from going any further. Then again, he had been quite an easy-going man who generally did not have a lot to apologise for. For Dominic, I had come to realise, saying sorry was simply a matter of practice makes perfect.

It seemed now, though, that he really meant it. His face looked pinched and his eyes were darting from my face to the train carriage to his own feet and I knew, I should have known after five years with him, that he was genuinely upset at the thought that his surprise for me, this thoughtfully organised trip, looked set to be just another of our travelling slanging matches. And I was not blameless. Dominic craved order and control, no doubt as a result of the chaos of his childhood, and I, who knew this, what did I do to help? I mislaid things, like keys. I forgot things, left them behind. I didn't focus on what I was meant to be doing, with the result that my mind was constantly walking into lamp posts.

I thought all this and finally, standing there on the platform, I was able to smile back at him.

'I'm sorry I didn't remember where I put the keys,' I said.

'You know how wound-up I get when I travel,' he said

again. His voice rose half an octave. 'It would just help if you could be a little more organised, that's all. Unlike you, I didn't sleep very well last night.' He managed to make a good night's sleep sound like an act of aggression.

'And lugging heavy cases down stairs and into the taxi and out again . . . How anyone can need quite so much for a three-day break.'

I glanced around me, hoping no one was listening.

'You offered to take the bags,' I said, speaking quietly, hoping he might do the same. 'I was bringing down my own case and you actually insisted on taking it.'

'I was *trying* to be helpful.'

'I know you were and I'm grateful . . .'

'I'm not asking you to be grateful but seeing that you seem intent on making a meal of this I am asking you to be a little more thoughtful of other people and not stuff your suitcase full to the brim . . .'

'That's why I wanted to carry it myself,' I explained. 'I know I've packed quite a lot —'

'Quite a lot?'

'And I didn't want you to suffer for it.'

'Suffer for it. You do over-exaggerate.' Exaggerate will do, I thought as he went on. 'No one's *suffering*, as you put it. I am simply suggesting to you, in passing, that you might wish to be more considerate of other people.'

'I didn't think that —'

'You don't think: that's your problem. If you had, you would have packed sensibly.'

'We should board.' I made a quick move towards my case but he got there first. 'No, let me,' I said. '*Please.*' It had been my turn to raise my voice.

'I told you it's not a problem.' He handed me his own lightweight duffel bag and grimaced as if in pain as he heaved my case on board.

He needed a cigarette. Making for the platform again, he felt his pockets.

'Damn, I've left the pack at home.' He turned round. 'I'll have to buy some.'

'We'll be leaving any minute,' I told him.

'Do you have to make a deal of *absolutely* everything? I'm exhausted and not, I have to say, in a good mood. I *need* a cigarette.' He glanced at his watch. 'There's plenty of time.'

I watched him stride off.

The last night in Paris I had stood for almost an hour on the balcony of the *pension* room; the air was warm and soft, rich with fumes and the smell of food from the restaurant below, where someone was playing the piano. On the pavement people passed, a parade of dressed-up dolls for my delectation, and all around me the night was blue.

Across from me on the train the woman was still reading. She had only a few pages left. By now Lucas, the novel's hero, a world-weary journalist, and Catherine, the pianist heroine, would be coming together, as the reader had always known they would, in spite of fate having done its best to prevent it.

'Stop, stop the train!' Dominic had actually said that, or rather shouted it, running down the platform waving his arms.

Maybe I should not have waved back. No, it had not been a nice thing to do, to lean out of the window with a smile and a wave as the train pulled away, leaving him behind.

The woman had finished her book. She gave a little snort of pleasure, blew her nose and closed the pages, absent-mindedly stroking the cover: a row of hazy houses against a background of golden-yellow and turquoise, the words *Suburbs of the Heart* by Rebecca Finch in raised gold.

Dominic said that he hoped my 'little trip away' had done me good.

I told him I thought it had.

'Well, I'm glad all that money wasn't entirely wasted.'

'Oh it wasn't.' I paused. 'But I am really sorry you didn't make it.'

'You didn't look sorry. I would have considered paying for another ticket and coming out on the next train but quite frankly the way you leant out of the window and waved at me, well, I thought, what would have been the point? Then when you didn't answer your mobile.' He shrugged.

In my mind I was busy formulating words like, No, I was simply encouraging you to run faster and, You might have thought I was smiling but I was actually fighting to hold back the tears, and, The battery ran out and I had forgotten my charger. But like George Washington I could not tell a lie, not any more.

'I'm having lunch with Angel-face tomorrow,' I said instead. 'What about you?'

He shrugged again.

'I'm visiting a client in Sussex.'

As he got up from the breakfast table I got up too and put my arms round him.

'I'm sorry,' I muttered.

Dominic stiffened and then he relaxed and kissed me.

'Maybe it did us good, having a couple of days apart,' he said. 'By the way; I hope you managed to arrange some sort of refund from the *pension*.'

I found it difficult to settle down to work so instead I decided to tidy my study. I was not a naturally neat person, but I had learnt through the years that if the room in which I worked was chaotic then my mind followed suit, whereas if, when I gazed up from my screen, the view was uncluttered and pleasingly ordered the words flowed easily. Of late the room had closed in around me. There were piles of paper on my desk and on the table by my armchair. On the bookshelf the books were placed anyoldhow, stacked and balanced on top of each other and mixed up with box files and magazines. The large corkboard above my desk was layered like an artichoke with leaves of cuttings and memos. In the drawer where I kept my old notebooks and diaries I found the blood-red leather-bound diary that I had kept during the days and months after I had first met Dominic. I had never consistently kept a diary although I had always liked the idea of doing so, starting yet another one when something momentous was occurring in my life or a pretty powder-blue spine and a small beribboned key caught my eye at a stationery shop. I would always start with a flourish and end, usually not many weeks later, with some dutiful jottings that seemed just a pointless distraction from my real task of writing books. But today I was glad that I had saved all these half-finished diaries, as suddenly I was curious to be reintroduced to the person I had been. I opened the covers of the diary and began to read:

'This time it's going to be different, I know it,' my darling told me this morning as we lay in bed together. And I know he's right. I love him, I love him, I love him, and he loves me and I could not give him up any more than a prisoner could turn his back on the sun and return to his dark cell.

I had to read this passage twice, paying special attention to the way the letters were formed to make sure they were written by me and not some teenage impostor.

On moving in together this half-witted girl wrote:

It's as if there had never been a house before this one: no other kitchen stove or television, bed or linen. This is the first Christmas. It is the first tree that we carry back together through the streets, which miraculously are dusted with the first snow.

And six months later she was still at it with her pink-tinted pen:

Last night I went to the Summer Party at the gallery. It's wonderful to see how well liked he is. Although there are of course people who are jealous of him, of his success and his easy charm. I was thrilled when the mother of his oldest friend and client embraced me saying, 'Bless you, my dear, I can't remember when I last saw the dear boy looking so happy.'

'He always looks happy in the beginning,' her companion said with a dismissive shrug. I meant to ask her what she meant by that but the two of them had moved on.

There were just a few entries after that, fading out into white virgin pages. What a waste of good paper, I thought. I sat down at my desk and started to write, filling in according to memory an evening a year later:

I didn't know it was the Summer Party until this morning. I approached him at breakfast, the note in my hand.

'I found this when I was tidying your bedside table: "Dearest Dominic, I can't wait till tonight. Mary tells me your parties are legendary. All love, Martha." Why haven't you asked me to the party? And who is Martha?' I asked while scarcely believing that it was me standing there in an unbecoming towelling dressing-gown, accusing, mouth set tight, arms folded across my chest.

'I didn't think you'd want to go. You're always complaining that you don't like parties and that we go out too much. For God's sake, I thought I was doing you a favour.'

'But this is your party. Of course I want to go to that.'

'Well, come then. But I won't be able to look after you. It's work for me. I have people I have to attend to.'

'Like Martha?'

'Don't be childish. Martha is a new client, that's all.'

I put my pen away and closed the diary. It was all going to be so different, we had said; we were going to be different, break the pattern with our everlasting, shining love. And in that, I thought, closing the drawer, we were just like everyone else.

Angel-face, my god-daughter, had just got engaged to Zac. The two of them had met at university and four years on they were planning their wedding. Bridget, Angel-face's mother, had at first worried that they were too young but had since got used to the idea. 'He truly loves her,' she had said to me. 'And he's got a good career ahead of him. Angel-face needs someone with a good career to look after her.'

I agreed with that. Angel-face was a potter. Not a potter who made mugs and butter dishes and other handy household goods that sold in their hundreds, but a maker of sometimes wonderful but never useful things such as bouquets of pottery tulips, birds of paradise and pots that were just too small for anything to fit inside.

Angel-face, as always, was on time and we went inside the restaurant together. I ordered pink champagne and smiled at her across the table. Angel-face did not smile back; instead her soft brown eyes bore a troubled look and her high forehead was creased in a frown.

The champagne arrived and I tried again.

'To Love.' I raised my glass.

Angel-face lifted her glass in reply, not with the forceful upward thrust of celebration but absent-mindedly, holding it just a little off the table, where it stayed as if she had already forgotten it was there.

'Mazel tov?' I said.

'What? Oh yes, mazel tov.'

'Angel-face, is everything OK?'

'I'm doing the right thing, aren't I, getting married?'

I put my glass back down and removed Angel-face's before it slipped from her fingers.

'That's quite some question. What's happened?'

'Nothing's happened.'

'Then I don't understand. You've just got engaged. Did you

not mean to?' That wasn't such a silly question when directed at Angel-face, who quite often ended up doing things she had not really set out to do. Although of course that usually meant things like having her hair coloured black when she'd booked a trim, or joining a month-long sailing trip round the Isle of Wight when she'd just been popping down for the weekend. Getting engaged without meaning to was an altogether bigger deal.

'Of course I meant to,' Angel-face said, sounding a little annoyed that I had felt the need to ask.

'And you love him?'

'Of course I love him.'

'Has he done something to upset you then? Has he been unkind to you?'

'No, of course not. Zac is the kindest man I've ever met.'

'Then I really don't understand,' I said again.

'Good,' Angel-face said.

'Good. What do you mean *good*?'

'I mean good as in you don't think it's inevitable.' Angel-face picked up her glass with more purpose this time and gulped down a healthy mouthful.

'*What* isn't inevitable?'

'That Zac and I will end up divorced like forty per cent of couples, fighting over custody of the children – or the cats. Fighting over the house. Slinging insults at each other across a mediation table. Or worse, still together like the Nicholsons but itching with pent-up resentments, nursing years of "wrongs", unable to say a single word to the other that isn't barbed or loaded.'

'It doesn't have to be like that,' I said. 'Look at your parents. How long have they been married? Almost thirty years?'

'Yes, look at them,' Angel-face said with a sour little twist of her full lips.

'They're all right, aren't they?' I asked her. I thought surely Bridget would have told me if there were problems. Then again, she always said that in her view a problem shared was a problem doubled.

Angel-face shrugged.

'Yeah, they're all right. And that's a worry in itself, don't you see? I mean is that the gold standard, the best I can hope for: being all right? And is all right even remotely all right or actually a complete betrayal of all one's earlier hopes and dreams? You know, Zac took me to see *Romeo and Juliet* at the Donmar last night. Oh Rebecca, it was awful.'

'Really? I read some excellent reviews.'

Again Angel-face waved my words away with an impatient flap of her hand.

'No, no, that's not at all what I meant.'

'Well, what *do* you mean, Angel-face?' I said. I was used to getting it wrong at home, I thought. When I was out I wanted a break.

'It was Juliet. There she was in her big scene trying to suck some poison from her beloved's lips and I wanted to stand up and shout, "No, no, Juliet, don't do it! Look around you first. Look at your parents and aunts and uncles before you decide to die for Romeo."' With that she handed me a handwritten page of dove-grey A4 paper (Angel-face never had got to grips with computers). It said 'Love – My Concerns', under-lined twice in red, and went on:

Can love ever last for ever? I know, not that first high, but the excitement that that beautiful, perfect person is really yours? Is it possible to go on really caring what the other feels and thinks, wanting to touch and caress easily, frequently, searching each other out still at parties? (This fear brought on by Daddy saying the other day in a restaurant, 'I didn't go out to dinner in order to have to sit next to my own wife.' He thought he was being funny but I would die if Zac ever said that kind of thing.)

Children! I admit there are a few couples worldwide who are madly in love after years of marriage but none of them have children. I want children AND passion.

Angel-face had watched me as I read, her eyes wide and expectant. I was getting upset. My god-daughter had come to me for advice. Like most people who knew very little about how to live their own life I was fond of giving advice to others. In fact in my early days as a writer I had supplemented my income by being a newspaper agony aunt. But sitting there, my glass of pink champagne in my hand like a balloon at a wake, I could think of nothing either wise or comforting to say.

Angel-face raised her little hand with its pink-tipped finger adorned with a ring of a deep-blue sapphire flanked by two diamonds.

'I know what you're going to say.'

Really? It was my turn to look expectant.

'You were going to say that the first flush of passion is bound to cool but that the love that takes its place is truer and deeper.'

Yes, I thought, that was exactly what I would have said, had I thought of it. I nodded encouragingly. Our food arrived. My pasta with clams was pungent with garlic, just the way I liked it. Angel-face, however, stared moodily at her cod in a salt and herb crust.

'Don't blame the cod,' I said. 'I bet that poor fish didn't even have a chance to get married, let alone divorced.'

Angel-face looked up at me with a frown, then her brow cleared.

'Oh, a joke.'

'Well, an attempt.' I coughed. 'You were saying?'

'I was saying that I know all that stuff about love changing but not for the worse. I know you were going to tell me how everyone when they're young looks at the older generation and thinks, I won't ever be like them, but then you get to that same age and you do become just like them but you don't actually mind . . .'

I was going to say all of that too? I nodded some more.

'But, Rebecca, if it were so, why the ennui and the quiet desperation, why the middle-aged affairs, why the hunger for your books? And why, why, Rebecca, does my mother look at me and Zac with such sad longing?'

I felt even more discomfited. Bridget was brisk and cheerful, competent and matter-of-fact. She said, 'Let's just get on with it,' where others lingered and debated. She had no business to look at anything with sad longing. And I knew my reaction was selfish, but wasn't that how it was? We depended on the daffy friend remaining daffy so we could exercise our practical side, and on our poor friend to remain poor so we could be generous. Our strong friend must thus remain so we could let go now and then and appear just as small and scared as we felt.

'I don't know why your mother looks at you that way,' I said finally. 'But it could be simple nostalgia as she remembers that wonderful feeling of being young and in love. It doesn't have to mean that she's dissatisfied with what she's got now.'

'Bollocks! It's got nothing to do with being young and everything to do with the place you're in. Look at Aunt Geraldine.'

'How *is* Geraldine?'

'She's fine. Blissed-out, in fact.'

'That's good. And *she's* married.'

Angel-face nodded.

'Oh yes. Aunt Geraldine is always married. It's just the husbands that vary. She's on her third.'

'Ah.'

'Ah indeed,' Angel-face said. 'The only woman of my parents' generation whose relationship is one to which I feel like aspiring is married for the third time. But, Rebecca, I want to be with Zac. And don't say, "And you are." Because if he's the love of my life it seems to me that the only way I can make sure he remains that way and that we end up happily ever after – with each other – is if I put *us* on hold and marry at least two other people first. And patently that would be absurd.'

I was thinking about that when Angel-face repeated, rather crossly, 'And patently that would be absurd?'

'Yes.' I nodded vigorously. 'Yes, of course it would be absurd. Anyway, Geraldine aside, divorce is usually a very painful and debilitating time with long-term consequences, especially if there are children involved.'

'Humph,' Angel-face said. 'Tell that to Bella's mother.'

'Your pretty red-haired friend Bella?'

'That's the one. Her parents are getting divorced . . .'

'Oh I'm sorry. Is she all right?'

'Sort of. She hasn't actually been living at home since uni, but of course it still gets to her. Now they're going to court fighting over the house and Katy . . .'

'Bella's got a sister?'

'Dog. Well, her parents' dog. And the house thing really upsets her because it will probably have to be sold in the end and even if she doesn't live there any more it's still her home, you know. It's still important that it's *there*.'

I nodded. I knew what she meant. When I left home I had expected my mother to remain for all eternity in the same flat where I had grown up, surrounded by the same furniture and pictures right down to the china ornament on her desk. I might be moving on; my mother, if I had my way, would live out her days preserved in aspic.

'Bella's father is miserable and stressed,' Angel-face continued, 'but her mother seems exhilarated more than anything. It's just all so disheartening.' She sighed and poked at her fish with the fork.

'It's not that bad, Angel-face, it really isn't. The world is full of people who are happy in long-term relationships.'

'Give me a list,' Angel-face said. 'How long were you married to Tim?'

'Eleven years.'

'Ha! Well, as it happens, that's actually the national average. That would bring me up to thirty-four for my first divorce. How long have you and Dominic been together?'

'About four years.'

'So you have a few years left.'

And for the first time, right then, at the lunch to celebrate my god-daughter's engagement, I wondered consciously if Dominic and I had much time left at all.

The waiter asked if we wanted another glass of champagne. Angel-face said no thank you but I nodded a yes. Sometimes I found that champagne actually alleviated a headache.

I lowered my glass to find Angel-face staring intently at me.

'Don't tell me *you're* not happy!'

'Oh darling, it's not as if I *want* to be unhappy.'

'So I'm right. You and Dominic aren't good, either.' Angel-face sat back, her arms folded across her chest, her pointed chin raised and a frightened look in her eyes.

Words were dangerous things. Once let out they took on a life of their own, pulling consequences along with them, reproducing, prompting reactions, making solid that which had been shadowy and only partially formed. Words, once spoken or written, chased your illusions away.

'No,' I said eventually. 'No, we're not very good.'

'That's it, I give up.'

'There's no point getting cross with me.'

Angel-face looked as stern as anyone with a face like hers could.

'I'm not sure there isn't. What was it they called you in the papers last week? The High Priestess of Romance, if I remember rightly.'

'You know what those headlines are like.'

Angel-face ignored the comment.

Instead, she said, 'I'm afraid it's people like you: poets, film-makers, ad-writers, wedding-magazine editors – romance-mongers the lot of you – who are to blame, who are absolutely responsible for little girls growing up still dreaming of finding the perfect love and marrying while wearing the perfect frock in the perfect venue and going on to live the perfect romance. Oh we pretend we're not. We tell ourselves and those around us that what matters is our careers and our independence and our darling girlfriends, but back in the privacy of our own minds we go on dreaming and planning and hoping and that's as much due to people like you as anything. Then when I come to you for some reassurance what do I get? Nothing. I mean how can you do it? How can you go on writing your books that you obviously don't believe in? *J'accuse*, Rebecca Finch, that's what I do.'

I tried to think of something to say, tried to untangle my thoughts and retrieve one at least that was straight and true and useful.

Angel-face went on, 'So what are you saying to people like me and Zac, young people about to embark on marriage?'

I opened my eyes wide. I shut them tight. I opened them wide again.

'Better luck next time?'

I walked fast down the Fulham Road towards home. The afternoon had turned chilly: April playing at winter, the wind chasing from the north making a nonsense of my short thin jacket and the flimsy skirt that blew and billowed around my legs exposing my thighs with every other step that I took. I walked as if I could outrun my own thoughts. When I had been a child I had been able to. If my mind was especially troubled I would shut the front door behind me and start running anywhere, as fast as I could, until I had reached the speed at which my mind was left behind. However, due to incipient middle age and a sedentary lifestyle, I wasn't so fast any more and my thoughts had no problem at all catching up with my feet: I had upset Angel-face on a day that was meant to be a celebration and I had heard myself say that I was in an *unhappy relationship*. Yet how could I be? I had promised myself that it would be different with Dominic and I had believed me. Right through the arguments and screaming matches, the insults and petty betrayals I had believed that ours was still a grand love affair. Until today when I heard myself state the opposite.

Back home I stripped off the outfit that had seemed so appropriate that morning but now seemed to mock me with its simpering prettiness and changed into a far more suitable pair of black trousers and an oversized jumper. Sitting down at my desk I proceeded not to work but to stare out of the window and on to my street. Usually the view soothed me. Soon the hydrangeas in the tiny communal front gardens would be in bloom, some pure pink, some veering towards blue as if they had decided to change but had been interrupted halfway through. Now, in spring, the multitude of blossom on the cherry trees made me feel as if I were living across the street from Mary Poppins and, as everyone knows, when she was around nothing bad could happen. Only it seemed that it had. I needed someone to talk to, someone to ask if sometimes they too looked out on a much-loved view only to find that the trees and houses looked liked cousins of the usual trees and houses, alike but not the same, and the cars did not appear like the everyday items they were but alien things, newcomers. I needed someone, not Angel-face, who took my words and pierced her own heart with them, not Dominic, who reacted to any attempt at conversation beyond small talk or quips like a virgin to an indecent proposal, and certainly not Vanessa, my mother. Vanessa, or daughter of Pangloss, as

I liked to call her, took bad news, any bad news, whomsoever it might relate to, as an unwarranted act of vandalism, graffiti scrawled across the pretty wall she had erected against the ugliness of life. Try telling her that all was not actually for the best in this the best of all possible worlds and she would tell you not to be naughty.

I thought of calling my friend Matilda.

'Hello, it's me. I know we spoke as usual at ten this morning but I just wanted to add that I'm not in the enviably romantic and passionate, although somewhat stormy, relationship I've led you to believe I was in, but that actually I'm unhappy. What's that? You're not surprised? You're telling me all the signs have been there: the constant bickering in public that made everyone around us uncomfortable. Goodness, you noticed? And you say that I seemed quieter, not my usual confident self when he was around. His constant flirting with other women, you say, and me just having had the best holiday in ages – in Paris. On my own. Well, yes, Matilda, those were all clues but it seems that I needed something more to make me see clearly. A cosh with the words "You are in a toxic relationship"? Well, thank you for offering that, Matilda, but I think I'm getting the message. Would I like to come round for supper and talk about it? No!'

Or I could call my agent.

'Hi, Gemma, it's me. Yes, I'm fine, work is going well. How is that gorgeous boyfriend of mine? He's well too, thank you. Abusive? Yes. Unhelpful and self-absorbed? Yes, bless. What is happening to my proposed article, "The Art of Everyday Love: How to Retain the Romance in Your Relationship", that was going to be so useful in publicising the paperback of *Suburbs of the Heart*? Well, seeing as you brought it up, it's fine; well, as fine as a piece of self-delusional garbage can ever be.'

Clowns are good listeners.

I looked behind me but of course there was no one there. I sat down resting my throbbing head against the kitchen table. A lorry rattled by, birds sang; apart from that there was silence. I shook myself and got up to make a cup of coffee. I needed to work. I was at least two pages away from my daily target of five.

Then came the discreet clearing of a throat.

I said clowns are good listeners.

Coco? There he was, preening. *What the hell are you doing here?*

Ah, you've missed me, that's nice.

I shook my head slowly from side to side like an old donkey trying to shake off a troublesome fly. I was not well. Obviously I was not well if Coco the manic-depressive clown . . .

Bipolar; these days we prefer the term bipolar, Coco interrupted, looking self-important.

. . . my childhood imaginary friend, whose last appearance at my grandfather's funeral I had put down to grief and stress and then all but forgotten about, had reappeared.

Actually, imaginary friend was stretching it. Coco had always been more of an imaginary bully. Of course I had tried to tell that to my grandfather and my mother. I had wanted them to help me get rid of him but it had been useless. They had been so determined in their desire for me to be special, imaginative, amusing that convincing them that all I actually wanted was a nice, cosy, ordered childhood with regular mealtimes and firm but fair discipline had been completely impossible.

Now he was back. People had warned me that I was working too hard. What they had not known, because I had not told them, was that although I was indeed working harder than ever I was actually achieving less. Sentences that would normally spring from my fingertips like children rushing out to play were hanging back, sulking in the doorway of my mind, and having to be coaxed out with bribes of coffee and wine and late-night television.

I wrote two thousand words a day. I always wrote two thousand words a day. It used to take me about five hours. Now that time had nearly doubled but I kept at it until my task was done. One day it might be the inscription on my gravestone, 'Say what you like about Rebecca Pearl Finch but she kept at it.'

Maybe I was ill. Perhaps I was having a small breakdown. In which case I could not be held responsible for those unhelpful comments I made to Angel-face. Not being well would also explain my overreaction to what was simply a bad patch in my and Dominic's relationship.

Patch? Coco slapped his thighs in mirth. *Patch?! And I suppose Australia is a smallholding?*

I would *not* let him distract me. All I needed was some rest, maybe a quick course of antidepressants and before I knew it everything would be back to normal.

And as I was sick and in need of a rest there would be nothing wrong with me having a bath, although it was the middle of the afternoon and I hadn't finished my two thousand words. If you're sick you're off the hook.

I caught sight of myself in the bathroom mirror and it was like being shown my face ten years on.

I'd sue the dermatologist, Coco said.

I undressed, bending down to pull off my tights, when a sharp pain stabbed me at the base of the spine.

Coco suggested suing the yoga teacher. I made a mental note to seek specialist advice.

I found Charlotte Jessop's number on the hall table in the silver box where I kept all those cards you pick up at parties and conferences when wine-induced bonhomie makes two strangers decide they are destined to be best friends, or landscape gardener and client, or cat breeder and cat owner, only to have forgotten all about it by the next morning. Charlotte and I had been introduced at the launch party for my friend Maggie Jacobs book, *If Fifty Is the New Forty and Forty Is the New Thirty Does that Mean I'm Twenty?* Charlotte, who was a therapist, had a special mention in the book and was also, Maggie told me, the relationship expert on *Good Evening, Britain.* While I was embarrassed at not remembering having seen her on television or even having heard of her, Charlotte Jessop was perfectly happy to admit that she had only read part of one of my novels and that was in order to get a handle on the mindset of 'a certain type of woman'.

'Why didn't you tell her to go stuff herself?' Maggie said afterwards.

I explained that as I had spent my entire professional life being patronised why should I start minding now?

I dialled Charlotte Jessop's number. Her receptionist told me that they were now taking appointments for the period beginning the 1st of June. From the tone of her voice – a mixture of pity, triumph and incredulity that anyone could be misguided enough to presume that Ms Jessop was easily available – I deduced that dashing people's hopes was the most satisfactory part of her job.

'I really do need to see her sooner than that.'

'I could put you on the list for cancellations but I have to warn you that there are already several people ahead of you, so the likelihood –'

'I think I'm having a breakdown. I'm already behaving irrationally and there's no telling what I might do next.'

'In the case of an acute condition you should go immediately to your local A & E.'

'When I say I'm behaving irrationally I mean I'm not being myself. I need help but it's not an emergency.'

'In the case if you'd like to call again on Monday when I will be starting the new appointment list –'

'I'm seeing clowns.'

'I beg your pardon.'

'I'm seeing manic . . .' Coco wagged his finger. 'I'm seeing bipolar clowns.'

'Please hold.'

I waited, then, 'This is Charlotte Jessop. How may I help?'

'Oh, hello. It's Rebecca Finch. We met a while back at Maggie Jacob's launch party.'

'Rebecca Finch? Oh yes, the romance writer. You say you're hearing voices too?'

I nodded into the receiver.

'Both. Just one voice, though.' It was important to be as clear as possible when speaking to a professional.

'Then I think you'd better go to your local A & E. Would you like me to arrange some transport or do you have a friend or relative who can take you?'

'No, no, it isn't at all like that. Coco is an old friend. OK, maybe not friend exactly . . . anyway, I know he's not real. He's there, which is why I'm calling you to make an appointment, but he's not *there*, if you see what I mean. I'm very tired. That's probably all it is. Exhaustion. I've heard that one can hallucinate from pure exhaustion, so that's probably it. I just felt that it would be a good idea . . .'

'Come to my rooms at six tomorrow evening. I'll hand you back over to Della and she'll take your details.'

There was a brisk click in my ear and, 'Right then, Mrs . . .'

'Ms Finch.'

'Right then, Ms Finch, you seem to have somehow got yourself an appointment.' There was a brief pause as her professionalism battled with her disappointment. 'Now if I could have your full name and address.'

Therapy, eh? Coco somersaulted down from the curtain rail, where he had been hanging upside down from his knees. *It won't work.*

Medication, I told him. *Against hallucinations.*

Coco could not go any whiter, his face-paints saw to that, but he was definitely shaken.

I felt better and more in control having made the appointment and as Dominic was in Sussex seeing a client I had the evening to myself to think things through. I decided I would phone Angel-face and tell her . . . tell her what?

I returned to my desk and sat down. As the little tune chimed and the screen of my laptop lit up I felt comforted, like a child when their musical box plays at bedtime. I created a new document and typed a heading. 'Angel-face: Reasons to

Marry and to Believe in Love and Happily Ever After'. I paused. Then I typed, 'Reason One'.

I sat back in the chair, thinking. Reason One. Reasons to believe in love. That shouldn't be too hard. I believe in love because . . .

You have to believe in love. Coco was standing at my shoulder. *In the same way you have to believe in imaginary bipolar clowns, because it exists.*

And that's supposed to be helpful?

Suit yourself.

'Reason One: love exists.' Obviously I needed something more. 'I love therefore I am.' Which sounded quite good but what did it actually *mean*? I tried, 'Reason Two: love is a good thing.'

Or was it? Yes, some love obviously was; the kind between parents and children and brothers and sisters and friends. But romantic love? The love in question right now, the love with which I dealt in my books, was it such a good thing? Had we invented romantic love simply as a way of placing our mating on a higher plane than the other animals? Was that why it so often ended badly, because it was just a construct? No, that couldn't be right because people had always indulged quite happily in sexual encounters with no pretence of love attached. So was romantic love there to make us settle for one person for long enough to bring up a family? That did make sense. It made sense but it usually didn't work. I wrote, 'Romantic love is a sensible emotion enabling stable parenting.' But lack of sense, of proportion and clear-sightedness was integral to the concept of romantic love. I tried, 'Romantic love is a senseless, muddled set of emotions enabling stable parenting.' Somehow that didn't look right.

'Reason One: romantic love is.'

Then I decided the best way to help Angel-face and undo some of the damage I had done by my thoughtless remarks was to find her some example of lasting love. I wrote, 'Ronald and Nancy Reagan, my mother's cousin Deborah and her husband Alistair . . .'

Adolf Hitler and Eva Braun, Coco chipped in.

I told him there was no evidence that Adolf Hitler loved anyone at all and that even if he had it wasn't in any way what one would call an encouraging example. Instead I wrote down, 'Héloise and Abelard.'

And that really did *end well*, Coco smirked.

An hour later I gave up and made myself some more tea.

At eight o'clock I phoned Bridget.

'Did Angel-face tell you about our lunch?'

'Ha!'

'Sorry, what's that?'

'Ha! I said ha! She's here now. In fact she's been here all evening talking about breaking off her engagement. Right now she's in her old room clutching her teddy. She's thinking of calling off the wedding.'

'Because of our lunch?'

The food was that bad? Coco looked concerned.

'Because of your conversation; yes, I'm afraid so. And you know you upset her or why else would you call?'

This was true but what was also true was that I had expected, in return, to be reassured that Angel-face was absolutely fine and that of course she hadn't taken anything I said to heart. The weight of responsibility descended upon me and out shot self-justification.

'But that's silly. She can't blow hot and cold like that, depending on the views of whoever she spoke to last.'

'You're not *whoever*, Rebecca, you're her godmother. Her favourite godmother, to whom she has looked up all her young life, a godmother who's given her signed first editions of every one of her novels about the wonders of love.'

'Oh God, I know, I know and I'm really sorry.'

'You said better luck next time. That's what you told her. At the lunch to celebrate her engagement.'

'God, I'm sorry.'

'You've already said that. By now God will be bored and asking you to do something about it. So have you?'

'I think so.'

'You think so? Well, why don't you come over here and share your insights with your god-daughter.'

'The thing is . . .' I paused, feeling my way through the conversation. 'These days, what with people living so long – I mean for example we don't die in childbirth the way we did previously . . . which of course is a tremendous thing.'

'I'm glad you see it that way.'

I laughed a little too uproariously.

'No, what I'm trying to say –'

'Yes, what *are* you trying to say?'

'OK, as we all know, back when marriage was in its heyday, people's chances, women's in particular, of surviving more than eleven years or so into the marriage were substantially slimmer. Add to that the fact that women no longer need marriage to achieve social standing and economic security and you see how the goalposts have moved. Until death us do part, for one – or two if we're talking goalposts, obviously. So I'm thinking maybe, just maybe, we should consider a first marriage at an early age as a sort of starter marriage.'

It was Bridget's turn to pause.

'What did you just say?'

'I said that maybe . . .'

'I know what you said. I just don't believe you did.'

'OK, I didn't.'

By now I was exhausted. It had been a long day. Actually, it had been a long forty-two years. Good ones, of course. I was a very lucky woman, who had been a very lucky child. Lucky lucky lucky not to be like my sister, stuck in a wheelchair, unable to talk or read, and dying when she was still in her thirties. Lucky not to be like my mother with her broken child and lost love. Lucky to be healthy – give or take the odd nervous breakdown and imaginary clown – lucky to be a perfectly attractive and successful novelist with a handsome and charming partner. So, Rebecca Pearl Finch, smile, even if you don't mean it. Smile with your lips and your face will smile with you. Smile with your face and your head will smile with you. Smile with your –

'Rebecca? Are you there?'

'Yes. Yes. Sorry. Yes, I am.'

'Let's be sensible here. Why don't you come over? We'll have a glass of wine and you can tell Zoe yourself. Cheer her up. Tell her she got it all wrong.'

'It's almost bedtime.'

'You've got a car.'

'Dominic's got it.'

'Then take the tube, or a cab.'

Bridget had put the phone down. I sat back and closed my eyes, straining to recall the state of mind and the thoughts that had made me able to write my books of happy-love-everlasting. It was like bobbing for apples: just as a loving memory was within my grasp it ducked away and I was left splashing about in the cold waters of my disillusionment.

I went across to the bookcase and brought out a copy of *Suburbs of the Heart*, turning to the last page and reading that final line: 'And as she lay in his arms a voice –'

I was interrupted by Coco appearing at the controls of an old biplane, wearing goggles and a leather airman's hat, and towing a sign that read 'Lies, All Lies.' He finished off with a neat loop-the-loop.

I closed the book with a bad-tempered slam.

I hope your pennant gets caught in the propeller.

The bridges, Chelsea and Albert, were lit up, as was the Embankment; the lamps reflected in the water, making the evening brighter than the gloomy day that had gone before it. Across the river in Battersea Park shadow-figures were running. I understood the value of exercise; for example, I always kept my twice-weekly appointment at the yoga studio, but generally I was a walker, not a runner. You missed so much when you were running. After all, we were made to run away from things or towards things but hardly just for the sake of it.

I found Angel-face sitting on the floor in her room, her back resting against her old bed, which was single and virginal white. I sat down next to her.

Angel-face did not look up.

'I'm thinking of breaking it off.'

'Your mother told me.'

36

Angel-face turned her huge, velvety-brown eyes on me, eyes that were confused and filled with anxiety.

'It's your fault.'

'I know. Your mother told me that too.'

'Today at lunch I asked you a question and at first you had no answer. Then when you did it was horrible.'

'I'm sorry.' I put my hand on her arm giving it a little rub. 'But, Angel-face, you have to make your own decisions, trust your own feelings. It really isn't fair to put all this on me. I'm hardly the first person to say these things.'

'No, you're not, but you are the first High Priestess of Romance to do so. And you know how I've always looked up to you. You can't just allow yourself to be looked up to and then deny any responsibility. So when you tell me that, in your view, there's no hope for me and Zac then I take it seriously.'

'Now you're exaggerating, Angel-face. I never said there was no hope. I expect I did say –'

'That the odds by and large were not in our favour.'

'Even if I did, you can't live your life like that, saying you won't do anything because it's a risk. And disappointment is relative to expectation. Some marriages obviously break up for good reasons: abuse, criminality . . . but many, in my view, end because of too high expectations.'

'And whose fault is it that we do have these expectations?' Angel-face asked.

I sighed; I could see the way we were heading.

'Mine, I expect. But, Angel-face, don't you see that I'm damned if I do and damned if I don't, because first you tell me I've ruined things for you by what I said at lunch and by not being all starry-eyed and romantic and then you tell me I've ruined things because I *am* starry-eyed and romantic.'

37

'That's right,' Angel-face said trying to look assertive but I could see that she was close to tears; her eyes were open wide and her lower lip was trembling.

I put my arm round her shoulders and the feel of them, so slight and a little bony, made me close to tears myself. I wanted to find something to tell her that would make her happy again.

Coco suggested saying that just because something was bound to end in disaster there was no reason not to give it a go. *I mean look at life*, he said. *Give me one example of a happy outcome – I am assuming here that most people don't see death as a happy ending – but hey, by and large people still give it a shot.*

'Romance isn't the be-all and end-all of a marriage,' I tried.

'I never said it was. I said that I would settle for ending up somewhere in the vicinity of my dreams and hopes. I said I would settle for not being sour or sad or disappointed or angry or divorced.'

'Tell her you're not well.' Bridget's voice reached us from the other side of the door. 'Tell her she's just having cold feet.'

'Come in, Mother,' Angel-face said in her new, tired voice.

'You're just having cold feet, Angel-face,' I said. 'And don't listen to me, I'm not myself.' I wondered if I should mention Coco. Maybe it would help Angel-face to see that I was not to be trusted right at that moment.

Bridget turned to her daughter.

'Youth wants and expects it all. And that's part of youth's charm.' She was smiling all of a sudden, a dreamy, reminiscing smile. 'I planned to be the first woman chef with her own three-Michelin-star restaurant. Bit by bit, however, I realised that, as good a cook as I was, I didn't have the talent, or the time and space, but I'm perfectly happy with my little catering business.'

'That's awful.' Angel-face looked as perturbed as any child realising that their parents had had dreams once too.

'It's not awful,' Bridget said. 'It's life.'

Angel-face looked as if in that case she might take it or leave it.

'One learns to be a little more realistic in one's expectations,' Bridget continued. 'Whether it's of love or of oneself.'

Angel-face was unconvinced.

'If all these hopes and dreams of love are just symptoms of youth, how does that explain Elizabeth Taylor?'

We all fell silent. Nothing could.

Finally Bridget said, 'Tell her she's just got cold feet.'

'You've said that already,' Angel-face snapped. 'And of course I've got cold feet. I mean what kind of an unthinking moron would I be if I didn't? I love Zac and he loves me, for now, but it seems pretty certain that, within the space of ten or so years, *if* we're still married, we will be just like all the couples we swore we would never be like, who in turn never thought they'd end up like that when *they* exchanged their vows. Oh no, they would have said, we'll be different. But no one ever is.'

'Tell her she's being defeatist,' Bridget said.

'You're being defeatist, Angel-face.'

'At least *try* to sound as if you believe it!' Bridget snapped.

'But you just told me I *should* be defeatist,' Angel-face said. 'Actually, you both have, in your different ways.' She turned to her mother. 'You just told me I should give up on my dreams, that it was part of growing up and I said that –'

'I said no such thing. I just told you that as life moves on your priorities change.'

'And *I* said that if they did to such an extent, if all the hopes and dreams were simply a symptom of youth, why do we have all these divorces and unhappy –'

'Look at it this way,' I interrupted. 'The one thing you *can* be sure of is that if you *don't* buy a lottery ticket then you'll never win.'

'Oh come on.'

'I was trying to be positive.'

'Well, don't.' Bridget glared at me. 'It's not very convincing.' She turned back to her daughter. 'If people will have ridiculous expectations of floating on cloud nine for the duration –'

'We don't,' Angel-face said. 'As I said to Rebecca, most of us would settle for ending up somewhere just in the *vicinity* of our dreams and hopes.'

'And maybe you will,' I said.

'You really believe that?' Angel-face brightened, gazing at me as if the map of her life was etched on to my face. I avoided her eyes.

'Rebecca?' Angel-face leant close.

'It's certainly not *impossible*,' I said.

'I think you're soured by your own experiences,' Bridget said.

And about time too, Coco said.

'I've noticed the tension between you and Dominic. Quite frankly, the way you let him speak to you –'

'Maybe things aren't so good between us . . . Anyway, I'm seeing someone, a therapist.'

'So it's a breakdown.' Bridget nodded and the set of her lips softened. It was easier to deal with things when they had a label. 'You know when I said you were soured by your experiences I didn't mean it unkindly.'

I did, Coco said.

'Oh shut up!' I realised I had spoken out loud.

Bridget's eyes widened as she opened her mouth then closed it again.

'Oh I didn't mean you, Bridget, or you, Angel-face. I was talking to myself. I was telling myself to shut up.'

'You really aren't very well, are you?' Bridget said. Now her expression was all kindness once more, motherly and concerned.

'I don't think I am.' I turned back to Angel-face. 'So really, don't pay any attention to anything I say at the moment.'

Angel-face perked up a tiny bit.

'Do you mean that? You really think this is all because you're not feeling well?'

I nodded, realising for the first time the joys of being Elizabeth Barrett Browning.

'I should probably go home and to my bed.'

Bridget, still with that friendly, concerned look on her face, agreed.

'Shall I call you a cab?'

'Maybe.' My voice sounded weak as I got up from the floor with my old woman's scrabbling movements, I, who only a week ago could get up from a prone position to standing in one smooth go.

Bridget turned to her daughter and a note of pleading crept into her voice.

'Look at Granny and Grandpa: they were happy.'

'Grandpa lived on the golf course and Grandma was surgically attached to the card table. Call me a silly old dreamer,' Angel-face said, 'but I was hoping for happy *together*.'

'And Aunt Hilary . . . no, maybe not. But the Taylors, now I'm not saying they haven't had their ups and downs –'

Angel-face interrupted.

'Personally, someone saying, "I don't care if he lives or dies but I love that house too much to risk it in a divorce," seems a little stronger than "ups and downs".'

'Kate didn't say that?'

'According to her daughter, she did, still does, frequently.'

Bridget made a final stand.

'Well, take Daddy and me then.'

Angel-face looked at her with something like pity.

'I think you've just lost the argument,' she said.

Mount Olympus

IN OUR FAMILY WE´RE always on the lookout for mortals who are an asset in our own particular field so when Rebecca Finch made it big with her latest romantic novel she really caught Mother's attention. We began tuning into her life, checking that she was OK, that everything was running smoothly, and possibly to show off – to Athene in particular. 'See,' Mother would say, 'just see how I'm worshipped. This woman's work is read by millions of women across the world.'

As I mentioned earlier, Mother and I could do with a boost. Our results have been pretty dire lately and it has become a talking point.

Mother, of course, defends herself: 'It depends how you define result,' she says. 'If you look at my 'Profane Love' portfolio you *could* argue that my results are up. People are coupling like never before. Adultery is perennially popular.'

'But isn't it all a question of balance, Aphrodite dear?' Athene has been speaking to Mother but her eyes are on Grandpa. 'In your case the balance between the profane and the sacred, is that not so, Zeus?'

Grandpa, as always, just loves being asked his opinion.

'Indeed it is,' he says. 'And I'm afraid that balance has been absent for some time. It pains me to criticise . . .'

No it doesn't, you old fart, you love it.

'But any fool . . .' Here everyone turns round and looks at me, which I think is just totally unfair. 'Any fool can get them to couple. It's ensuring that they remain in a strong, loving and worshipful relationship that is the challenge.'

'It's this "life meaning life" business that's so difficult,' Mother grumbles. 'They're around for so much longer, for a start.'

'You're supposed to be a goddess,' Athene says. 'Build a bridge and get over it.'

Mother's eyes have already turned to thunder-grey and now they go black, which personally always makes me extremely nervous.

But she keeps her voice low as she says, 'We all have our problems. Your own cult, for example, Athene, is hardly flourishing. Look at who they chose to lead them. I mean Ares hasn't had it so good for a long while. And look at what entertains them. I'm as open to new things as anyone but honestly, where there used to be Euripides and Shakespeare, Voltaire and Ibsen, Strindberg and Chekhov, even that funny little man in a dressing-gown, there's now hours and hours and hours of watching extremely foolish people stuck between four walls . . .'

'Pinter isn't that bad,' Hera objects.

'I was talking about *Big Brother*,' Mother says. 'And look at their icons. Look at who they worship. Very thin women with bandy legs who eat through their noses. Men with guitars who say what everyone knows already. And then actors, don't start me on actors; these days people seem to be fascinated by their *off*-stage opinions. No, Athene, look at the state of your own cult before you criticise mine.'

'Hurrah and well said.' I clap my hands.

'Oh do be quiet, boy,' Athene snaps.

It would be nice if Mother stood up for me but she's too busy fluttering her eyelashes at Grandpa. It's pathetic how they all suck up to him.

Then Mother switches on London again and watches as Rebecca Finch is given the news that her latest book is topping the charts on both sides of the Atlantic.

'Oh she's lovely,' Mother says. 'A perfect example of the quality of my acolytes: bright, kind-hearted, hard-working, modest, faithful . . .'

'There is that small matter of her divorce,' Athene says. 'And wasn't there some adultery?'

'Oh that was ages ago. And it wasn't her fault anyway. No, this woman has dedicated her life to the cult of love, my cult . . .'

Mother and I are very pleased with Rebecca Finch.

Rebecca

THE ESTATE AGENT TOLD me that the flat by the river had not been on the market since 1955. Not that I had any plans to move. In fact, had anyone asked me, I would have said that I expected to live the rest of my life in my pretty house on the tree-lined street – or at least until I was no longer able to get up the stairs. (It hadn't been possible to install a lift because of the configuration of the hall and landings – I had checked with the builder when we first bought it. This had amused Dominic, who said, 'You're thirty-eight, why do you need to ask about lifts?' I explained that I wanted to feel that I was settled at last.)

I had first noticed the flat for sale on one of my walks along the Embankment. I had taken to going for long walks in an attempt to clear my head and refill it with inspiration, but although I had found that I enjoyed the walking it had so far failed to inspire my work. I fell in love with the river. It might not have had the showy charm of the sea but it was such a reliable, helpful thing, and standing on the banks, just watch-ing, I could see the imprint of the centuries on its tranquil surface. At first I used to wish it had been bluer; how spectacular it would be if the Thames flowed through the city the colour of the Aegean. After a while, though, I discovered that if you looked long enough and attentively enough at sludge-brown all manner of shades and colours would appear to surprise and please you.

This particular evening, the last Thursday of April, the lowering sun was turning the sky orange above deep-purple trees and the river itself responded by stretching pink stabbed through with gold. The scene lasted for just a few moments before the sun shifted its gaze a fraction and the colours evaporated. It seemed that no one else, not the dog walkers or the courting couples or the panting joggers, seemed to have noticed the miracle of colours so maybe it had just been some kind of mirage: my eyes, tired from fruitless hours staring at the computer screen, playing tricks. I turned to walk on and it was then that I noticed the 'For Sale' sign fixed to the railings of the fourth-floor balcony across the road.

A week later I was outside the flat once more, in a cab this time. We had been inching through the evening rush-hour traffic and when I realised exactly where I was I paid my fare and stepped out. Just then a young man in a tight-fitting pinstriped suit left the building. As he went up to the Smart Car with the name of an estate agent emblazoned in mock graffiti on its side, I hailed him from across the road and he paused and waited for me.

'The flat.' I pointed upwards. 'May I view it? Now, perhaps?'

By the time I returned Dominic was already home from the gallery. I knew he was back because the canvas satchel he used in place of a briefcase (briefcases being, he said, for 'boring little businessmen and city types') was slung on the hall chair.

'Guess what?' I called out, unsurprised when there was no reply.

I found him, as usual, in his study.

'I had my meeting today and guess –'

'Oh, it's you.'

He was seated in his Victorian winged armchair reading an exhibition catalogue, a glass of whisky on the small table by his side. He hadn't looked up. I remained in the doorway, my excitement sucked away by his indifference; it had happened so often lately I imagined I had a tidemark somewhere in the area of my neck.

I said, sounding like the kind of woman I never thought I'd become, 'Can't you even pretend to be interested?'

'Don't start.'

'Don't start what? Communicating? I felt happy. I wanted to share my good news with you. Is that a crime?'

'I said *don't* start. I'm extremely fragile today.' He put the catalogue down and looked at me for the first time. 'I don't think you understand just how exhausted I get.'

'Oh yes I do.'

'No, Rebecca, I don't think you do. And why should you? It's all right for you being at home all day. But you try fighting your way across this godforsaken city . . .'

'It's not a godforsaken city, it's a wonderful city.'

'You see, cloud cuckoo land. You have no idea what it's like out there in the real world. Then again, I should be used to it by now.'

'Used to what?' I don't know why I asked when I knew the answer would be a heap of criticism, but I did.

'Used to you living in your own little world completely undisturbed by reality. You have no idea, though, how grating it is to live with someone like that.'

'Where did all this come from? I arrive home all happy and full of good news and suddenly I'm public enemy number one and –'

'God, not more self-serving, self-pitying crap . . .'

The scene was so familiar. We played it out night after night so I knew it by heart. Dominic would grow ever more venomous as I became tearful and reproachful and increasingly like someone I did not wish to know, let alone be. Not tonight, not any more.

'You know,' I said contemplating him, 'your whole face seems to shrink when you're being spiteful. It kind of narrows and becomes mean. It's really most extraordinary. Even your eyes grow closer together.'

'Go away. Fuck off!'

'Don't speak to me that way.'

'I said go away!'

I sat at the kitchen table reading a magazine interview with myself. The copy had arrived that morning but I had not had time to look at it until now. I tended to approach these things, articles, interviews, with the slightly queasy fascination of someone watching a reality show. Who *was* this woman? Why had she agreed to it? Who *cared*?

As I read on I saw that I lived with my partner in a charming 1920s house that would not seem out of place in a quiet cul-de-sac in some genteel provincial town although it was only a short walk from London's fashionable Fulham Road. My kitchen, with its clotted-cream and buttercup-yellow hues, was warm and welcoming and filled with flowers.

I looked around me. Yes, that was true: it was. In fact the tulips on the table in front of me were particularly beautiful in shades from shell-pink to mauve, and miraculously for tulips they had remained upright instead of tipping over the rim of the vase as if they were thinking of ending it all.

I read on to find that my own real-life romance sounded so perfect that it might have been taken from the pages of one of my delightful novels.

I thought back to that first meeting some five years ago at the Affordable Arts Fair in Battersea. I had been separated from Tim for about six months. I was living in the country in a rented cottage in the same village I had lived in when still married. Our separation and subsequent divorce had been amicable inasmuch as we both admitted that our love was a rather pallid affair with our feelings for each other more akin to that of brother and sister than lovers. Where we had differed was on what to do about it.

Tim had felt that we should remain married, as we 'got on', and there was no overwhelming reason to go our separate ways.

'We share interests, we enjoy our home and our friends; hell, we even like each other. How many other married people can say the same?'

I had looked at him, exasperated.

'It's not enough,' I had told him. 'Surely you can see that?'

He said he didn't and could I please try to explain.

I had not been able to, not even to myself, until that day when I stepped back from a painting and straight into the arms of Dominic Townsend. I had turned round to apologise and looked straight into a pair of small but unusually bright eyes fringed with long dark lashes.

He spoke first.

'And we haven't even been introduced.'

We had wandered round the exhibition together, then as there was so much to talk about we had gone for a walk in the park and ended up kissing in the dappled shade of a large beech tree.

I was interrupted in my reverie by Coco, who was perching on the top shelf of the dresser, his stripy legs dangling as he dabbed at his eyes with a huge red-and-white spotty handkerchief.

That article was right, he said. *It's just amazing the way your life mirrors your art; cliché upon cliché.*

Piss off, Coco. I looked at him again. *Anyway, how come your make-up doesn't run?*

Imaginary Max Factor, he said. *You simply can't beat it for staying power.*

I wanted to return to my reminiscences. It was cold and lonely where I was now. I wanted to dream myself back into happiness but Coco had spoilt the mood. In an attempt to get it back I brought out my box of mementos from the cupboard underneath the stairs. I looked through birthday and Valentine cards, photos and letters and the countless little notes Dominic used to leave for me to find in the mornings.

I recalled how Dominic's partner at the gallery had told me, 'People think he's a philanderer – well, you know the score, the ex-wives, the girlfriends – but what no one seems to realise is that the poor boy is just a hopeless romantic. He's on a quest to find that perfect one and he can't bear to be disappointed.'

I reminded myself of all the reasons Dominic had for being difficult. He had been picked on at school for being small and artistic. His army father had bullied him and neither parent had understood his need 'to soar and fly', always preferring his older, sporty and uncomplicated sister. His first wife, and the mother of his grown-up daughter, had been a shopaholic and his second wife had turned hard and bitter when he had insisted they stick to their initial agreement not to have children.

Had he actually used that expression 'to soar and fly'? He had. And I had still taken him seriously? What was wrong with me?

You were in love, Coco said.

Dominic and his partner Archie ran a gallery that specialised in Victorian and Edwardian watercolours. Dominic always said he would have preferred to have lived back then. The world today, he said, was ugly.

I did not agree.

'The world is beautiful: it's just some of the things in it that are ugly.'

'Cloud cuckoo land.' He had waved my words away.

'As an Edwardian you would have the First World War coming – think about that. And you hate going to the dentist as it is, so just imagine having a root-canal filling without decent anaesthetic. There were no antibiotics either and your own daughter would have died from appendicitis. Of course, we wouldn't be together because divorce would most probably have been out of the question.'

'You have no soul,' Dominic had replied.

I put on some rice to boil and placed some chicken breasts in an ovenproof dish with a yoghurt and garlic sauce and prepared some salad. While I cooked I thought that there was much for which I had Dominic to thank. For example . . .

Come on, come on, Coco prompted me some ten minutes later, *we haven't got all night.*

There was the way he used to look at me, as if I were his sweetest dream made flesh. The way his voice softened like churned butter when directed at me. He had made me believe that just being myself was enough to deserve being loved.

The bully giveth, Coco said, *and the bully taketh away*.

It was true. The adoration had waned and I had watched it happen, helpless to halt the decline. I had tried to, heaven knows I had tried to, remembering the particular things he had said he loved best about me and trying to be those things even more. But it seemed the rules had changed and what had once been good was now irritating, silly, stupid, or simply wrong. Of course had I been counselling a friend my advice would have been a robust, 'Just be yourself and if that's not good enough, well, that's just tough.' And, 'What is *he* doing to try to please *you*?' And, 'Are you a woman or a mouse?' But as this was about me, none of that worked.

Coco nodded and tried to look wise.

Oh yes, as Mary Poppins would say, 'When Mrs Self comes through the door Miss Sense flies out of the window.'

I was pretty sure Mary Poppins had said nothing of the sort but I wasn't going to argue with my own hallucinations.

I thought Charlotte Jessop told you I wasn't a hallucination, Coco reminded me.

Indeed she had. Coco was a reaction to long-term stress, an escape valve, she had said. With therapy and rest he'd disappear.

But could therapy cure disappointment? Could rest give you back your trust? I thought it unlikely. I put my head in my hands and asked, how had Dominic and I come to this? I remember him looking deep into my eyes way back then and saying, 'For us failure is not an option.' I had believed it too.

We had learnt from our broken relationships, had we not? We knew what we wanted: each other, and we knew how to nurture our love to make it grow and endure.

There was a thump as Coco, who had been laughing so much, toppled from the dresser and on to the floor.

Once upon a time I had brushed the lock of hair from Dominic's forehead and traced his sensitive –

Weak, Coco said. He had brushed himself down and was lying like a draught-excluder across the doorway of the French windows, his arms behind his head.

Sensitive.

Weak.

Sensitive.

Weak.

– *sensitive* mouth with the tip of my index finger.

'If I wrote you,' I had told him back then, 'I would be accused of exaggerating.'

And how right you are, Coco said, *but for completely different reasons.*

Go away, Coco! Bugger off back to childhood, where you belong.

Coco leapt to his feet and squared up to me, hands on hips.

I call that really unfair, he said. *You spend years putting up with the jerk upstairs but a perfectly decent imaginary clown you want gone after a few days.*

I had to agree that he had a point.

When Dominic finally appeared I could see by the way he braced himself, straightening his shoulders, flexing his neck and moving the corners of his mouth upwards, that he was determined to *make an effort*.

I watched him toy with his food.

'Don't you like it?'

'It's fine.' He made a show of eating a small mouthful. 'But you know I always say that simple is best.' He pointed to the chicken breast on his plate. 'Trust your main ingredients. Then you don't have to smother everything in sauces. And before you start taking offence, I'm not being unkind, I'm simply thinking of you. You make so much work for yourself and for not very much return, it has to be said.' He looked up at me and forced a smile. 'So how was your day?'

'Good, thank you.'

'Good, thank you: is that all? Nothing else to tell? You seemed to be pretty excited about something when you came home. Come on, you're not still sulking?'

I tried to coax back some of my earlier excitement but I had become shy of displaying enthusiasm. I started small.

'At the meeting today they told me about all these plans and ideas for the marketing of the next book. The publicity department had some really good ideas too.'

'Well, that's good. Oh, I meant to tell you, I was speaking to Jenna, you know Jenna at the gallery? We were talking about books; she's amazingly knowledgeable about the whole literature scene.'

'Is she?'

'Absolutely. And she made a really good point saying that, although obviously she didn't read romantic fiction herself, heaps of women did and that by reaching audiences that weren't natural readers you were doing literacy a great service.'

'Hmm,' I said, 'crap that mysteriously manages to penetrate the thick heads of the masses. Bit like Enid Blyton really.'

He slammed his glass down.

'God, you take yourself seriously, don't you?'

'No, I take my work seriously. There is a difference, you know.'

'You're always complaining that we don't talk but when we do, when I make an effort all you do is whinge. Is it any wonder that I get bored, eh?'

'Maybe,' I said, 'if you approached having a conversation with me as less of an effort . . .'

He got to his feet.

'Much as I'd love to stay and listen to you drone on I have work to do, so if you'll excuse me.'

I remained at the table finishing my supper. It took some time; every part of my body seemed heavy, my head had difficulty staying upright and my arms found the weight of my hands hard to support. Then Dominic reappeared, sitting back down opposite me, toying with his cold food.

Suddenly he smiled at me and reached out, putting his hand on mine.

'I'm glad you had a good meeting.'

I was so tired of fighting.

'Guess what?' I said.

His smile stiffened.

'You know how annoying I find that phrase.'

'Sorry. Anyway, *Suburbs of the Heart* is going to be number one this weekend – here *and* in the States. Dorothy opened a bottle of champagne and well, all kinds of people joined us, toasting our success, toasting me, actually. It was exciting. You know the kind of thing I used to fantasise about when I was starting out.' As I relived the afternoon I began to feel genuinely elated. I grinned at him. 'The whole thing: it was a writer's wet dream.'

'They've spent enough money on promoting it. Of course they're pleased it's paid off.'

'I suppose my book must be pretty good too,' I said. 'That's the best thing of all: I think I might have written a really good book.'

'You shouldn't confuse popular appeal with quality,' he said.

'I know that, but it is good.'

He looked at me and there was a light in his eyes.

'I wouldn't know,' he said. 'I haven't read it.'

I returned his gaze, taking in every feature of his face.

'What?' He shifted in his chair. 'Why are you looking at me like that?'

I picked up our plates and got to my feet. I stacked the dishwasher and put the kettle on.

'No pud?' He deployed his best boyish smile.

'No.'

He got up from the table.

'Becca, don't be like that. Don't be a grump.' He pulled me close and I smelt the familiar mix of aftershave and cigarette smoke and something else, something that was uniquely him, and I closed my eyes and for a moment, as I relaxed in his arms, everything was all right.

He pulled away and smiled down at me with that same rueful little-boy expression.

'I know, I know, it's probably all my fault. It's just that . . . well, you just seem to know how to irritate me.' He stroked my hair. 'You just have to learn to handle me a bit better.'

I shrugged free.

'Handle you? What the hell are you? Radioactive waste?'

His mouth pursed.

'Don't start.'

'And by the way, I'm buying a flat.'

'What do you mean you're buying a flat? When? What for? We're not moving.'

I sat back down at the kitchen table and poured myself the last of the wine. I turned and looked up at him.

'What I mean is, I'm buying a flat. It's a wonderful flat and I've fallen in love with it. I decided to buy it . . .' – I looked at my watch – '. . . about two minutes ago. Or maybe a little earlier when you could not bring yourself to be happy for me. Or perhaps it was when you were rude about my cooking. Or maybe it was when you told me to fuck off although I had done nothing to deserve it. Yes, I believe that was it, the fuck off, if you like, that broke the camel's back. Then again maybe it was when I got home and you heard me in the hall but you decided not to acknowledge me. Who knows? Who knows when something actually begins, seeing as everything is connected and one thing always leads to another? But quite simply I've had enough of being the butt of your foul temper. I'm exhausted and on edge from your criticising, your lack of respect or even basic civility. I'm tired of being humiliated in front of our friends, tired of trying to constantly appease you. Appeasement never works. With you, all one can be sure of is that you never want what you have and that if you're given what you think you want you end up wanting something else. You're a toddler, a terrorist . . .'

A will-o'-the-wisp, a clown, Coco sang to the tune of 'How Do You Solve a Problem Like Maria'.

I started laughing and Dominic, who had been looking scared, relaxed and walked over to the table, putting his hand out and touching my cheek.

'Come on, Becca. Don't be a drama queen.'

I had stopped laughing and I said instead, 'Do you know that when I hear your key in the lock my heart starts thumping . . .'

Dominic started smiling and his hand slipped down to my left breast.

'Me too,' he said. 'In spite of everything, that's how I feel too.'

I pushed away his hand.

'With fear,' I said.

His smile shrank, bringing his cheeks with it.

'Fear? Don't be ridiculous.'

'You're right, it *is* ridiculous that in the twenty-first century a grown woman of independent means should allow herself to be bullied and controlled and demeaned in her own home by the man who is supposed to be her best friend and lover, so, Dominic, I'm through with playing red rag to your bull. I'm buying a flat for me, just me.'

And me, Coco chirped.

I laughed again.

'Have you lost your mind completely?' Dominic said.

I considered the question: it was important to be fair, to look at things from every angle and viewpoint, especially when making decisions that affected other people.

'No,' I said finally. 'I admit there are some signs . . .' – Coco waved encouragingly – '. . . but no, I don't think I have.'

Dominic stood in front of me, his arms crossed over his chest.

'And how are you going to pay for this flat, may I ask?'

'Oh didn't I tell you . . . Gemma's negotiated this big – enormous actually – advance. It will be enough for a downpayment. With my share of this place and a bigger mortgage obviously it should be fine, tight but manageable.'

'You think they're going to increase your mortgage? You don't have a steady income. One swallow doesn't make a summer, you know.'

'Didn't I tell you that either? I've got a three-book contract. That should do it, I reckon. Now, where did I put those tea bags?'

Mount Olympus

'EROS, EROS, WHAT'S GOING on?' Mother has been watching the screen but now she's turning round, calling me.

I have been minding my own business at the other end of the room, listening to some music, chilling.

'What?'

'Eros, take off those silly earmuff things and come over here *now*.'

I sigh but do as I am told, removing my headphones and sitting down next to her.

'Can we watch the States?'

'No, we cannot. You watch far too much North America. You're even beginning to talk like one of them.' She points at the screen. 'Now *what* is going on?'

'Someone's moving home,' I tell her.

'I can see that. I do have eyes in my head. But can't you see who that someone is? It's Rebecca Finch. Why is she moving? Didn't you get her together with what's-his-name just the other day? Wasn't that supposed to be the big romance, the great all-conquering love?'

I shrug.

'Dunno. But mortals don't need long to muck things up. What really pisses me off –'

'Don't use that vulgar language up here, Eros. Don't you understand the gravity of the situation?'

What's-his-name comes out of the front door waving his arms around and I think he's shouting. (It's hard to tell as Mother's turned the sound right down. I expect she doesn't want the others to hear.) The removal guys try to carry on as if they're not noticing. Two of them are pushing a huge piano up the ramp to the van, while Rebecca Finch fusses around as if she's worried they'll damage it. She's crying. She's obviously trying to pretend she isn't but she's definitely crying. The shouting guy – I still can't remember his name – has stopped yelling and is just standing there on the doorstep, his arms slack at his sides, watching.

Rebecca Finch walks off towards her car.

'I can't believe it,' I say to Mother. 'The woman's driving a bloody Skoda.'

'Don't swear. And concentrate.'

What on? I mean nothing's happening. What's-his-name's still looking gormless and Rebecca Finch just stands there by the lame car staring at the house as if she were counting each brick. *Finally* she gets into the driver's seat and heads off, leading the way for the van.

Mother has calmed down and is saying that, as Rebecca Finch and What's-his-name weren't actually married, there will be no increase in the divorce statistics, and Harmonia points out that, as there were no kids either, the whole thing isn't a big deal. And I agree with them totally. But there's always someone, isn't there? With us that someone is usually Ate.

Before long she slides up to Mother and says, 'If only things were so simple.'

We've all got Ate sussed by now and Mother says, in this really clipped voice, 'What is it you are trying to say, Ate?'

And Ate says, 'Maybe you missed it, Aphrodite, but only the other day your mortal, your favoured acolyte, counselled a young woman against love, against marriage.'

'What are you talking about?' Mother snaps.

'Your favourite, Rebecca Finch. A vulnerable young girl comes to her for reassurance and instead she gets a giant bucket of cold water poured over her hopes and dreams. Now that, I think you will agree, is a worry.'

'Oh just piss off, Ate,' I tell her. 'Anyway, you're not even meant to be up here.'

For once Mother doesn't tell me off for using bad language. Ate smirks.

'And you are? So when did you become a member of the mighty twelve? Or have you forgotten: you got demoted.' She gives Mother a sideways glance. 'Looks like someone else might be in line for the same treatment, the way things are going.'

I tell you, if Mother hadn't been there I would have shoved her off the summit, but as it is I keep my cool.

'Mother's invited me,' I say. 'Who invited you?'

'Oh stop it, the two of you,' Mother cries, 'or I'll have you both removed.'

'What do you mean both of us? *I* am actually trying to help. *I* am your son.' I state that last bit with more conviction than I actually feel.

But Mother isn't listening. Clad in thunder rather than her usual golden aura she paces the floor, muttering to herself.

'This is most annoying. What is Rebecca Finch thinking of? And she's not getting on with her new book. No, this won't do, it really won't. She's got responsibilities, to her readers, to *me*.

Athene seemed totally engrossed in her embroidery but it turns out she's been listening: she's really creepy like that, Athene.

'Maybe your mortal's seen sense at last?'

Mother stops pacing.

'And what is that supposed to mean?'

'Don't get exercised, Aphrodite dear,' Athene says in that reasonable voice which totally freaks me. 'I'm simply pointing out the possibility that your mortal might have come to realise the grave problems your cult causes.'

'Problems? Problems? How can that possibly be? How can love ever be a problem, tell me that, eh?' Mother's eyes darken from sky-blue to teal but Athene isn't phased.

'The kind of love portrayed in those books,' she says, 'does nothing but foster impossible expectations and foolish notions, which in turn lead to many of the ills the rest of us have to contend with, such as broken families, social disorder, juvenile delinquency, poverty.'

'And you blame all that on my mortal? Well, you might as well blame it on me while you're at it.'

There is a pause while Athene executes some weird sewing stuff then she looks up at Mother.

'Well, you said it, dear.'

And what does Zeus do through all of this? He just sits there stroking his beard and trying to look wise.

Then Mother appeals to him.

'And Zeus, does he agree with this . . . this extraordinary analysis?' And because you can usually get round the old man with flattery, however gross, she adds, 'Does someone as wise, as experienced as Zeus actually agree that *love* is a problem?'

Zeus strokes his beard some more and then he delivers his bombshell.

'I do believe that love is being brought into disrepute, yes, I'm afraid I do.'

Of course Mother goes ballistic. Back in her own rooms she shouts and curses and paces and guess what, she blames it all on me. Since she was demoted from Aphrodite Urania to Aphrodite Pandemos she has lived in fear of being demoted further, possibly ending up having to move down from the summit like I did. Personally I don't think that would be so bad because then we could hang out more but Mother just hates the idea.

I have been about to go up to her and maybe put my arm around her, comfort her a bit but she turns and gives me this really mean sea-green look.

'Why did you have to go and get her together with that Townsend person, eh? Surely you could see that relationship had no future?'

'That's so unfair.' I back away. 'You didn't say anything against it at the time. In fact you told me just to get on with it.'

'That's called *delegating*, Eros. You're supposed to be able to handle such things by yourself, but oh no, someone's become sloppy, careless, shooting off his arrows blindly in every direction with no thought about even basic compatibility or suitability.'

'That's so unfair.'

'Oh do stop saying that.'

'You stop being unfair,' I say, but so quietly that she can't hear. 'Anyway,' I say louder now, 'I'm not meant to think about those things: I'm just a boy.'

Mother sinks down on her bed. She seems too tired even to rant. Instead she sighs; I hate it when she sighs.

'Oh Eros, you're always just a boy.'

'And that's my fault? Anyway, you're supposed to be in charge of strategy.' But even as I protest I know she's right to be pissed at me. My heart just hasn't been in the job lately.

Truth is, I'm bored. So obviously it shows in the results. You should see my pending tray: man, it is stacked high. But think about it from my perspective. I work really hard getting people paired off; I mean I could just hang out with my friends and have a nice time but no, I work. And it feels thankless. I shoot – the person lights up as if they've just had a hundred-volt light bulb shoved up their arse. *She* loses weight. *He* walks around saying he's finally realised what's important in life. They love each other like no one's ever loved before and next time I look they've cocked up.

'You're right,' Mother says suddenly. 'I shouldn't blame you. You do what's in your nature. But Eros' – she puts her hand out so I go over and take it – 'Eros, I'm terribly afraid that they'll demote me. I'm telling you, I couldn't go through that, not again.'

Everyone thinks Mother's so strong but she isn't really. Actually, she hasn't been the same since that business with Adonis. She needs someone to lean on. I'd like that someone to be me but I know I'm not enough. I pat her hand.

'There there,' I say. 'It might not be that bad.'

She snatches her hand away from mine.

'What do you mean it might not be that bad?' Her eyes have turned granite, yielding nothing. It scares me when she goes blank on me like we were strangers, as if I'm nothing to her. And she starts to list all the stuff that would follow from demotion: loss of status and power, laughing stock, unbearable humiliation, the satisfaction given to Athene, not to mention Hera. She finishes off with, 'And there would be no more family dinners for you, do you hear?'

That really got to me. You might ask why. Guys my age don't usually go out of their way to spend time with the olds. But it's different for me. Being up here, having dinner with Mother and Grandpa and the others, sitting on those shithard gold thrones means you're someone, that you belong. And that's actually what I need right now, to belong. Truth is, I had a bit of a shock recently. I haven't talked to Mother about it; as you might have worked out we don't really have that kind of relationship. Still, it makes me laugh, it really does, when I watch the screen and hear people bleat on about their dysfunctional families and stuff. Well, try this for size: you've got used to the fact that no one, least of all your mother, seems to know who your father is. There are a few candidates for the post, chief amongst them Hermes and Ares. I'm not overly impressed by either of them but if I was forced to choose I'd go for Hermes; he might be an arsehole but at least he's not *aggressive*. Then there's the rumour, which is like beyond sick, that Zeus's the guy. I mean he's my grandpa! So, if all that's not gross enough, I'm told by Ate, who else, that there's a theory around that Mother isn't even my mother, that I was hatched from an egg laid by Nyx and that actually I'm not a person at all but a kind of primeval force, a fucking phenomenon! For a moment there I was flattered; I mean being a phenomenon sounds pretty cool but then I thought about it some more and I felt really sad. I still do actually. Aphrodite might not be everyone's idea of a mother but she's *my* mother, or so I thought. OK, so you can't always rely on her but I've got pretty good at relying on myself. Now I can't even do that because if this latest theory is anything to go by I don't exist.

I know everyone has those kinds of thoughts: Who am I? Where do I come from? Why am I here? It's sort of an intellectual exercise. Not for me, though, not any more.

Mother says she wants to be alone so I go down to the woods. I thought Pan might be there, we could play some music and stuff, but I can't find him so I just sit by the water. Just as well I'm on my own, because when I think about everything, about who I am, or who I'm *not*, more like, and about demotion and maybe no more family dinners and all that I get really upset. I sit there on the edge of the pool looking down, and then these tears fall and break the surface of the water, shattering my reflection.

Rebecca

WHEN I TOLD THE removal men that this was the last time I would ever move, the foreman laughed.

'That's what everyone says, madam, but it's hardly ever the case, is it now?' He sipped his tea as he leant against the kitchen workbench. 'Family break-ups are what earn us most of our money these days. Like in your case, if you don't mind me saying, madam. I saw from our records that we moved you into your current property five years ago more or less to the day. And here we are, moving you out. I expect we will be moving Mr Townsend somewhere else in the near future too. It's a big place just for one.'

I stood looking out of my brand-new window; of course the window itself was not new but it, like the flat and the view, was new to me. A barge moved downstream, seemingly deserted with just a few crates on deck and no human being in sight. The day had been overcast and it was beginning to rain. A white plastic sheet had been blown into the branches of a tree, where it flapped like a trashed bridal veil. Dusk was falling. I didn't like dusk, that no-man's-land between day's slick brightness and the dark shield of night. I imagined myself standing by this same window as the seasons changed and I changed with them, lined and greying, increasingly stooped, until one day I was carried out in my coffin.

'All right, madam?' The foreman appeared in the doorway.

I said to him, 'This really is the last time I move.' And, before he had a chance to give me his knowing smile, I added, 'Remember I'm moving in here on my own. You can't break up what isn't there.'

'Oh you won't be on your own for long, madam.'

He meant it as compliment, a comfort and an encouragement, but he needn't have worried. Alone in my flat, my own flat bought by me, for me, with my own money, gazing out of the window at the view, a view that would soon be as familiar to me as my own face in the mirror, and listening to the sounds of the passing traffic, a sound that would soon be so familiar I would hear it no more unless an exception occurred, a crash or a faulty exhaust. I felt at peace for the first time in a long while.

'Books in here, madam?' The foreman pointed to the sitting room. I went to join him. 'I couldn't help noticing when we packed up your old place that your name was on a lot of them books.'

I nodded. As usual in these circumstances I could feel the slight modest smile on my face. This was rather annoying, I know; after all, you didn't find lawyers or bankers or even firemen and doctors looking bashful and pleased when asked about their chosen careers, so why did I feel the need to acknowledge the fact that I wrote books in the manner of someone accepting an award?

'So what are they about then, your books?'

'Oh about life and people and love.'

'Romances then.'

'Romantic fiction,' I said.

'Oh yeah. Is there a difference then?'

'Sometimes,' I muttered.

'I moved another lady who wrote romances last year. You two might know each other: Sally Kendall, her name was. Then again maybe she wrote under another name.'

I shook my head.

'I don't know her, I'm afraid.'

'She's written hundreds of books. All love stories. She was a lady on her own just like you; funny that, when you think about it.'

I had bought a new bed but I still kept to my side. The first night my ex-husband and I shared a bed he asked to sleep on the right-hand side; he said that way his sword arm was free. I remember thinking that would have to depend on whether Tim slept on his back or his side and then on which side but I hadn't argued because it had been a nice idea. Since then, throughout my marriage, after its break-up and during my five years with Dominic, I had remained sleeping on the left-hand side. Maybe only when I woke up one morning sprawled across the middle of a king-sized bed would I be truly a free woman.

Mount Olympus

EVERY TIME I SEE Mother she seems more stressed. Nothing seems to be going right. Another Hollywood marriage gone bust, another high-profile adultery involving a politician, another mindless crime committed by some kid from a broken home. And all of it blamed on us, on Mother and me.

Athene said that if Mother could not keep one mortal, a favoured mortal to boot, in line then could she really be trusted running her own cult? Of course no one told Athene to wind it in, instead Zeus sat there looking wise, Hera smirked – she's always been jealous of Mother – and even Harmonia looked away without saying anything. Mother went as white as alabaster, her eyes turning the colour of a frozen sea. I ran up to her; she was standing up at the time and I thought she might collapse. She turned to me with this tiny smile and put her hand on my shoulder for support. I was gutted for her obviously, but at the same time I couldn't help feeling kind of happy because at least now she needed me.

Today she hasn't even left her room so I go in to check on her. She's slumped on her couch, barely looking up as I enter, but she says, 'That wretched girl Ate was right about Rebecca Finch. I've gone over some of the tapes and there she is, clearly seen counselling a young girl against marriage, pouring scorn on the idea of love everlasting.'

'I suppose she has a point. I mean it doesn't last usually, not even for you and you're the goddess for fuck's sake.'

'Don't *swear*, Eros! Anyway that's different, completely different. All those things, fidelity, family stability, coupling for life, those were not invented for *us*. They, *mortals*, need boundaries, rules and strictures, or there's anarchy. They don't have the wherewithal to cope with the freedoms we up here take for granted. As for Athene, she is intolerably smug and quite intentionally hurtful, but as I said to her, she would do well to put her own cult in order before she criticises someone else's.'

'Atta girl. You show the bitch.' Mother gives me a green look so I quickly say, 'I mean you show Aunt Athene how it's done – properly – kind of thing . . . anyway . . .'

Mother says, 'There is no doubt that Rebecca Finch has been letting me down and letting me down badly. She still hasn't delivered her new book. Her heart is not in her work at all. The other day she mumbled and fumbled her way though a talk at a very high-profile literary event when she was meant to shine as a representative of her craft. No, Eros, that kind of behaviour cannot be tolerated, it really cannot.'

'So what do we do about it?' I ask.

'We get her back on track, that's what we do.'

'How?' I am about to sit down next to her but she gives me a look so I remain standing.

'It's obvious, isn't it? We make her love again, that's how, and this time it has to be permanent.'

'It sounds so easy,' I say, 'but I thought I did a pretty good job with what's-his-name – Mother stops me with another of those mean dark looks. 'OK, maybe not that good but what

73

I'm saying is that it's not my fault. All right then, it might be partly but –'

'Oh, do stop drivelling. The fact is that Rebecca Finch has failed in love. If she isn't capable of learning from her mistakes and finding love again then we must do it for her. And as we all know the child is the father of the man so if you'd kindly fetch me the box set of her life and meet me next door.'

'She's a woman so shouldn't it be the girl is the mother of the woman –'

'Can you not do what you're asked to without arguing, just for once?'

'I wish we could change to DVDs,' I mutter as I dump this huge pile of tapes on the table.

'You know I can't work those things,' Mother says. 'Now stop complaining and watch.' She pats the seat next to her on the sofa. 'Right, *cherchez l'enfant*!'

As the first video starts playing I sit down next to her. I rest my head on her shoulder just lightly, sort of expecting her to shrug me off but she doesn't, so with a sigh I fold my wings and snuggle closer.

'Is your mother always sad?' Matilda asked Rebecca.

Rebecca nodded.

'Pretty well.'

'Why?'

'Because her heart's broken.'

'Does it hurt?'

'Duh.'

'How did it happen?'

'It happened when they put my daddy's coffin in the ground. He was in it.'

'Was she underneath?'

'No. No, of course not. They only put dead people in graves. Didn't you know that?'

Matilda felt stupid, and trying to recover she countered, 'Not if they're zombies.'

'My mother isn't a zombie and she wasn't in the grave.' Rebecca too was getting upset.

Matilda put two strong little arms around her friend and gave her a hug.

Then she said, 'Can our hearts break too?'

Rebecca nodded again.

'When our husbands die.'

'They don't always die, you know. Mrs Nicholson's, for example, just left for Canada.'

Mother presses the pause button and says, 'An early pre-occupation with mortality. There could be something there. Wasn't her sister sick too?'

I shrug. I mean how should I know?

'Well, forward it on that fast-slow thing until we find out.'

'Why don't we just do it?' I say.

'Do what, Eros?'

'Get her in a room with a good-looking guy and . . . ping' – I act out shooting off one of my arrows – 'we're in business.'

'Don't be an idiot.'

'I'm not. Why do you say that? I was only . . .'

Mother rests her head in her hands for a moment before looking up.

'Don't you see, Eros? It's that kind of short-sighted beha-viour that's landed us into trouble in the first place; just getting mortals together willy-nilly with no thought to whether there's any true compatibility, any real chance of lasting love and respect. And before you say anything' – Mother raises her hand – 'I know that sometimes there's a place for the short term-affair. I know that there have even been times when I have positively encouraged you to cause mischief with your arrows, but we can't afford that kind of behaviour now. This time we have to get it right. Now, if you would be so kind as to fast-forward just a couple of years or so.'

When Rebecca was younger she did somersaults and cartwheels when people visited. Nowadays she was more subtle. This afternoon the Cadwells were coming for tea. Tom Cadwell was Laura's friend. He couldn't walk or talk either.

By the time the doorbell rang to let in Tom and his parents, Rebecca was already in position, perched in the drawing-room alcove engrossed in her book. It would look good, she thought, a mere child reading *Voltaire*. As it happened no one took any notice of her but by then she was enjoying the book so it didn't really matter. That is, she had been enjoying it but then *Dr Pangloss* opened his big mouth and said, '"All is for the best in this, the best of all possible worlds."' She reread those words, as stricken as when Dennis, her grandfather, had admitted the truth about Father Christmas; in fact, she felt worse. Her father was dead, her mother's heart was broken and her only sister, aged fourteen, was stuck in a wheelchair for the rest of her life, and *this* was the best there was?

'All right, Rebecca?' her mother asked as she passed with a plate of scones.

Rebecca opened her mouth to cry out, 'No. No, I'm not all right. Just read this and tell me it isn't true,' but her mother had already moved on. No wonder, Rebecca thought, that she turned to her imaginary friend; he was the only one as interested in her as she was herself.

Bloody hell, Coco. What if it's true. What if this really is the best there is? Laura would never get wings and be God's special angel and Rebecca would not be rewarded for being such a good sister. Shit! And she gazed out of the window as dusk enveloped the high street and the buildings opposite. She didn't like dusk. It made her sad even when there was nothing in particular to feel sad about. Usually she would turn away from the window and read a book but this book was no help at all. She decided not to carry on with it. She slipped down from her seat and went into her room picking out *The House at Pooh Corner* from her bookshelf.

'Rebecca, where are you, Rebecca!' It was her mother calling.

It made you wonder, Rebecca thought, being noticed when she *wasn't* somewhere rather than when she was.

At breakfast the next morning she turned to her mother.

'You could say we've been lucky with Laura.'

Her mother frowned at her piece of toast − a tiny buttered triangle with no crust, covered neatly from edge to edge in home-made marmalade − as if *it* had been speaking and not her youngest child.

Maybe her mother's toast did have the gift of speech, Rebecca thought. It wouldn't be altogether surprising. She herself quite liked the crust as long as it wasn't burnt, and she actually preferred jam to bitter-orange marmalade, but still she coveted her mother's toast. It always looked so especially delicious, as if it belonged to a whole different species from that which everyone else ate.

Her mother was still frowning although she was biting into her toast now. Rebecca tilted her head towards it, listening for its screams.

Toast always suffers in silence, Coco informed her. *It's one of the reasons it's such a popular breakfast food.*

'What are you talking about, Rebecca?' her grandmother asked.

Rebecca looked at her sister, whose perfect features were scrunched up in one of her involuntary grimaces.

'Laura, I'm talking about Laura. I'm saying that we're very lucky and all is for the best in this . . .'

Her mother had put the remaining piece of toast back on her plate and now her large blue eyes filled with tears.

Rebecca's grandmother got to her feet and went across to her daughter-in-law, who was sobbing.

'Let's go and lie down, shall we?' she said, leaving Rebecca to bathe in her grandfather's disappointed gaze.

'What did I say? I mean it's Voltaire. You always say how Daddy loved Voltaire.'

'Never mind, Rebecca.' He too got to his feet. 'Help Laura finish her breakfast, will you, there's a good girl.'

'Where are you going?' Rebecca's voice was shrill. She couldn't bear to be excluded.

'I'm taking the dog for a walk.'

They didn't own a dog. This was her grandfather's way of saying he needed to get away from them all for a while.

'So much for a nice family breakfast,' Rebecca said as he shut the dining-room door behind him.

She looked at Laura and as she looked she felt herself growing meaner.

'Oh, so you're still here?' She stuck her tongue out.

She was sorry right away. None of this was Laura's fault. Nothing was ever Laura's fault. Her poor arms jerked and her withered legs kicked as she tried to conquer her disobedient features. Rebecca could see that she was trying to smile by the way her mouth lifted in one corner only to collapse then lift at the other in a lopsided grimace.

Rebecca, from a mixture of guilt and pity, got even crosser.

'Oh give up, why don't you. You can't do it. You can't do anything.'

Laura was trying to say something. There were times when she could make herself understood, at least to her family, but instead of trying to decipher the words Rebecca just sat there, arms crossed over her thin chest, enveloped in meanness as if it were a cloud of sulphur. Laura, in her effort to make herself understood, leant further and further in her chair until finally she toppled over on to the carpet. She lay there, silent. Laura never cried. Rebecca stared at her in horror then rushed up from her seat and across to Laura, pulling her back up, hugging her close and staying that way until her sister's heartbeat had slowed into a steady rhythm.

Their mother returned to see her two girls hugging.

You're a good kind girl, Rebecca, and I'm sorry I got upset with you.' She put her hand on Rebecca's shoulder briefly as she passed. 'But I rely on you, you know, with everything . . .' Her voice trailed off as she picked up the magazine she had been reading over breakfast and was gone once more.

Rebecca let go of Laura and stared at the closed door. Had her mother still been in the room she would have told her no, pleaded with her to believe that Rebecca was neither particularly kind nor sweet and nor could she always be relied upon. In the best possible world her mother would then have taken her in her arms and told her it was all right, she loved Rebecca anyway. But her mother wasn't there so Rebecca said nothing at all, which was probably just as well. To her grandparents, who had lost their only son, and to her mother, who had lost the husband she adored and whose firstborn child was a broken doll that could never be mended, Rebecca was a comfort and a joy, that's what they told her. It was an important job and today she had failed. If Rebecca was the light, Laura was their angel. On a bad day Rebecca thought that angels had it pretty easy. They didn't have to do anything other than just be because it was all in their nature: that's why they were angels.

That evening she sat in Laura's room until her sister's eyelids drooped and she fell asleep. They all loved watching Laura sleep because then her features relaxed, allowing the perfect beauty that was Laura's face to show, and her lips moved in symmetry the way they never managed to when she was awake. Rebecca wondered what the dreams were that made her sister smile so sweetly. But

Laura, of course, could not tell. Rebecca stayed and imagined herself a dream-stealer. With steps as soft as night she would enter children's rooms and hovering above their beds like a giant hummingbird she would steal the dreams right from their lips.

The door opened: it was their mother. She didn't see Rebecca, who was seated on the floor away from the night light. She perched on the edge of the bed stroking Laura's hair, humming softly. Rebecca didn't have to see to know the look in her mother's eyes. It was a look that said she wanted nothing but to wrap her oldest child in velvet and put her in her pocket so that she could carry her safely with her always.

That would be the look exactly, Rebecca thought, that her husband would have when gazing at her, his darling wife.

As I watch the poor kid I tell myself that if I ever have any myself, kids, that is, which doesn't seem all that likely seeing as I'm stuck in this early-adolescensce phase for what seems like for ever, I'll do something really radical and actually listen to them. Not pretend to while I'm thinking about something else. Not think I am because I am so convinced that I know best, but actually listen.

Mother waves her hand at the video player.

'I've learnt all I need to from her childhood: please fast-forward to her teens.'

It was the summer they were all in love. Seeing that they were pupils at an all-girls' school, finding objects for their ardour was a challenge but one that, being teenage girls, they were equal to. Caroline was in love with Amy's brother, Andrew. Amy was in love with her cousin, John. Leonora was in love with Mr McCall, the new physics teacher. Matilda was in love with Adam Ant and Rebecca was in love with Jean-Luc Régnier, her French pen pal.

It was morning break and seated on the grass in the furthest playing field the girls were busy with their needles, scratching the initials of their beloveds on their wrists. Matilda was the bravest; she had done this before and within minutes tiny ruby beads rose to the surface of her skin to form the letter A. Leonora was dithering because she had just realised that she didn't know Mr McCall's first name.

'Do an S, for sir,' Rebecca suggested and was rewarded with a shove that sent her flat on to the grass.

'Anyway,' Leonora said, as Rebecca scrambled back into a sitting position, 'at least I've met him.'

Amy looked at Rebecca, her eyes open wide in a show of astonishment.

'You haven't *met* Jean-Luc?'

'Of course she hasn't,' Matilda said. 'That would spoil all the fun.'

Mother asks me, 'Did she ever meet that boy, the one from France?'

'Dunno.'

'Well, of course you don't. I don't know why I bother asking you anything. But I have to tell you that it's exactly that attitude that will ensure that you remain a minor figure, and you have no one to blame but yourself.'

'That's so unfair . . .'

'It's perfectly fair, I'm afraid.' Mother points to the remote. 'I believe she got married very young, barely twenty, yes? Forward to the time leading up to her marriage. You must have had your reasons for bringing her together with Tim Lodge.'

I'm feeling just a tad uneasy. It's all pretty hazy but I'm beginning to think that I've cocked up somewhere along the line; I'm just not sure when or how.

It was New Year's Eve and the girls were getting ready in the second bathroom of Amy's parents' cottage in the country. Amy and her brother Andrew were giving a party, together with Lance Cooper, who lived next door.

'Has he got a girlfriend?'

Amy lowered her mascara wand and turned to Rebecca.

'Who?'

'Lance.'

'Do you like him?'

Rebecca shrugged.

Then she said, 'Maybe.' Then she blushed. 'Actually, we kind of have a date for this evening. Do you think I'm his type?'

'Sure. I mean he usually goes for blondes but you're almost blonde, aren't you?'

Rebecca was gazing into the mirror trying to decide whether to wear her hair up.

Now she sighed impatiently.

'Laura's the one with the amazing hair. You've seen it; all gold and ringlets.'

Rebecca's hair, although thick and wavy, was that annoying in-between colour that was neither truly brunette nor quite fair enough to pass for blonde. Once, a couple of years back, she had said to her mother in a moment of despair that she wished she looked like Laura. Her mother had asked her if she wished she had been dealt the rest of the hand that Laura had been dealt as well.

'But why could I not have her looks and my life? Why is it always one or the other? Why does everyone your age always seem so pleased when they can say you can't have it both ways? I want it both ways. That's going to be my aim in life, to have it both ways.'

So far, she thought, she had not got very far in her ambition.

'Have you still got that bleach kit?' She turned to Amy.

Amy disappeared into the bathroom, returning with a bottle and a pair of rubber gloves.

'How long should I leave it in for?'

'I've lost the instructions, but about half an hour should do it.'

'Is your cousin coming?'

'John?'

Rebecca nodded, almost dropping the towel wrapped around her head.

'He's supposed to be,' Amy said, 'if Aunt Violet lets him.'

'If she *lets* him? How old is he?'

'Do you know the difference between my Aunt Violet and a Rottweiler?'

'No. What *is* the difference between your Aunt Violet and a Rottweiler?'

'A Rottweiler eventually lets go.'

'Do you still fancy him?'

'When you see him you'll get why I did, but he's my cousin. It'd feel weird if anything actually happened. Pity, though. He's gorgeous.' Amy looked appraisingly at Rebecca. 'You should have a go.'

'I like Lance,' Rebecca said, sounding prim.

The party was well under way when Rebecca finally arrived. Her hair had taken rather a long time to style as somehow the bleach had made it quite a lot wavier as well as drier; on the other hand it had turned really blonde. Standing in the doorway she gazed out across the vast room, peering through the cigarette smoke. Amy was by the drinks table with Matilda and Leonora, handing out cups of fizzy white-wine punch.

When she spotted Rebecca she said, 'Wow!'

'You really think it suits me?'

'Yeah. Don't you think it's good, Matty?'

Matilda nodded.

'You know, you actually look a little like the blonde one in ABBA, but curly.'

'Lance will love it,' Amy said.

'Where is he?'

'I don't know. I haven't seen him for a while, actually.'

There was still no sign of him when Robert came up to her and asked her to dance. She nodded and downed her drink. She danced as if Lance was watching her. He wasn't. After three tracks she excused herself and went back to the trestle table, pulling out a bottle of Bacardi from beneath the long tablecloth and tipping some of it into her glass of punch. She downed the drink as she pushed her way through the throng.

'There you are,' Matilda said, barring her way. 'You're pissed.'

Rebecca shrugged.

'Have you seen Lance?'

'You still haven't found him?'

Rebecca shook her head.

Matilda looked at her friend's shiny bright eyes and flushed cheeks.

'You sit down,' she said, pointing at one of the bales of hay left behind as seats. 'I'll go and find him.'

Rebecca grabbed Matilda's arm.

'Don't tell him I asked you to.'

She waited a full ten minutes and finally Matilda returned. Rebecca knew from the look on her face, pity mixed with the tiniest bit of excitement, that the news would be bad.

'Bastard.' Matilda sat down next to Rebecca and picked out two Marlboros from the packet in her pocket. She lit them both and handed one to Rebecca. 'Bastard,' she said again.

'Why?' The word came out in a squeak.

'He's with that slag, Julie.'

'With Julie? What are they doing?'

Matilda gave her a pitying look.

'Oh.' It was a long oh, said in a small voice.

They each inhaled deep on their cigarettes.

'Oh,' Rebecca exhaled. She got to her feet.

'Now where are you going?'

'Out,' Rebecca said and weaved her way across the

dance floor towards the exit, pushing through the gyrating, stomping, hip-swinging, hand-waving crowd, grabbing her coat and her red woolly hat from the seat where she had left them. She pulled on the hat but dropped her coat to the floor as she spotted Lance locked in an embrace with Julie FitzGerald.

Her feet thumped the frosty ground and she got into a rhythm, her breath creating little cloudbursts. She kept on running as the track turned into a road. She turned a corner and ran straight into the headlights of an oncoming car. There was a screech of tyres as it slid to a halt no more than a foot away from her. She stood where she was, half blinded still by the lights. The driver was young, her own age or there-abouts, fair-haired, white-faced. That was all she saw.

The headlights dimmed and the door opened.

'Are you OK?'

Rebecca didn't reply. The shock had sobered her enough to know exactly how stupid she had been; she did not intend to hang around to be told as much. Instead she turned and headed back to where she had come from, slip-sliding down the bank and on to the farm track, hurrying off into the night.

'Are you OK?' the boy called again.

The church bells started to chime midnight.

Without looking back or stopping she raised two fingers to the starry sky and yelled, 'And a Happy fucking New Year to you too!'

The next morning she woke with a headache and a . . .

'Stop! Stop the tape right there,' Mother orders. I do what I'm told. 'Rewind,' she says. 'No, stop. What's that, in the top left-hand corner?' We both stare. 'Goodness, Eros, it's you. What are you doing there? Forward. No stop. You're shooting! You've shot the girl Rebecca . . . forward . . . and she stumbles and then the car . . . you shot the boy as he was driving. So that's it: their eyes never meet. Oh for heaven's sake, Eros, what were you thinking of? Who is the boy? Had I asked you to shoot him or was this one of your own harebrained little schemes?'

I try to remember. It wasn't long ago by our reckoning, but still . . . who the hell was he and why had I shot at him, and her?

'Yes?' Mother demands, her arms folded across her chest, her eyes opaque.

'I'm *trying* to remember.' I lean back on the chaise longue, closing my eyes. New Year's Eve . . . I check the tape box . . . 1981, their reckoning. What had I been doing? Party – that was it. I'd been partying with Dionysus and some of the other guys. Had a bit too much to drink, head hurting, wings sore . . .' I sit up. 'I must have . . .'

'Yes?' Mother's voice is low and deceptively mild and I know I'm in for a bollocking.

'No. I can't remember. I'm sorry, OK?'

'No, Eros, it is most assuredly not OK.'

'I told you I wasn't feeling too good that night.'

Mother is livid.

'No wonder things have gone so badly for the pair of them,' she says. 'Think about it, Eros – although sometimes I do wonder if you are actually capable of coherent thought – as a result of your incompetence or lack of care, those two will have wandered through life searching for someone, not knowing who, leaving discord in their wake. Anyway, who is the boy?'

John

YEARS LATER HE WAS to tell people that he became a barrister because without law there can be no civil society, but actually it was to please his mother.

His mother's love, though great, was of the tearful variety. When John was little she would fold him in her arms with a grip that was surprisingly strong for such a fragile-looking woman and then she would cry. She cried when he made his prep school's first fifteen at rugby and when he passed grade eight on the trumpet. She cried when he got his twelve O levels and her pretty squirrel-brown eyes were red-rimmed for days after he received his offer to study law at Cambridge. Three years later, on the morning of his graduation, he knew when he returned to his rooms from breakfast that his mother had already arrived because of the trail of coloured Kleenex on the stairs.

John's very first memory was rising to the sky on a friend's garden swing. His second was of his mother pulling him down off the swing, shaking him one moment and hugging him the next, and saying, 'Never forget, my darling, that you're Mummy's everything. Always remember you are my world.'

Mostly she chose not to notice the rituals her darling boy was beginning to develop, such as pulling a door shut behind him and not letting go until he had counted to a hundred and having to start again if he got into a muddle, or swimming out to the furthest buoy in the sea every day on holiday even when the temperature of the water was no more than 13 centigrade and it had dropped to 15 outside. Even when she had the evidence thrust before her, a skinny eight-year-old trembling with cold and with lips the colour of blueberries refusing to get out of the steel-grey sea, she shook her head and smiled at his 'perfectionism' and 'funny little ways'. He was crying out for help, in need of it as surely as if he were drowning in that cold sea, but to his doting mother he was just waving.

And then there was the time a year or so later when he fell in love with the stories about Biggles, the fearless flying ace. He had cycled to the library to return the first volume in the series, heady with the knowledge that there was an entire shelf of further thrills waiting for him. But he knew it was all over when, scanning the shelves, a thought so quick it was more of an impression shot through his mind. It went something like this: unless he wanted something terrible to happen to his mother he would have to read his way through the alphabet, an author for each letter, before he could finally settle on J for W.E. John, his hero's creator. The elation from just a few minutes ago drained from him leaving him cold with despair. He was trapped. Helpless. A small yelp of distress escaped his lips and an elderly man lifted his gaze from the tome in front of him to glare. John tried to retrieve the thought in order to unthink it. But it was too late. The challenge had been issued and the smile of anticipation had been replaced by the anxious set to his jaw his mother saw as determination. Nine books would take him the rest of the holiday to read. And he was only allowed to take three out at a time. The cycle ride alone took half an hour each way. But he had a choice: either he read his way through those nine books or he did not get to read about Biggles again, ever. He squared his shoulders. At least he could pick the shortest ones.

'Darling, you have to go outside. It's not healthy to stay inside with your nose stuck in a book all day. And what's that you're reading? *Nora's Ballet Shoes*? Oh.'

At the progressive co-educational school his mother had picked for him, John walked the whole way along the narrow wall enclosing the stairwell at the back of the school gym block, continuing even when the drop down to the concrete got to ten feet. He was the only one in his year to dive from the highest diving board, and he alone tracked the Dirty Old Man all the way to his lair in the woods, when the rest of his friends were too scared, yet nothing would have made him skip straight to J on that library shelf.

As he grew older it was lucky he was such a handsome boy, or the girls would have fallen about laughing when they saw his lanky figure striding towards them in the corridor, his eyes fixed on the floor, his feet side-stepping, nimble as a boxer's. Instead they sighed and swooned and forgave him everything and not even a titter passed their eager lips the time he walked into the open locker-door. No, as he looked up through his one good eye the other was bleeding, from inside or just above no one could tell at first; all he saw was a flock of anxious gazes boring down on him and strong small hands wiping and dabbing, accompanied by high soft voices clucking.

The boys too accepted his odd ways on account of his undoubted, though somewhat unreliable, skill on the sports field. And though he had only a few really close friends, most of his peers, if asked, would refer to him as 'an OK bloke'.

He read a book by a psychologist, Roger W. Pointer. Pointer equated laziness with evil. It was a variation on the theme of 'the devil makes work for idle hands', but whereas homespun wisdom barely registered, the argument put forward by Roger W. Pointer, that there were few evils in this world, mental or physical, that could not be put down to laziness of the body or spirit, resonated with the truth of a perfectly pitched note. So John got to work at being busy. Not because he always wished to be, not because he was not so tired at times that putting one foot before the other seemed like a trek to the moon but because it was the best way he knew to keep from falling off the edge of reason.

He made treaties and he bargained. If I cut my time over a mile by twenty seconds then I'm allowed to pass the school noticeboard without reading every single sentence of every notice posted. If I do ten one-handed press-ups I won't cock up my exams. Two nights without once falling asleep and my mother won't get cancer. If I happen to read a sentence containing the word 'cancer', touching wood seven times will prove I don't wish it on anyone.

On and on his busy brain laboured, wheeling and dealing, bribing and bartering as if it were a politician or a hawker in some Middle Eastern bazaar. It was exhausting. This boy, although strong and fit, was always tired. But he couldn't stop because the alternative to all this activity was a slow drowning in the quagmire of his mind.

*   *   *

93

On New Year's Eve he had stayed to have dinner with his mother but had told her that he would have to leave by eleven at the latest in order to make the party. When that time came his mother, eyes welling up with the inevitable tears, had thanked him for caring about a lonely old woman and reassured him, unasked, that he was not to worry about her being left to see in the New Year on her own as she was very happy with her wireless.

'At least watch the goddamn TV,' John snapped.

'Oh darling, don't get cross.' His mother reached for her lace handkerchief. 'I'm grateful, you know I am.'

'I don't want you to be grateful.' He put his arm around her shoulders and winced at how slight she felt. 'I've enjoyed our evening. And it wasn't a sacrifice. I wanted to have dinner with you. I just get . . . oh I don't know. I'm sorry I upset you.' He sighed, raking his long-fingered hands through his fair hair until it stood up at the front like plumage. 'But I have to go now, though, I really do. The others are expecting me. I'll call you at midnight, or just after anyway.'

His mother dabbed at her eyes and gave him the kind of smile you might put on when you're about to go Over the Top.

'Of course you mustn't keep your friends waiting.' She raised a paper-dry hand. 'No, I mean it. There's a girl, isn't there? How could your old mother possibly compete?'

'No girl,' he said. And he thought nor will there be the way things were panning out. It was gone half-past eleven before he made it out through the front door and into his car.

His mother had given him a five-year-old Volvo 343 when he got his place at Cambridge. A Volvo was so uncool, but she trusted it to keep her darling boy safe. He knew that beggars could not be choosers, he knew not to look a gift-horse in the mouth and he also knew that a car was a car; and it could have been worse, it could have been new. Anyway, by now he was too old to worry about peer-pressure.

'You, of all people,' his mother had said at the time of giving it to him, 'do not have to worry about *image*.' She might have been pronouncing the word 'image' as if tasting a newfangled dish, but she was right. This boy had been blessed by the gods: tall, athletic, with wheat-blond hair and dark-lashed velvet-brown eyes. His square chin even had a dimple. And he was bright and kind and strong: truly, he was a golden boy. And he knew it and tried his best to level the odds. Inside his lovely head ran a train loaded with junk. Unlike those of British Rail, this train ran night and day and it was always on time. It did not stop other than to refuel and take on more junk: count to three five times and shake your head – but careful so no one sees – and the bad thing might never happen; wipe your feet twenty times on the left foot, always the left foot first, then twenty for the right and then ten on each again and your bad thoughts are rendered harmless; ask forgiveness to that judge and jury in your head for the thought that flew through your mind so swiftly you did not know your wilful brain had fired it; plead and whisper over and over again that you did not mean it, you did not mean to think the thought you could barely remember thinking. Plead that it won't shoot through the membranes of your brain and reach God the creator up on high. God, who might (because such is the hubris of this poor boy's mind) hear his inadvertent prayers and act upon them. 'Sorry never, sorry never, sorry never.' Three times, always three times, for each bad thought.

He had not driven more than two hundred yards when he began feeling guilty. Why could he not have been nicer to his mother when he was home? She had made such an effort over dinner. 'All your favourites.' Of course even that had irritated him: these were dishes that had been his favourites when he was twelve.

As he drove through the snow-silenced countryside the thought went through his mind that if his mother was dead he would be free, free of guilt, free to go, free to be. He regretted it immediately. He loved his mother. He would never wish her any harm. Sorry never, sorry never, sorry never.

In response, his unruly mind conjured up a picture of his mother at the top of the stairs taking a tearful step down towards him, arms outstretched and then falling, falling.

Sorry never, sorry never, sorry never.

The country lane wound round to the right before it started the climb. The girl with long fairy-tale hair was running down the hill track, unsteady on her feet, her red knitted hat pulled down low. As the church bells started to chime mid-night she tilted her head right back, lifting her eyes to the star-stained night sky. Then she wobbled, clutching at her chest as if in pain.

He, far away in his land of private nightmares, had come close to running her down. Something brought him back just in time to slam on the brakes, sending him skidding to a halt in front of her. He felt a sudden pain in his chest making him think he must have hurt himself on the steering wheel but he was more concerned for the girl. He opened the car door and called out to her, asking if she was all right, but she was heading down the dirt track, tall, slender, a flight of hair under a red knitted hat.

He got out of the car and called after her again.

She didn't turn round but raised two defiant fingers to the starry night sky. Her voice was high and clear.

'And a Happy fucking New Year to you too!'

Mount Olympus

MOTHER IS TELLING EVERYONE that I stuffed up.

'Of course I was right: everything was there in Rebecca's past. She was meant for another all along. Someone' – here she casts a sideways glance at me but I pretend not to notice – 'someone had her and a perfect young man in his sights, then . . .' Now she goes all theatrical, rolling her eyes and raising her palms to the skies. '. . . Makes a complete mess of the whole affair. Our would-be lovers are shot within each other's presence, but for reasons only someone knows they don't in fact lock eyes. Instead they're sent off into the world like unguided missiles of frustrated love with predictably disastrous results. *She* marries the first decent man who asks her and *he* moves from woman to woman searching for he's not quite sure who, and ends up a one-man divorce factory.'

I make out like I'm not listening but actually I can't believe Mother. I mean yesterday Athene was public enemy number one and now the two of them are sitting thick as thieves, shaking their heads and rolling their eyes at you-know-who. It hurts, actually. I would never dump on Mother like that, never. I'm not going to let her see she's upset me, though, so I pretend to be concentrating on the screen, laughing at some joke, that kind of thing.

Mother looks across the room at me.

'And you can stop smirking, Eros. Really, I don't know what to do about you. You just don't care, do you? Well, luckily I do.' She turns back to the others, nodding at Athene. 'And you'll all be glad to hear that I have come up with a rather good plan to solve our little problem.'

'That's excellent, Aphrodite dear. And just to clarify, when you say *our* problem, you are meaning yours and Eros's, not ours as in all of us?' Athene says, totally showing her true colours.

Speaking of colours, Mother's face goes chalk-white and her eyes are tarmac, but her voice remains calm.

'Very well, I assume full responsibility. I'm used to it. It's not as if I've ever been able to count on anyone but myself, anyhow.'

I assume she's having another dig at me but actually she's directing her mean look at my stepfather Hephaestus. He, of course, doesn't react, probably being deep in some wet dream about his next DIY job.

'No, *I'm* sorry,' Athene purrs. 'I think we've all been guilty of placing too much responsibility on your slender shoulders.'

Mother walks straight into it.

'Well, thank you for your concern,' she says, looking somewhat surprised.

'Yes, we have all been expecting too much,' Athene goes on, her voice so silky it slides through her lips. 'I suggest' – here she turns and looks at Grandpa – 'I suggest that we consider relieving Aphrodite of the onerous task of looking after the sacred aspect of love and leave her with what she does best, the profane.'

That's it. I've had enough. I switch off the screen although it's a really serious ball game on and I turn and give Athene one of my stares. She doesn't seem to notice so I tell her straight.

'You'd like that, wouldn't you? It would suit you just fine if Mother and I gave up on that other stuff, but I'm telling you it ain't gonna happen and if you think—' I feel the hand of Zeus on my neck and the next thing I know I'm back down in my own room, sent there, literally, by one swipe of his hand.

I can hear his voice booming down at me like thunder.

'And don't let me see you up here again until you're ready to apologise to your aunt.'

I totally hate the way they can just evict me whenever it suits them. It's humiliating.

'I'm sorry, Athene, I shouldn't have spoke to you that way.'

'That's all right, Eros. Just don't let it happen again.'

Of course, you'd think from that that she was being all gracious but what do you know, just moments later I hear her whisper to Hera, 'What can one expect? Feckless mother . . . no real father figure . . . stepfather not interested . . . countless lovers.'

Mother just doesn't have a clue.

They're watching France – again.

'Do we have to?' I ask. It's so *slow*. OK, so the photography is pretty cool and some of the cars, but essentially it's *pointless*; essentially it's just a lot of people dressed in black, eating stuff and talking and talking and talking – I mean is that all they ever do there, talk?

I get another lecture, from Hera this time, about watching too much USA.

So I tell her, 'The United States of America is the Mount Olympus of the mortal world.' And I feel pretty bright saying it too.

Then Zeus does this really lame Bush imitation.

'This is not what this great country of ours is all about but a misunderestimate.' It's not even funny but obviously everyone laughs and Zeus looks around him with this pleased little smile. I tell you no flattery is too gross for him to swallow.

The talk turns again to Mother's great plan.

'Hand me the remote, will you, Eros.'

She flicks through the channels until she gets London, Great Britain. She's not that good on the digital aspects of the screen but eventually she finds what she wants – a guy in a collarless shirt with the sleeves rolled up. He's sitting at a large desk in a complete dump of a room – underground, shelves stacked with files, desk stacked with files, more files in boxes on the floor. I tell you, if yours truly left his room in that kind of a state Mother would come down on me like a ton of bricks, but not when it's this guy, oh no. Instead she just smiles and rolls her eyes in this indulgent way.

'Nice arms,' Hera mutters.

'Well, this is he,' Mother says, 'John Sterling, our one-man divorce factory.'

She clicks on the archive function and up pops a picture of our guy flanked by a couple of grinning females. The caption reads, 'Landmark victory for ex-wives'. We move on to another picture with another grinning woman and this time it says, 'Record settlement for stay-at-home wife.'

Now you would have thought that Mother would be totally against that kind of activity. I mean this guy is doing serious damage to our cause. Instead she's got this soppy look on her face and it hits me: the guy is a dead ringer for Adonis, or at least Adonis's older brother who's not slept for a while. The similarities are uncanny: same blond locks, same dark eyes and chiselled features, hell yes, this guy even has a dimple in his chin.

This is *not* good. Adonis is the one guy Mother really cared about, I reckon. I remember the day they met. Mother must have been in a particularly good mood because we were playing catch in the fields, just larking around. I was standing still to catch my breath for a second and she bends down and grabs me from behind, playfully, putting her arms round me and that's when the point of one of my arrows scratches her chest just above her heart. She pushes me away but the wound is quite deep and before it's had time to heal completely she's clamped eyes on him, Adonis, who was guarding his flock or whatever just a little distance away, and that was that. She goes completely la la; follows him everywhere, leaving home for like ages at a time, which was quite hard for me because although I've always been able to look after myself it felt weird not having her there at all. In fact, it was like she had forgotten all about me and all the stuff we always do together. For example, I sent her a message saying that Elizabeth Taylor was getting married – we always watch Elizabeth Taylor getting married together – and she didn't even reply.

Then the guy, Adonis, gets himself gored by a boar – who, some say, was actually Ares, which would not surprise me at all seeing he once got me banned from the summit for an entire decade completely out of spite as I did *not*, I repeat *not*, shoot an arrow at the wrong woman just so that he would be pursued all over the place by this total minger instead of her gorgeous sister – but anyway, Adonis lay there bleeding from this huge wound in his side and Mother freaked. She knelt by his side and raged at the Fates (which, as we all know, is completely pointless as those old biddies listen to nobody and I mean *nobody*!). Adonis kept bleeding and . . . well, it was horrible. Mother wept and wept and he bled and bled and with each drop falling to the ground a crimson rose grew.

Mother lamented, 'Stay, Adonis, stay, ill-fated Adonis, so I may hold you for the last time, embrace you and mingle my lips with yours. Awake, Adonis sweet love, for a little, kiss me one last time, kiss me as long as the kiss has life, till your spirit passes into my mouth and your breath flows into my liver . . .' On and on she went and I just knew that there was nothing I could do to make it better.

It would have been nice if there had been, but she said the best thing I could do right then would be to leave her alone, so I did, going back to my place, just hanging out, playing my lyre, waiting for when Mother would need me again. She didn't for ages.

In the end, of course, she did perk up, although she wasn't really her old self. Still isn't, actually, so when I see this other guy looking a bit like A and Mother taking a really close interest, you can't blame me for getting worried.

I make my voice all casual as I ask, 'Does John Sterling remind you of anyone?'

'No,' she says but like too quickly.

So Athene says, 'You know, Eros is right – for once; your John Sterling does remind me a little of that boy you were so fond of, the one who got himself gored, what was his name? Adonis? Yes, that's it, Adonis.'

Mother makes a big show of peering at the screen and eventually she concedes.

'Maybe a little. Still, what matters is uniting the two of them, John Sterling and Rebecca Finch, two people who have, and I say this with sadness rather than condemnation, turned out to be a great disappointment to me. Yet by having them love each other' – she pauses as she turns to Athene and her eyes turn a brilliant green – 'for the rest of their lives, I will again demonstrate the power of the great goddess of love . . .'

'Where? Who?' Ate makes a show of searching, including getting down on her hands and knees to look under the table – I mean how juvenile can you get?

Mother wisely ignores her.

'Thereby demonstrating the power and might of *love*.'

'I give them five years,' Athene says. 'Tops.'

Once we're on our own Mother drops the act.

'It's not going to be easy,' she says.

'You're telling me.'

'Everything is so much more difficult these days when people don't believe in one. Where to start, where to start?' She paces the room and then she stops. 'We need a link. Find the Amy person? Get her back in touch with Rebecca? Yes. I know – she should give another party inviting her cousin. Yes, yes, Eros, I'm buzzing with ideas . . .'

I return and tell her the bad news.

'Amy whatsit's in New Zealand.'

'Damn!'

So I bring out my trump card.

'*I've* got a link.'

Mother looks at me, her eyes a heavenly blue.

'Do you, Eros, do you really?'

I nod and annoyingly my face turns bright pink.

'Yup. He's nuts. She's nuts. They're both nuts!'

'Oh Eros, so what? Show me a mortal who isn't.'

'No, I mean really nuts. As in seeing a shrink. They both are.'

Mother brightens.

'The same one?'

I pull a face.

'No.'

'Oh Eros, how is that going to help us then?'

I kick at a boulder. It curses: I'd forgotten about Prometheus.

'I don't know how it's going to help, all right? I just thought it was a start.'

PART TWO

PART TWO

John

JOHN HAD BEGUN THERAPY at the behest of his girlfriend, Melanie Ingram, who had informed him, as they were cooking supper one evening, that he was 'an emotionally stunted workaholic commitment-phobe'.

'Is that all?' he had replied, causing Melanie to throw a loaf of sliced bread at him.

As he picked the slices of organic wholemeal off his shoulders John realised that he was no longer in love. Yet he was tired of running. And maybe he asked too much of relationships? Maybe this, what he had with Melanie, was as good as it got? She wasn't always angry, and when she wasn't she was great fun. She was certainly pretty with her pert jogging body, clear blue eyes that looked confidently straight at you, her glossy blonde bob and her wide smile. She was bright too, and energetic. It was the energy that had first attracted him to her. John did not discount the possibility that she was right to be angry with him, yet part of him felt hard done by. Take work, for example; when they first met he had told her that he was aware that one of the problems he had when it came to maintaining a relationship was that between his work and seeing his daughter there was not a lot of time left for anything or anyone else.

Melanie had looked him in the eyes with that straight, earnest gaze of hers and said, 'I couldn't be with a man who wasn't absorbed by his work. It's a sign of passion, isn't it?' Her voice had gone down a note as she said the word 'passion' but her gaze had remained fixed on his. 'I have friends who never stop complaining about their husbands or boyfriends coming home late or working weekends or whatever. I mean have they no lives of their own? I'm probably too independent but honestly I couldn't cope with a guy who hung around all the time.' As for him spending time with Susannah, Melanie had told him she thought there was nothing sexier than a man who was a good father.

John had spoken in earnest. He had assumed that Melanie had been equally candid. Yet these days when she sulked because he never seemed to get home from Chambers before nine or because he couldn't join her to visit friends at the weekend because he was working or because Susannah was coming to stay and he reminded her of those early-day conversations she would stare at him, seemingly exasperated at his denseness.

'For God's sake, John, can't you see that things were different then?'

When he told her that he did not feel that to be in any way a satisfactory reply, she rolled her eyes and said, 'John, at least try to be human: we're not in court now and I'm not some witness for you to cross-examine.' Then she suggested therapy.

John wanted very much to be human. The suggestion that he was somehow not had been made a few too many times by his mother, his ex-wife, opponents in court and now Melanie for him not to consider that they might have a point. Maybe therapy *would* help. Maybe it would give him the missing part, the part that would stop women looking at him, at first with adoration and then with increasing frustration, before telling him he was not quite human.

Melanie thought he should see Rupert Daly. Rupert, she said, had worked with several of her friends, and everyone spoke highly of him. John had told her he would prefer to do some research and to find someone himself, but he had ended up submerged in a case so seeing Rupert Daly had seemed the simplest way forward. At the first session John had explained that what really concerned him when it came to relationships was that the women he had loved, and who had professed to love him, all seemed to end up disappointed.

'So you have been left many times?'

'No. They don't leave, they stay and complain.'

'I sense some anger here.'

'Anger? No, I don't think I'm angry.'

Rupert Daly did not pursue the point; instead, while scribbling on his notes, he said, 'So you leave them?'

'Sometimes parting is a mutual decision.'

'But often it is you who instigates the parting?'

'Yes, yes, I suppose so.'

'In fact you have a habit of running away from conflict.'

John gave a dry laugh.

'Hardly, I'm a barrister.'

Rupert Daly looked up from his writing.

'I'm not talking about your work but about your private life. You find it hard to handle disappointment and anger at a personal level so instead you leave.'

'I terminate . . .' He paused, realising how clinical, inhuman you might say, that word sounded in the context. He tried again.

'I end a relationship if I feel that the benefits are outweighed by the problems.' That did not sound much better. 'I don't think I'm one of these men who change once I'm secure in a relationship. I don't take people for granted or stop making an effort. I even shower at the weekends.' He smiled and got a small smile back. 'I am aware of my faults. I don't pretend to be someone I'm not. I explain that my work often does come first and that I'm single-minded. I tell them that when I'm working up to a big case I shut off from everything else; I have to, in order to do my job properly. I admit that I'm useless at the romantic stuff . . . gosh, the list is endless . . . and they appear to listen, only to feel angry and let down when what I always told them turns out to be so.'

'And how does that make you feel?'

'Puzzled.'

'I mean emotionally.'

John searched for clues in the therapist's face but finding none he tried again.

'Confused?'

Following this somewhat unpromising start the therapy sessions had begun to have a use beyond keeping Melanie happy. Halfway through their second meeting John had made a jokey reference to being obsessive.

Rupert Daly had not laughed.

Instead he had looked John deep in his eyes and said, 'I was wondering when we would come to that.'

'I'm not sure I follow . . .'

'I was wondering when we would come to the real reason you're here. Do you feel that your obsessive-compulsive disorder is the main obstacle to your attempts at achieving a lasting loving partnership?'

'I'm familiar with the condition to which you're referring,' John said sitting back, an easy smile on his lips, though his fingers gripped the arms of his chair. 'Howard Hughes, Dr Johnson . . . however, I really don't think I can be accused of suffering from a full-blown mental illness.'

'And I would never *accuse* anyone of suffering from any kind of illness.'

'All right, I get your point. Still, as I mentioned last time, none of the women I've been with have had a problem expressing their concerns and being obsessive has only come up as a point of conflict in relation to my work. I of course would always make the point that I was merely being thorough.'

'That's a good little speech.'

'I thought so.'

'But actually I'm not interested in whether or not OCD is a problem for other people but whether it is a problem for you.'

John had been about to say that he still did not accept that he suffered from OCD when he found himself saying instead, slowly as if each word had to be fetched from a place far away, 'Yes, it is. It's a terrible problem.'

John did not find it easy to fit in the regular appointments but he managed, most of the time. In between he tried to apply the techniques shown to him by the therapist.

'Don't engage in a dialogue with your obsessions. Don't carry out the rituals. Resist, resist, resist. You will feel uncomfortable, panicked even, but the more you don't give in the fainter the discomfort. Think of it as going cold turkey. OCD is a form of addictive behaviour and should be treated as such. Now, if you were to find the time to join my six-week intensive programme . . . all right, I can see you can't, but if you were to, you would find recovering alcoholics, sex addicts, drug addicts, food addicts, as well as people with OCD. Now I know this is a somewhat controversial take on the subject, but I have achieved some truly excellent results.'

But progress was slow and John was growing impatient. He was pan-frying some sea bass in the kitchen of his two-up two-down in Primrose Hill, a house that seemed to have received all the makeovers his girlfriends would have loved to give him. (Right now the interior of the house was a tranquil space of dark wood and soft creams and whites, or, as his ex-wife called it, a triumph of beige over imagination.)

As he tipped the fillets on to the pre-heated plates he said, 'I don't know, darling. I really feel as if I've gone as far as I can with the therapy.' As Melanie's eyes narrowed and her mouth moved to speak, he added quickly, 'Of course it's taught me a lot, but that's just it.' He brightened. 'I feel I've got the . . . the coping mechanisms now to manage myself.' Then he made the mistake of adding, 'And I really can't keep going off in the middle of the afternoon like that.'

'Five o'clock is hardly the middle of the afternoon. In fact, it's at the end of most normal people's working day.'

'Well, it's not at the end of mine.'

'And that's exactly why you need to go on seeing Rupert. You won't tell me what the two of you discuss but I can't believe that he hasn't identified your total obsession with work as a serious obstacle to any kind of a normal, happy home life.'

John sighed. His working day had started at six, at ten he had gone into court, remaining there for most of the day, and then there had been a tricky conference with a new client. He had driven home hopeful that this evening Melanie might be a little less angry, a little less unhappy and resentful and that he would be able to sit down with a drink and relax, chat without having to search each word as if it might contain explosives.

'I don't think our home life is unhappy or especially abnormal,' he said.

'Well, that just shows how removed you are from reality.'

He slammed his fork down on his plate.

'For Christ's sake, Melanie, we've been through this a million times. You knew when we met that I worked long hours. What really gets me is that at the time you positively approved.'

'Don't raise your voice at me.'

'I wasn't . . .' He stopped as, to his horror, she started crying. He wanted to go across to her and hold her and say he was sorry he'd upset her. But instead he just sat there looking over her shoulder at the fridge door as if his lines were written on the brushed-steel door.

'You always bring that up,' Melanie sobbed. 'Why don't you try to understand how I feel *now*, and respect those feelings instead of trying to . . . well, I don't know . . . out-argue me. I mean don't you want us to spend more time together?'

'Well, of course I do. And that's another reason why I want to stop these sessions: to give me more time.'

Melanie blew her nose noisily, looking at him over the tissue with moist, mascara-smudged eyes.

'That's just stupid. As if you'd spend that time with me rather than staying on in Chambers!'

John reached across the table and took her hands in his.

'I'm sorry,' he said. 'I'll carry on with the sessions if it means so much to you.'

She pulled free.

'Don't do me any favours.'

He quelled an impulse to snap at her, saying instead in his mildest voice, 'I know it's for my own sake and I'm grateful to you for pushing me to do it. You're very good for me.'

'What do you mean I'm good for you? How bloody patronising can you get?'

He met her angry gaze with a small smile and an expression of polite interest.

'A lot more, I assure you.'

Her eyes overflowed once again and, pushing the plate with the uneaten sea bass away, she told him that he was hopeless and that their relationship was hopeless too.

He looked mournfully at her abandoned fish. It was getting cold and he had really made an effort, trying out a new recipe involving a freshly made warm tomato relish and some deep-fried parsley.

'So you have nothing to say?' Melanie picked up a piece of buttered leek with her fingers and put it into her mouth.

'About what?'

'About what we've been talking about. About how you're never home. I mean do you realise that you've been working for the past two weekends, and the weekend before that you were with Susannah?'

'We went to the cinema last Saturday.'

'That was three weeks ago and the film was about furry creatures living in a magic wood.'

'Susannah is six; what would you have taken her to? *The Lives of Others*?'

'That was on ages ago.'

'Was it?'

'Is that all you've got to say?' Melanie asked him again.

'I'm sorry if I've upset you, but . . .' The sight of Melanie picking at the leeks and leaving the fish uneaten irritated him so that instead of apologising, which had been his plan, he said, '. . . Well, *someone* has to pay the mortgage.'

Melanie opened her bright eyes wide and shook her head.

'You're unbelievable, do you know that? Unbelievable: rubbing my nose in the fact that you're the main earner. I mean do you think I enjoy being financially beholden to you? Do you?'

'I don't know,' he said, finishing his fish and speaking in a low, reasonable voice. 'But I bet it beats working for a living.'

He was put on notice.

'If you want us to have *any* chance of surviving as a couple then there'd better be some changes, fast.'

As the restless night turned into a wakeful dawn he decided he was not ready to give up on his relationship with Melanie. He had been so sure when they had first got together that this time it would work out and that Melanie would be the woman with whom he would build the next phase of his life. He had imagined them having children, brothers and sisters for Susannah. He had loved her energy and resolve, her willingness to try new things, her way of confronting problems head on, banner flying. This time, he had told himself, he would only have himself to blame if it did not work out.

So was it him? Was Melanie right? Not just a little bit right about little things but was she generally right about him and his shortcomings? Maybe the truth was that if he could not make even this relationship work then he might as well resign himself to being on his own.

He got up, determined to stick with his therapy and to work on what Rupert Daly termed his 'relationship skills'. There, he thought, as he shampooed his hair under the shower, he had even managed to use that phrase with only the barest hint of irony. He rinsed his hair, finished showering, dressed and walked off whistling towards the tube.

Then a letter arrived from Rupert Daly saying that he had received an offer to work at a world-renowned clinic in Houston, and that he had decided to accept. It was all rather sudden, he acknowledged, 'But I'm pleased to recommend my successor, Dr Angie Bliss, bla bla bla . . .'

'That seems to be it then,' John told Melanie.

'What do you mean that seems to be it? We've been through all this. And if this other person is as good as Rupert says she is then there's no reason not to continue with the sessions.' She was on her way to the kitchen window box with the watering can and she paused briefly to give him a smile and to push his hair back from his forehead. 'Don't look so worried. I really feel we're getting somewhere at last.'

John left his room in Chambers to walk the few blocks to his therapist's offices. He strode along the Strand, his gaze raised, as if he were scanning some faraway horizon, not just a London street in the afternoon rush hour. Quite a few women and a couple of men glanced as they passed him on the pavement. John did not notice: as usual he was deep in thought. The sessions with Rupert Daly had increased his ability to control his OCD but there were still times, usually when he was allowing himself to relax, read something not work-related, watch some TV, catch up on the newspapers, that he would be sucked down the drain of obsessive thoughts. When he surfaced, exhausted and frustrated, he would find that a whole precious hour had passed whilst he was weighing up the likelihood of having caused an epidemic of blindness in children by failing to remove the large dog turd deposited outside his gate.

Right at this moment, however, he was deep in what he termed 'legitimate thought', going over the meeting he had just had with a new client. He tried to do at least one case a year for the Bar pro bono unit, although it was getting increasingly difficult to find the time; his recent and public successes had meant that more instructions for ever bigger cases were coming in than he could possibly deal with and the clerks were not best pleased when he turned some down in favour of the unpaid work. 'You've done your bit,' they kept telling him. 'More than most, in fact.'

And John would mutter something about how you could never do enough for those in need. But it was all about his own private trade-off: doing unpaid work bought him immunity from OCD. In his mind it went something like this: ten hours spent working for free for someone unable to afford to pay his fees allowed him to ignore the dog-turd-blinded-children, the little-old-ladies-run-over-by-his-big-car-without-him-noticing, the danger-to-Susan-nah-from-his-reliance-on-the-wireless-network, and the rest of the pack of feral thoughts that invaded his mind; allowed him to shove them to the back of his brain, where they belonged – for a while at least. But try explaining that to your clerks.

The latest case he was doing pro bono involved a father, Derek O'Connor, whose ex-wife maintained that the couple's three children, all girls, no longer wished to visit their father and his new girlfriend. The father was convinced that his ex-wife was poisoning the children's minds and was appealing a judgment awarding his former wife sole custody.

Mr O'Connor had left his wife for another woman with whom he had now set up home. Mrs O'Connor was seeking to block her husband's access to their three daughters unless he agreed not to bring them into contact with his girlfriend, *ever*, claiming that the girls returned from visits to their father's home in 'a hysterical state' pleading with their mother not to make them return. Mr O'Connor argued that the reason the girls were hysterical was because their mother had painted such a negative picture of his girlfriend, and lately himself. 'So they would be, wouldn't they?'

Mrs O'Connor was a pretty woman, slim with a neat haircut and pleasantly dressed in black trousers and a dark-pink jacket, but the moment the name of her ex-husband's girlfriend was brought into the conversation her eyes turned into black bullets and her chin jutted, causing two deep lines to form on either side of her mouth.

'I'm not having that woman, that tart, contaminating my children.'

John looked away. He never quite got used to the visceral quality of the anger of someone whose illusions had been shattered. Abigail O'Connor was crying now, hoarse shuddering sobs, and her husband, his client, barely looked at her, turning instead to the file in front of him, making some notes and passing them to John. That was another thing he found hard to get used to: the way you could end up so far removed from the person you had once loved, the person you had promised your entire life to, the person in whose arms you went to sleep at night and wished to see first in the morning, that their deep distress blended into the white noise of everyday life.

Mrs O'Connor had stopped crying and blew her nose.

'The man I knew would not have been capable of doing such a thing.'

They all said it: the person to whom I gave my heart and my trust and who alone knew each and every soft part of my soul could not have done this to me. It was *that* woman/man/trollop/bastard.

This time, however, John's sympathy was tempered by the particulars of the case. He had to stop himself pointing out that her husband's betrayal should not be a complete surprise, seeing that he had begun his relationship with her when he was still married to the *first* Mrs O'Connor.

'And that bitch, with no conscience, no morals . . .' She turned directly to John, 'You're saying I should put my little girls in the care of someone like that?'

It was Mr O'Connor who replied.

'I won't have you talk about Roxy like that.'

This was not the wisest thing he could have said, John thought. To defend your new love against your old betrayed and wounded one was not a good idea, not if you wanted to make peace.

'Ah, poor, defenceless little Roxy. What kind of name is that anyway? *Roxy*. Then again I suppose it was just right for the lap-dancing club where you found her.'

'She is not a lap-dancer, as you well know.' He turned to John. 'Roxy is a dance teacher. She teaches children. She's very experienced with young people, actually.'

'Very experienced, full stop,' Mrs O'Connor snarled. 'Maybe I should let the parents of those children know exactly what kind of —'

'You see?' Her ex-husband had slammed his fist down on the table. 'This is the kind of rubbish she feeds our daughters.'

'The truth hurts. She is a tart and a home-wrecker and if you think you and your fancy lawyer are going to be able to silence me —'

Her own counsel put a steadying hand on her arm.

'No one's trying to silence you, Abigail.'

John said, 'Love, or should that be infatuation, does have a way of making us forget our principles.'

Mrs O'Connor looked at him as if he had just dropped a rat at her feet.

'I can see what you're thinking. I suppose you've heard all about it from *him*.' She turned her gaze on her husband; mixed with the dislike was something soft. 'Yes,' she said, her eyes still fixed on him, 'he *was* married when we met. And now he's trying to convince himself and everyone else that what this woman is doing is no different from what I did back then. But it was, it was . . .' She started sobbing again. 'It was completely different. For a start, everyone knew their relationship was on the rocks. This, us, was totally different. We were happy until she came along. We were happy until she took it all away.'

John sighed. Of course it's different when the pain's your own.

The new therapist, Angie Bliss, was running late. Rupert never ran late. As John waited, leafing through the *Standard*, he was already regretting having come. Apart from the fact that he could ill afford the time, he was annoyed at having to see someone new. It had taken him months to get on top of the sessions with Rupert.

Melanie, when he mentioned this, had turned on him, exasperated.

'You're not supposed to be *on top* of it. That's the point: for once you're supposed *not* to be in control. God, you're such a *freak*.'

So he waited.

Finally the door to the consulting room opened and a man about John's own age appeared. His face bore a glazed look making John wonder if he was on some kind of medication. He had little sympathy with the mentally afflicted. That, at least, was normal, he thought, not nice but normal; you most dislike the flaw in others that you recognise in yourself.

The new therapist appeared. Her voice as she called his name was melodious with a slight, untraceable accent. He got to his feet, looking pointedly at his watch, but the therapist did not seem to notice.

Angie Bliss wore glasses, heavy-framed and rectangular, which made John think of Clark Kent. Her fair hair was scraped back in a ponytail and she wore no make-up.

He followed her into the room.

'You've redecorated?'

Rupert's warm sunshine-yellow had been substituted for a bright Aegean-blue, the chairs were reupholstered in jade-green and a vase of red roses was placed on the desk next to a large bowl of fragrant apples.

The therapist looked around her with faint surprise.

'Have I?'

'Someone has,' John said. The woman was a complete space cadet.

Angie Bliss had seated herself on the desk chair rather than the armchair Rupert Daly had favoured. She glanced at some papers in front of her then swivelled round to face him.

'Do you not think it's time you stopped flitting from relationship to relationship?'

John had been sitting back, practising his courtroom faces, currently exaggerated attentiveness with one eyebrow raised. He had been about to change to ill-concealed boredom with stifled yawn but instead he sat forward in the chair, his jaw dropping in surprise.

The therapist continued.

'You're forty-three years old. Aren't you risking becoming an object of ridicule, as well as setting a very poor example for your children?'

John, still taken aback by the turn the session was taking, could only retort with a, 'Child. One. Daughter,' while casting a meaningful glance at the open folder in front of her, which he assumed contained his notes and therefore all the relevant information as to family status, number of children etc. But he was wasting meaningful glances.

'Whatever,' she said, inspecting her shell-pink nails. What she saw seemed to please her. She brought her attention back to John. Crossing one sleek bare leg over the other, she asked, 'Is it sexual, your problem?'

He raised an eyebrow to feign incredulity but this had no effect other than to make the therapist ask her question again.

This time he replied with a simple, 'No.'

'Well, that *is* good.' She seemed relieved. 'So what is it, do you think?'

'I don't think that I have such a lot of problems, actually, other than the OCD, which, as I'm sure my notes say, could be worked on further and my handling of it improved. And I believe Melanie and I are getting back on track.'

'It won't last.'

'Excuse me?'

'I said it won't last. You'll be at each other's throats again before you can say break-up. She'll be weeping or threatening or both. You'll be alternately defensive and apologetic then cold and sarcastic. It's going to end so why not save time and further misery by getting on with it?'

'Did Rupert tell you all of that?'

'Rupert? Oh Rupert. No. Yes.'

'I wasn't aware I had put things in that way.'

'Well, there you are.'

'Anyway,' John said, 'the sessions with Rupert had moved on – I'm sure that's in my notes too. We were dealing mainly with my OCD.' He paused.

'And you think your OCE –'

'D. It's OCD. I presume you are familiar with the condition?'

Angie Bliss gave a little laugh, high and clear.

'Of course I am. But I would like to hear how you experience it. So why do you think your DCT is affecting your ability to maintain a decent long-term relationship?'

'OCD. You are trained in that area, are you not?'

'Of course I am. Would you like to see my diplomas?'

On receiving the letter from Rupert Daly, John had spoken briefly to him and Rupert had told him, 'Don't be fooled by first impressions. She might come across as a bit ditzy but trust me: her qualifications are amongst the most impressive I've ever seen.'

John was no stranger to the unorthodoxy in his own work. It could be that Angie Bliss's apparent flakiness was actually part of a deliberate strategy. He decided to relax and go with her for the rest of the session.

The therapist was engrossed in reading what he assumed were his notes. It was all very well to trust her but surely she should have been better prepared? To him, not to be prepared was the worst kind of professional solecism.

'You are familiar with OCD?' he asked again.

Angie Bliss swivelled back round.

'Of course I am familiar with it. After all, is it not elementary in today's thinking on these matters?'

He was about to ask, 'Which matters, exactly?' but he could hear Melanie's voice in his head. 'For God's sake, you're not in court now.'

Angie Bliss continued.

'*Obsessive-compulsive disorder*' – There followed the briefest of pauses, as, looking pleased with herself, she cocked her head to one side as if she were listening for something, applause, perhaps? – 'and the way it affects your relationships is, however, something that I need to approach in my own way.' She relaxed back in the chair, kicking off her gold ballerina shoes.

'As I told Rupert, I don't involve my partner in my

problems. If I have difficulties maintaining relationships it's not because of the OCD.'

The therapist was smiling at him in the manner of a fond mother watching her child playing make-believe and, disconcerted, he continued, 'I might be a little more tense because of it and that perhaps has a kick-back effect on my behaviour and I suppose one of the ways I deal with it is to keep busy, to work hard and not waste time. But all those things fall within the boundaries of normal . . .'

'I can't believe you have any difficulties picking up women.'

'What? No. Not as a rule.'

'So it's keeping them that's the problem?'

'No. No, I don't think it is, not in that way. As it happens I tend to be the one who leaves.'

The therapist clapped her slender pale hands together.

'Well, aren't we a big clever boy.'

At this point he laughed, he couldn't help it. He decided that Angie Bliss was really rather attractive although not his type; he preferred the more athletic, gamine look to the therapist's voluptuous, Pre-Raphaelite one. Again, he heard Melanie taking him to task, for being sexist, lookist and probably patronising.

'One thing leads to another and all roads, in the end, lead to the same place,' the therapist said. 'Now, wouldn't you like to find your soul-mate and settle down?'

'Of course I would.'

'Tell me what you are looking for.'

John leant back in his chair, a small smile softening his square jaw.

'Someone who is a true partner, someone who understands what I'm trying to do and who would support me in reaching my goals. Someone who had her own goals and dreams and who would appreciate *my* support in that same way. Someone to share it all with, the rewards and the struggles.' He stopped, surprised at how much he had ended up saying.

'And this Melanie isn't her, now is she?'

With a slight sigh he said, 'I thought she might have been.'

'But now you know better?'

He raised his chin.

'Not necessarily.'

'Fine. You're in denial. We can work with that.' She paused and giggled behind a slender hand. 'De-nial is a river in Egypt.'

He looked at her.

'Oh. Right. Yes.' He laughed politely.

'Does she need to be beautiful, this woman, your ideal?' the therapist asked in the alert yet efficient voice of a shop assistant offering to pick out your perfect suit.

'Beautiful? No, not really. It would be nice if she was good-looking, obviously. And I think enthusiasm is vital, passion – for something; it almost doesn't matter what. I don't like blasé or passivity. I like women who are self-sufficient, who don't wait for me to make all the decisions. Someone who likes challenges and won't stagnate.' He paused to find Angie Bliss smiling and nodding her approval. Next she'll stick a gold star next to my notes, he thought, not displeased. Melanie called him a try-hard. She was right, as it happened.

'So, if we find you such a woman then you might do better?'

'I was not aware that I had signed up to a dating agency. Anyway, I am still in a relationship.'

'OK, OK.' The therapist raised both hands in the air. 'But basically you don't want to face up to the gaping void in your life so you're here fussing about this O . . . OCD.'

'I'm fussing over it, as you call it, because I was encouraged to do so by your predecessor and because it's a pain, a real pain. I don't need the distraction. What I do need is to find a way of being able to give one hundred per cent to whatever I'm doing without these ridiculous, I mean really *ridiculous*, thoughts.'

'But there's no problem sexually?'

'No, I've told you that already.' He forgot about feeling awkward as he gazed into her eyes that were the turquoise of a Caribbean sea. He said, hesitating at first, 'At least, there never used to be a problem but I suppose that lately . . . well, it could be better. I just put it down to the other problems we're having at the moment. I'm pretty confident that it's not a, well a . . . medical problem.'

'Now that *is* a relief, isn't it? Again I'm sure' – she paused and looked him up and down – 'I'm sure,' she said again, 'that you will have no problems once you're with the right woman. Now, let's see . . . yes, your mother: would you say she was possessive when you grew up and that this might have something to do with your problems in forming intimate, long-lasting relationships?'

'I suppose she was a bit possessive, yes, but that's under-standable as it was just the two of us. My father left before I was born. He died not long afterwards. Anyway, I got the impression from Rupert that the key to OCD lies in the simple fact of brain chemistry rather than in childhood experiences and such things. He did mention Prozac or some other SSRI.'

Angie Bliss's eyes turned the colour of thunder clouds.

'Well, if you know so much about it why are you here seeing me? And I certainly would not recommend Prozac.

Have you not heard about the side-effects? Reduction of sex drive, inability to climax. Would you like to add those to your list of problems?' Then she smiled again and her amazing eyes softened to dove-grey. 'I'm not saying that Rupert is wrong, only that opinion is divided. I would say that the very latest findings suggest that . . .' She frowned and seemed to search for a word. 'Yes, that regression therapy can be helpful . . . in some cases. That means we delve into your past –'

'– Subconscious,' John filled in. He had to remind himself again that the woman sitting opposite him was a renowned expert in her field.

'But first we'll just regress via your conscious,' Angie Bliss said and there was renewed authority in her voice. 'Now, your childhood.'

'My childhood,' John Sterling said. 'There's nothing much to tell. Nothing I haven't been through with Rupert already.'

Angie Bliss frowned.

'Well, I want to hear it for myself. And don't roll your eyes. How old are you, twelve?'

John pulled a face.

'There's honestly not much to tell. I was born, on time more or less, so I believe, healthy and wanted.'

'Your father didn't want you.'

John's amiable smile remained in place but his voice was icy.

'What makes you say that?'

'He left before you were born. I would say that was a fair indication that he was not very keen on the idea of you.'

John coloured slightly but his voice was as controlled as ever when he replied, 'All right, so maybe I was wanted by one instead of the more customary two parents. And yes, there was a time that this bothered me. But I was fortunate in other things so in the end it seemed like rather a petty concern. Then again, we humans distinguish ourselves by our petty concerns, don't you agree, whereas the other animals confine their fretting to the real stuff: how to get fed, how to get laid, how to stay alive.' He paused and looked at his watch. 'Oh dear, my hour is up.'

'That's all right. No hurry.'

But John was already on his way to the door.

'I'm sure you have other people to see?'

'So I do.' Angie Bliss swivelled the chair round so that her back was turned. 'I've got you down for the same time next week.'

John was about to make some excuse but as he met the therapist's azure gaze he found himself nodding and saying, 'Yes, absolutely.'

On his way out, a good-looking young boy standing by the water cooler stopped him and asked in a faint American accent, 'She free?'

John nodded.

'Is she any good?'

'I can't really tell.'

'That figures,' the boy said. 'I'd give her another go, though.'

'Would you now?' John said. He smiled. 'Maybe I shall too then.'

Rebecca

I SLEPT WELL IN my new flat and awoke refreshed. I had put on some weight. 'You look really well,' my friends told me. 'Relaxed, more your old self.'

Coco agreed.

That cowed look is just so last year.

And yet.

And yet what? Coco snapped. *What's there to and yet about? You're free of the bastard.*

Don't call him a bastard.

What would you like me to call him?

I thought about it.

Oh I don't know, just go away.

'What do you mean and yet?' Matilda asked.

We were sitting at the kitchen table; through the window I watched a pale autumn sun setting behind Albert Bridge.

'Last week you were telling everyone that you'd never been more content. You said you woke every morning while the builders were in thanking God that you weren't having to cope with Dominic going ballistic at every little thing, especially when they broke the teapot. The freedom, you said, not answering to anyone: you loved it. The relief, you said, of not being watched and harangued at every turn. What's changed?'

I pushed one of the mugs of tea across the table top towards her and picked up the plate.

'Iced bun?'

'Don't change the topic,' Matilda said.

'OK. I'm sorry. And I don't suppose it's him I miss, not exactly. But I miss *something*. Maybe it's my dreams. The future is like a doily with all these cut-outs: the ski holiday planned for the new year, the weekends with his friends in the Cotswolds, his nephew's wedding in France. I mean it's not as if I can't travel without him, it's just, oh I'm not sure what the issue is exactly other than that I feel so very sad.'

'That's understandable,' Matilda said, her hand hovering above the plate of sticky buns, retreating then swooping down like a bird of prey. She bit into the bun, eating fast as if that way there would be fewer calories. 'But you will find someone else eventually, someone nice even.'

'That's part of the sadness, I reckon. I might well find someone, but then what do I do with him? Sleep with him, yes. And then what? Because eventually it would end the way it always does, in disillusionment and ugly strife.'

'Come on, it doesn't *have* to be like that.'

I sighed.

'I wish I could believe that. I can't work, Matilda. I can't go on writing my nice books about nice people meeting other nice people and falling in love and living happily ever after. From where I am now I simply can't imagine how I ever could. It all seems so long ago. But without my work I feel naked and chilly to the bone. No, worse, I feel pointless. I have no purpose. I can't live without purpose. I wonder if that's what you'd feel if you had lived all your life in Soviet Russia or Communist Poland when the whole idea of Communism collapsed? I've often wondered what it must have been like. There you are, having worked and sacrificed and suffered all in the belief that you were serving a higher purpose, creating Utopia for your children and their children –'

'Did anyone actually think that?'

'I think so. And then one day you're told that actually it was all a huge mistake and, as if that's not bad enough, you're supposed to go out there and dance around the square or hacked-down wall or whatever, celebrating the fact that your entire life's been a sham.'

'I'm not sure I would equate romance with Communism.'

At midnight the phone went.

'I know I promised not to call but, darling, I miss you.'

I sat up against the pillows.

'Dominic.'

'I'm sorry, did I wake you?'

'Yes, sort of. But it's all right.'

'*I'm* not all right,' he said. 'I know it serves me right. I've been a pig. I don't deserve you but, darling, I'm just lost without you.' His voice was low and intimate. It was the voice of a lover.

I didn't know what to say so I said nothing.

He continued, 'Darling, don't you miss me even a little bit?'

'Yes.' And with that yes I stepped back into my life and the time away seemed just like a dream.

I opened the door and watched him stride up the stairs. At the sight of me he paused then he smiled, penitent, jubilant, his arms wide open to clasp me to him.

Coco appeared in front of me frenetically rowing a lifeboat, calling my name. I turned my back on him and led Dominic inside. I opened a bottle of red wine. I wasn't sure why I did that when I knew perfectly well that he preferred white.

He looked at the red liquid as he took the glass from me. 'Red. Very nice. Thanks, darling.'

He stayed the night in my bed. Coco spent the night locked in the walk-in-wardrobe.

'It's like coming home,' Dominic said after we had made love again the next morning. 'Oh my darling. Oh my love, my life.'

Back in the early days he used to whisper those words and I had felt like a special being, anointed by love. I wanted to feel that way again. I tried hard. But instead I felt as if I were watching a love scene in the company of my mother.

As it was Saturday, I suggested we visit the local farmers' market. I was in two minds about those markets. I enjoyed the experience of walking between the stalls with a hand-woven basket in the crook of my arm. I liked the open air and the way the other shoppers bustled around smiling instead of shuffling and shoving their way along crowded supermarket aisles. Yet in some way I felt I was just a victim of another trend. 'Darling, how lovely, shit-covered eggs straight from the hen's bottom.' And, 'Unpasteurised cheese with real flies, how marvellously geniune.'

As a rule I valued solitude, but weekends on my own had made me feel lonely. Walking around the market with Dominic I enjoyed being part of a couple again, shopping for lunch for two, handing him a taster of cheese and discussing how much was needed of the Beaufort and how much of the Stilton. Other than the cheese we bought a couple of dressed crabs, which led me to wonder, as always, why a shellfish broken into its constituent parts was known as 'dressed'. As usual, I decided not to ask. I had a feeling there was an obvious answer that everyone knew but me.

Dominic disappeared only to return a few minutes later with a bunch of red roses.

'Roses for a rose,' he said, laughing at his cheesy joke, and all around us people were smiling. Babies in prams, puppies and lovers were all part of a delightful breed adored by, well, by most people, other than those who found the sight of any of these quite sick-making.

On our way home we passed the Bathroom Shop.

I stopped.

'I need one of those shelf things you put across the bath tub for soaps and sponges and stuff,' I said. 'Do you mind?'

He said he would wait outside in the fresh air.

'Leave the basket with me,' he added.

Inside there were several of those shelves to choose from. There was also an entire section with soaps and one with soap dishes and toothbrush-holders and such like. I went to the door and signalled to Dominic to join me but he shook his head and held up a lit cigarette. Following a very interesting discussion with the shop assistant about soap versus gels I was given two samples of each kind. I then bought a soap dish, a rose-scented soap and a honeysuckle shower-gel.

Outside Dominic was finishing a cigarette. He glared at me as he flicked the butt to the ground.

'Have you no idea of time?'

'Why didn't you come inside? There were some lovely things.'

'You know I don't share your love of shopping. Anyway, I had this.' He picked up the basket and the bags from around his feet. 'So can we go now? I'm cold and I'm hungry.'

'I'm sorry,' I said as I tried to relieve him of the basket. 'They were just so nice in there and had such nice —'

'You said.' He glanced at the small bag in my hand. 'So did you get the bath-tub shelf, or whatever you call it?'

I looked down at the bag myself.

'No, no, I didn't.' I laughed. 'Silly me.'

He sighed, a sigh so deep it could be heard above the roaring traffic on Chelsea Bridge Road.

Once we had eaten the crab and cheeses Dominic was in a better mood.

Looking around him he said, 'You really have done well with this place, darling.' He sat down next to me on the sofa with his mug of coffee. 'I feel really at home.'

My smile froze. My back stiffened and I put my mug down on the table.

Dominic leant back against the cushions with an air of belonging.

Was that banging I heard from my bedroom? One final smash and Coco came bounding past, out of breath and with his hair in disarray, carrying a half-closed suitcase with a pair of striped trouser-legs trailing the ground.

Save yourself while you can, he called over his shoulders.

Dominic opened his eyes and smiled fuzzily at me.

'Yes, I really feel at home here.'

I got to my feet.

'I have to go out now,' I told Dominic. 'I'll lock up behind you, shall I?'

*　　*　　*

When I saw Charlotte Jessop next I was anxious to find out whether she believed that my decision to break up with Dominic and not to rekindle our relationship might be a result, not of logic or even the dictates of the heart, but because of the clown.

'What do *you* think?' Charlotte Jessop asked.

'My gut instinct tells me that it's common sense and self-preservation kicking in at long last. But then again, is it just coincidence that Coco reappeared during this time?'

'I would like you to consider the possibility that Coco's reappearance was a necessary component in the process of you freeing yourself from what was, in fact, a textbook toxic relationship.'

'You mean he's some sort of enabler?' Like most clowns there was nothing Coco liked better than to be taken seriously.

Right now he was sitting on a stool in the corner of the room, his stripy legs crossed, a pair of spectacles perched on his red nose, and as Charlotte and I spoke he rested his chin in his hand and nodded.

'As long as we are both clear that he is simply another facet of your personality, another side of your internal dialogue,' Charlotte said.

I smiled and nodded.

'Of course.'

It was the end of the session and as I walked out of the room Coco followed me, crowing three times and hissing, *Judas*.

The cockerel crowed three times to Peter, not Judas, I told him. *And, Coco, you are an imaginary clown*, not *the Messiah*.

There, I thought, Charlotte Jessop had nothing to worry about on my account.

At lunch later on that day, Bridget said in a voice elongated with thought, 'You really have been very clever, Geraldine.'

'How do you mean, I've been clever?'

'Because you have it all before you to enjoy . . . for the third time: new love, sexual excitement, setting up a home together. It's as if you are living a romantic groundhog day.'

I didn't know Bridget's husband's cousin very well but I remembered Angel-face telling me that she had recently got married again. It was hard not to notice that, at fifty-one, the same age as Bridget, Geraldine looked much younger. Not because she was especially unlined, although she did have a good complexion, but because of the light in her eyes, the easy laughter, the languid movements, which all spoke of a woman who had woken up next to her lover that morning. Bridget, on the other hand, had woken up next to her very nice decent husband of almost thirty years. As for myself, I exuded the nervous energy of someone in turmoil. I had noticed that morning that this was not so good for the complexion.

'Do you think Robert Mugabe is at peace with himself?' I asked. 'There he is, tyrant of the year, destroying his country, impoverishing and imprisoning his people, torturing his opponents and yet, and yet he has the most incredible skin for a man in his mid-eighties.'

The other two ignored me; rightly so, I supposed.

Geraldine said, 'But I always envy *you*, Bridget. There's something intensely romantic about a lasting love affair.'

'I wouldn't say that your cousin and I are in the throes of a love affair; I mean I can't believe that anyone is after thirty years, other than in books.' As she said 'books' she gave a perfunctory nod in my direction. 'But we do get on very well; I mean I wouldn't change him. OK, perhaps for George Clooney. No, we rub along very well, we really do. But . . . well, I suppose it would be a more unusual couple than Neil and I who could still surprise each other at this stage. So it's predictable. We know the answers to each other. That's comfortable and secure, but . . .' Bridget's voice trailed off.

'. . . The problem is, it's the questions that are so exciting,' I said.

'Are you working on a new book?' Geraldine asked.

I nodded.

'Trying to.'

'Oh but you must hurry up and finish it. I'm such a fan. You know it's partly through reading you that I plucked up the courage to get out of my first marriage. You feel very lonely when you're unhappy, don't you? And I was unhappy. Not because Charles was nasty, or a bully like your ex-boyfriend . . . no' – she raised her hand to stop me from speaking – 'you don't have to say anything. As I said before, Bridget's told me everything. No, Charles was, *is*, a nice man, and he's the father of my children, but it wasn't right. For a long time it wasn't right. I felt such a lack at the very centre of my life, a big void where there should be warmth and comradeship and sex . . . and your books, well, they put into words what it was that was missing; it's as simple as that.'

'Oh my God,' I said.

'What?'

'It makes me feel responsible to think that someone made such an important decision based partly on my books.'

'You put your stories out there in the public domain for people to read,' Bridget said. 'Of course you influence people.'

'Proust influences people,' I said.

Geraldine, who was a very pretty woman with her creamy complexion, black hair and bright blue eyes, beamed a smile at me.

'I'm happy now, though.' She grew serious. 'But one must never forget how hard a divorce is for everyone involved, children in particular. My three have come out of it all in pretty good shape but there was a lot of heartache along the way. I have to ask myself if it's been worth it, causing such pain and upheaval.'

Looking at the light in her eyes and the way her lips turned up at the corners even when she was serious, I said, 'Do you, though, do you really ask yourself that?' Charlotte Jessop had told me that being forthright was not the same as being rude. I wasn't sure that this was true but I felt that paying a hundred pounds an hour to ignore someone's advice was just plain foolish.

It seemed the therapist was right because Geraldine did not take offence, instead she thought for a moment before saying, 'No, that's the thing, I don't. I *am* genuinely sorry for the pain I've caused and it's been pretty hard for me too. In fact at times it's been very hard, but if you asked me if I'd do it all again, I'm afraid the answer would be yes. Which, no doubt, means I'll go to hell.' Speaking of hell she turned to me. 'What about you, Rebecca? Any regrets?'

The other day I had read an interview with a famous actress, who lived off the land at her huge ranch somewhere in the US. When she wasn't cultivating her vegetable garden she rode, bareback, no doubt, through the wilderness or hiked the eight miles to the nearest small town. She had said, 'Regret is a completely wasted emotion.' I lived off takeouts and walked on tarmac and my life was definitely too short for all the regrets I was beginning to harbour.

'Regrets,' I said. 'Now and then.'

Bridget went into her kitchen and fetched the main course.

While she was away I said to Geraldine, 'Just after Zoe got engaged, I took her out for lunch and I'm afraid I upset her. She was worried about things, mainly about the chances of her marriage, actually any marriage, lasting more than a few years. She turned to me for reassurance, because of my books, and I let her down.'

Geraldine nodded.

'I heard about that. But she's a grown woman, who makes her own decisions, so you shouldn't feel responsible.'

'I do, though. But the other day I had an idea of how I could make things better. Instead of inventing stories about happily ever after, I would go out and find some real-life examples, talk to people who had made a really good go of it and write down their stories for Angel-face to read and be inspired by. *Recipes for a Happy Marriage: A Small Book of Inspiration*. Something like that. If it works I might even show it to my publisher.'

'What a good idea.' Bridget had reappeared with a laden dish. 'No, I mean it. Almost everything you read these days that purports to be real life is unrelentingly miserable: miserable marriages, miserable childhoods. No, I really think it's a wonderful idea and something that will be a real help and inspiration to Zoe.'

Basking in the approval (it had been a while), I helped myself to two lamb chops from the dish held out to me.

'Now all I need to do is find some happy couples.'

I got my chance a few days later. I was being interviewed for an Internet book page and the journalist, Nick Fuller, was wearing a wedding band and looked old enough to have been married for a good ten years. He had a sleek, contented look about him and he referred to his children on a couple of occasions. We spent quite some time on the interview itself and as darkness fell outside and the street lights were reflected in the river I opened a bottle of wine.

'I enjoyed your book,' he said. 'To be honest, I didn't expect it to be my thing but I enjoyed it. It's cheery.'

'Off the record and all that,' I said, 'I haven't really lived the way I preach. I told myself that I had, but I was deceiving myself, and others, including my newly engaged god-daughter. Not good. So I've set myself a task: I'm going to find ten happily married people whose stories I will write down and give to my god-daughter as a pre-wedding present to inspire and encourage her.' I paused and glanced meaningfully at his wedding band. 'You're married.'

He gave a joyless bark of a laugh and twirled the ring.

'Force of habit.'

'No! You're not serious? You're meant to be my first selected-at-random happily married person.'

'Sorry, no can do.'

'Damn,' I said, pouring us each another glass of wine. 'Damn, damn, damn.'

'I'm sorry,' Nick Fuller said again.

I sighed.

'What happened?'

'God, I don't know. Women, I suppose. It's this chimera thing.'

I laughed.

'Being a fire-breathing monster – part lion, part goat, part serpent? You're sure you weren't thinking of a chameleon?'

He grinned.

'Probably. Whichever, it's bloody confusing.'

There was a Lion, a Serpent and a Goat . . .

We met at work, a local paper in North London. Vicky was PA to the editor and I was a reporter. I was living with someone at the time but we weren't happy. Vicky was bright and pretty and funny, up for anything from white-water rafting to antique-hunting. And she seemed to really get me. She even liked my collection of cartoons – I'm not talking comic books here but framed pictures. We laughed at the same jokes, liked the same books and films; it was as if we really had that soul-mate thing going on. We started talking about having kids, in the abstract at first, and she said she wanted them but not so much that it was a deal-breaker if I didn't. So I told her I didn't. I just don't have the paternal gene, I guess, and I thought the responsible thing was to make that clear from the outset. And she was cool about it, saying how it was her idea of hell to spend her weekends picnicking in Battersea Park with a baby in a Baby Björn sling.

As our relationship developed she didn't give any indication of having changed her mind about having kids; in fact if anything she seemed even more against the idea. There was one time we were in a country pub and suddenly there was braying and crashing and banging and this group arrived: daddies in Barbours and yummy bloody mummies clunking past our table with pushchairs and bottles and wellington boots shaped like frogs, the whole catastrophe, and within minutes a peaceful Sunday lunch had turned into open day at kindergarten. You know the kind of thing. Try saying something like, 'Please could you tell the little guy that if he has to scream could he maybe do it a little less piercingly or else go outside?' or, 'Yes I do mind junior having his nappy changed on the table next to me while I'm trying to enjoy my mussels,' and you might as well have been dining on hamster fritters the way they react. Vicky and I completely agreed that these people symbolised everything we didn't want to be.

Anyway, we got married and no more than six months later I had the first intimation of what was to come. It was Sunday afternoon in London: July, warm but not hot, hazy sunshine, lazy side-streets and all the residents at the pub or in the country. We'd had lunch at this French fish restaurant around the corner from where we lived and we were walking back home, my arm round her shoulders. I was thinking sex.

She snapped to a halt then retreated a couple of steps, pulling me with her.

'Oh look, how cute. Isn't that just totally adorable?' She was pointing at a shop window filled with baby clothes.

'Very nice,' I said. I reckoned there was some godchild or niece having a birthday but that wasn't it at all.

She just stood in front of that shop window looking straight at it but with a faraway look in her eyes. When finally she decided to walk on she was really quiet. We'd had a fair amount to drink and white wine in particular could make her weepy or a bit aggressive so I decided that was all it was.

We got home and I tried to jolly her up.

Then I said, 'Let's go to bed.'

And she turned on me. Suddenly I'm a sex addict, juvenile, irresponsible, refusing to grow up. I didn't make things better by saying that what she needed was a good fuck. I know that that makes me sound like the stereotypical crass insensitive male but usually she liked that kind of banter. It was one of the really good things between us: she liked that side of things as much as I did. Or she said she did. Now I wonder if that was all an act too.

Anyway, she calmed down, looking at me in this superior pitying way as if I'm a scruffy schoolboy she's found with his hand down his trousers.

'Have you ever thought, even for a moment, about what the sex act is all about?'

'Well, there's a question,' I said, as I reckoned that whatever answer I gave would be the wrong one.

'Procreation,' she says. 'It's for making babies.'

A year later Eddie was born. And I was happy. It wasn't what I had planned but when he arrived of course I loved him. And Vicky was really happy, as if this, having Eddie, was what she had been waiting for all her life. So for a year or so everything was good. And I'm not one of these pathetic guys who gets jealous when his wife's attention goes to the kid. I mean obviously the baby has to come first. But with Vicky it was as if she was becoming a different woman. This new Vicky lived on Planet Baby and there was room for Eddie and Eddie's little friends and their mothers and her mother and the whole bloody playschool parent committee but not for me or for any of the things we used to like to do together. If I suggested we get her mother to look after the baby while we had an evening out or, dare I say, went away for a few days, just the two of us, she would look at me as if I had asked her if we could have a threesome with her best friend.

My mother told me it was natural: Eddie was still a baby after all and Vicky would get back to normal eventually. And I didn't need anyone else to tell me she was a great mother. So when she suggested another baby I thought we might as well get that stage over with in one go, more or less. And obviously it would be great for Eddie to have a little brother or sister. Ben was born and I spent more time with Eddie because Vicky was busy with the new baby, so we bonded and I really enjoyed the whole experience. And this time I knew what to expect so I just got into the whole family thing and if I wanted to do something else, like catch an exhibition or something, I did it on my own.

For our fifth wedding anniversary I booked a trip to Paris. Not very original but we'd never actually been to Paris together. And it was not too far so we could be away for just a couple of days. I had it all organised, the boys staying with my mother, the neighbour feeding the cat, so that there could be no suggestion that I assumed she could just drop everything and take off.

When I told her she seemed pleased. We got on the plane and she started asking me if I had told my mother how Eddie had no road sense and that Ben could only eat the white of the egg and so on. I told her we had written the list of instructions together and that last time I checked my mother could both read and write, quite apart from the fact that she had brought up three healthy, well-adjusted children. But Vicky just pursed her lips and I noticed this little double chin she'd developed. And before you say anything, I'm not that shallow. I accept that a woman's body changes with childbirth and I had no problems with the stretch marks and the varicose veins or the weight gain; I realise she went through all of that for the two of us. Of course a busy mother doesn't have time to look like a centrefold but couldn't she just make an effort now and then, for me? A bit of lipstick, a skirt and some heels, just to show I was maybe worth it.

We sat there on the plane, not talking, and I hated her. I hated her smug complacency, the single black hair that grew from a mole on her neck that she always forgot to pluck, hated her wash-and-go crop and the fact that she thought baggy brown cords and a sweater with sheep on was a nice outfit to go to Paris in. Some men might think all that's great: a woman who doesn't waste hours in the bathroom or hundreds of pounds on clothes and shoes and stuff. But you see, I wouldn't have minded that. I've always had a soft spot for high-maintenance women. Vicky was one of those when we first met. It probably makes me a complete Neanderthal but part of me always fancied being that guy in a 1950s comedy, shaking his head in mock exasperation as his wife comes home looking cute and guilty with her arms full of bags and boxes. Just so I can take her in my arms and tell her she deserves it all and that I love her looking so pretty.

Then I felt guilty so I was extra nice and she cheered up a bit until the pilot announced that we were about to land. She started crying and when I asked her what the matter was she said she missed the boys. And I sympathised, but I have to admit I was pretty hurt as well. Sometimes I think women believe they have a monopoly on feelings. Anyway, we arrived at our hotel, which was bijou and romantic, and we had an OK evening and an OK day the next day but it was obvious she was fretting so we changed our flights and came back home a day early.

Life went on as before. Vicky agreed that two kids were enough, especially as we wanted to educate them privately. So when both boys were at school full-time I suggested she might like to go back to work. It'd be a great help. And she got really angry. What kind of father was I? Did I want our children to be latch-key kids? And all the time she had this aura, like she was the sacred keeper of the offspring. I argued that she could work part-time or we could get an au pair and she accused me of being obsessed with money. I told her too right I was, with an eighty per cent mortgage and school fees to pay for.

I felt I had gone along with pretty well everything. The kids, the estate car, the move out of London and the commute – but still I was the bad guy.

It all came to a head one evening. She was always telling me I should be home in time to read the boys a story. I could make that on a Friday but the rest of the time it was not an option. While we were living in London, which incidentally is where I had wanted us to remain, I could be home by seven-thirty most of the time but with an hour and a half commute it just wasn't possible. Anyway, I had received an invitation to the preview of this really interesting exhibition and of course I hadn't been able to make it, rushing to catch the early train instead.

But this evening, at the end of a really tough week, I walked past the gallery and saw that it was the last day. I decided to go in. I just thought, why the hell shouldn't I? Why shouldn't I spend some time on something just for me, nothing to do with work or Vicky or even the kids but just for me? I mean Vicky had 'me' time every Wednesday night but apparently my 'me' time was all day every day at work.

OK, so I'm getting whingey, but that's how I felt: hard done by and put-upon.

Anyway, this exhibition . . . one of the artists was actually there and we got talking and it turned out we both liked these two really obscure French cartoonists. I was really enjoying myself talking to this guy. I told him about my collection and he asked if I had any of his; I told him they were a little out of my league. Before I know it he's gone off to have a word with the gallery owner and then they come out and offer me one that I had been admiring for what amounted to half-price.

The train was packed, the carriage smelling of the usual mix of BO and cheese-and-onion Pringles but, as I stood there with this small package under my arm, I actually felt happy.

I continued to feel good right through the saga of how the boys were getting naughty, probably in protest at not seeing their father enough, and how the tumble dryer had broken down again, which was just perfect, wasn't it, with the weather being the way it was and Ben having started to wet the bed again, and did I have any idea how tough it could be being at home all day with young kids and no adult conversation or outside stimulants?

I did sympathise, I really did, which is partly why I had suggested she go back to work.

Anyway, we were about to eat and I brought in the picture to show her, and she lost it. How could I tell her to go back to work because we needed the money and then go and spend a fortune on a bloody cartoon? And how come I had time to mooch around galleries but couldn't make it home in time to say goodnight to my own children?

I tried to explain that I had missed the train anyway – which was true, and that the picture was practically a gift.

'And I thought you'd be pleased: you've always liked my cartoons.'

I tell you, she gave this complete pantomime-villain laugh, tossing her head and flashing her eyes.

'Like them?! I can't stand them. Never could. God, if you want to know what I really think, they're a juvenile waste of space and money and if I had my way I'd get rid of every last one of them.' With that she leapt forward and grabbed the picture from my hands, smashing it against the edge of the sink, breaking the glass and gashing the actual paper.

I remember kneeling on the floor picking up the broken glass. Then I heard Eddie calling down to us, asking what was happening. The speed with which Vicky turned from gimlet-eyed harridan to soft mummy as she moved to the bottom of the stairs and called back that everything was fine, silly old Daddy had just dropped a glass was extraordinary. And I watched her, her broad back and low-slung arse in those goddamn awful corduroy trousers, and listened as she spilled out her convenient little lies. I thought, is that all she does, to all of us, lie? She turned back and walked right up to me, this triumphant little look on her face. I could count the flakes of dandruff at her temples, just where some grey was coming through. I took my picture and brought it with me up to the spare room.

Of course we didn't split over that. We muddled along for a while. Then I had an affair with a woman at work. It wasn't that serious for either of us but Vicky found out. Some note of Sarah's in the pocket of my suit jacket, the usual cliché. Vicky confronted me and I realised that she wasn't actually that upset; if anything she seemed almost gratified. She stood there, arms folded across her chest, telling me what I was jeopardising: two fabulous boys, a great wife and mother, our beautiful home. Then she listed her conditions for forgiving me. I would make sure 'the Trollop' left the office. I would have to start playing a 'proper part' in family life and, when I pointed out that paying the mortgage and the school fees is playing quite a big part, she told me I was a bloody idiot if I thought that was what mattered in life. The list went on and I listened and then, when she'd finally finished, I went upstairs and packed my bags.

Rebecca

`I FEEL SO ROOTLESS,´ I said to Charlotte Jessop at our next session, 'like a priest who's lost his faith. The framework to my entire existence is crumbling and I barely know who I am.' I brought out the printed version of the Internet interview and handed it to her. 'I read this and I ask, who is this person?'

Nick Fuller meets Rebecca Finch

I don't know what I had expected when I turned up for my interview with our new Queen of Romantic Fiction. A floaty Kate Bush, perhaps? Or a mature lady in florals reclining on a couch surrounded by yapping Pekes? But the woman greeting me at the door to her Central London flat looks as if she would be more at home in a Left Bank café worshipping at the feet of Jean-Paul Sartre. Rebecca Finch is tall and slender, dressed in black cigarette pants and a fitted black polo-neck. Her light-brown hair, lustrous and wavy, is pulled back into a careless plait and her hazel eyes, slanting slightly upwards at the outer corners, are emphasised by black eye-liner. I notice she is barefoot and that her toenails are painted a bright red to match her lips.

Nor is her home what I had expected. Airy and large with huge, curtainless windows facing the river; there are no flowery chintzes in sight. Instead what I find is an eclectic mix of old and modern. The furnishing is sparse but there's nothing minimalist about the colours, vibrant greens and cornflower-blues mixed with – yes, here we have it at last – some pink. When I comment on the colour she laughs – the fine mesh of lines around her almond-shaped eyes is the only giveaway that she has turned forty – and tells me pink is a colour that makes her happy 'every time'.

Over coffee by the fire in her book-lined study I ask her if she ever has writer's block; her output is prodigious by anyone's standards.

Rebecca curls up in her large armchair and takes a sip of her coffee. She shakes her head and a glossy curl of soft brown hair escapes and falls across her pale face.

'I don't really understand writer's block,' she says. 'I see myself as a jobbing writer; I have needed to write for so long now, needed it for my sanity as well as for my financial support. At the start of my career I'd turn my hand at pretty well anything: poetry, plays, short stories, articles, anything. It's not that I find writing easy. It's just that the alternative, i.e., not writing, is a lot harder. And there's no mystique, no hanging around waiting for the muse. In my view she's about as punctual as a Hollywood starlet. To quote George Bernard Shaw, the secret of inspiration is "applying the seat of one's pants to the seat of the chair".

'I'm usually up by seven and at my desk by eight after a breakfast of Cheerios with a sliced banana and a large mug of strong sweet milky tea. I stay there until lunch, which is a sandwich and some fruit juice, while I catch up on the news. I usually go for a brisk walk across the bridge to Battersea Park, or do some shopping along the King's Road before being back at my desk, where I stay until I've reached my daily target of five printed pages.'

I waited until Charlotte had finished reading and then I said, 'That's not me.'

'It probably isn't,' the therapist said. 'These kinds of interviews are famously misleading.'

'No, I think, to be fair, I did say those things. I had to say something. I mean you can't say yes to an interview and have some poor journalist and a photographer with all that equipment slog halfway across London and then sit there and say nothing. So I said the things I would have said back when I was my old self; I had to because I really don't know who my new self is.'

'Well, that's what we're here for, isn't it? To find out.'

'You are quite sure I'm not mad, or say, psychotic?'

Charlotte Jessop just kept looking at me with a bright and interested expression, her neat head a little to one side.

Old shrink trick, Coco said. *She's waiting for you to incriminate yourself further.*

'I'm not am I, insane?'

'You don't need to ask me,' Charlotte said.

'Yes, I do. I absolutely need to ask you. I need reassurance.'

'If you already know that my reply will be reassuring then why do you need to ask the question?'

Devilishly cunning, Coco said.

I told him to remove his deerstalker hat. *Anyway, you should be wearing a red curly wig.*

I hate those wigs, Coco said. *They're common.*

'Are you talking to Coco now?'

'Not *talking* exactly.'

Charlotte just nodded and made some notes in the file on her lap.

'It's not schizophrenia, is it?'

'No. However, we have made huge advances in the treatment of that condition.'

'But I'm not schizophrenic?'

'No, you're not.'

'I'm sorry, I'm being very boring.'

'You're not here to entertain me. You have an exaggerated need to apologise and to please. We need to look at that.'

'I think I'm getting better, though, or worse, depending on which way you look at it. Sorry, I'm being muddled. Do you think I might need some medication?'

Coco's face had been looming, disembodied like the Cheshire cat's grin. At the word medication it shrank like a balloon when the air's been let out, rocketing across the room and hitting the door, where it bounced, ending up on the floor, a flat wizened version of itself.

'We should see how we get along without it,' Charlotte Jessop said.

In the corner of the room a small gloved hand rose and made a V for victory sign.

While I waited to hear from Charlotte Jessop I decided to continue my search for happy couples myself. 'Historical persons and hearsay don't count,' I explained to Bridget. 'Perhaps I should advertise in the press: "Happily married? Call embittered romantic novelist on 0207 3526 . . . etc etc."'

'I don't think Zoe is going to be fussy as to whom you chose as your examples, as long as they're real.' Pulling a face a bit like Coco's when he didn't wish to admit to feeling sad, she added, 'I don't quite understand why she doesn't feel that her father and I would do.'

'Oh children,' I said quickly. 'Their worst fear is to emulate their parents.'

'Do you think that's all it is?'

I nodded a bit too emphatically.

'I'm sure of it.'

'You could try Matilda.'

'I don't know if that particular story would impress Angelface. I mean Matilda's never made it a secret that she wasn't in love with Chris when they married.'

'I know. Leonora.'

'Leonora Baxendale?'

'Walters now. And yes, I saw her and her husband at a party last Christmas. She couldn't stop telling me about her wonderful life.'

'Won't she think it a bit odd if I call up out of the blue? "Hi, remember me, your old schoolfriend? I heard that you were happily married – care to talk about it?"'

'Don't be silly. She'll be delighted to hear from you. She asked very fondly after you. You have to understand that since you became successful people are a bit shy of you.'

The thought was gratifying.

'Do you reckon?'

'*Yes*. Let me give you her number.'

* * *

157

'You really haven't changed much at all,' Leonora said after we hugged each other hello.

'Neither have you,' I said, and it was a return nicety but a true one.

Her face, although showing a few lines around the eyes and lips, was still round and pretty and her cheeks still turned bright pink at the slightest provocation. These days her wide green eyes were not hidden beneath glasses and her thick straight hair was streaked blonde and cut short. Maybe her strong little body was a stone or so heavier, but you would always have known her from the girl she had been twenty years before.

'Sit down.' Leonora gesticulated at the rose chintz sofa. 'I'll bring us some tea.'

She returned with a tray and put it down on the coffee table before sitting down herself. She poured the tea and handed me a cup.

Smiling at me she said, 'I know about your writing. I read the first two and I must say I really enjoyed them.'

Thanking her, I suppressed the urge to ask why, if she had enjoyed the first two so much, she had not read the others, saying instead, 'Bridget didn't tell me much about what you were doing other than that you were blissfully happy, which sounds pretty satisfactory.' My voice trailed off as Leonora's smiling face assumed a peculiar look. Had I said something wrong? Should I know what she did? Maybe Bridget had told me or maybe she was well known in her field. 'I mean what better achievement than a happy marriage,' I said. 'I might have done OK professionally, but my personal life . . .'

At this point Leonora burst into tears.

'Is this some cruel joke? You were always a little different but never cruel.' She fished out a tissue from a pocket and dabbed at her eyes. 'I know I shouldn't have told Lance Cooper that you were too intense for him but goodness, Rebecca, it was a long time ago.'

'What are you talking about?'

Leonora had stopped sobbing and now she cleared her throat and poured herself some more tea.

'Coming here after all these years, tormenting me about my "happy marriage".'

'What do you mean I'm tormenting you? It seemed like such a good idea: seeing you again after all this time *and* getting another recipe for Zoe's book. Didn't Bridget tell you?'

'Bridget left a message on my answerphone saying you were doing research for your book and would call, that was all. She didn't say anything about a cookery book.'

I leant forward and took Leonora's hands in mine. The right one still clutched the damp tissue.

'We'd better start again. What's going on?'

'I'll make a fresh pot,' Leonora got to her feet.

Left on my own I looked around the room. I should have noticed right away how it bore obvious signs of upheaval. The large Chinese vase in the window alcove had been one of a pair; I remembered them from her childhood home. Above the upright piano a small watercolour landscape was trying in vain to fill the space left by a much larger frame, the outline of which could be clearly seen picked out in a paler shade of cream untouched by London grime. There were other such virgin spaces where only an empty picture hook was left in the pale expanse. Leonora had been sitting in what was, in fact, a desk chair, and the chair opposite looked like an upmarket deckchair. At first I had thought it simply a fashionable piece of furniture, I had seen something very like it at Liberty's the other day, but on closer inspection I saw it really was just a garden chair.

Leonora returned to see me studying the room.

'Division of the spoils,' she said. 'It's what happens at the end of a war and as in all wars everyone ends up the poorer.'

Another Carefree Girl

The worst thing, the thing I mind the most, is that I've lost my best friend. God, I feel so *unoriginal*; I mean my husband running off with his assistant. Trust Matthew and me to be conventional right until the bitter end.

I think I realised something was seriously wrong when he used the sat nav to drive back home from my mother's. I was talking to him, and he put his finger out – I noticed how, well, *sausagey* his fingers had become lately – and he pressed the button and punched in the route. That ridiculous computer voice came on: 'Your route of twelve miles will take you on main roads and local roads. Turn left . . .'

'Why do you need that thing?' I asked him. 'You know where you're going. You've done this route a thousand times, at least.'

And he turned to me and I'll never forget the expression in his eyes; he looked like that vile little boy Giles Hardy when he dangled my gerbil over the balcony rail.

'Because she is more interesting than you,' he said. 'She can navigate *and* she shuts up when she's got nothing to say.'

Mercifully the children were plugged into their iPods. Matthew and I had always prided ourselves on keeping a civil tone between us at all times. We had our disagreements of course, but we didn't ever see the need to descend into insults and rudeness. Well, not until then anyway.

Supper was awful. I felt a real sense of doom as I went through the motions of serving up, telling the children off for squabbling and making normal-seeming conversation. Once they were in bed I confronted him. I told him, in a calm and grown-up way, how hurt I was by his behaviour and that, now we were talking about it, I felt he had been rather off with me for some time. I reminded him of how much value we both placed on respect and good manners. I even told him, which I had sworn I wouldn't, that two of my girlfriends had said that they felt he'd been picking on me lately.

While I spoke he just sat there, leaning back in his chair looking at me as if I were a snail about to attack his hostas.

'Have you nothing to say to me?'

'No.'

'But we're talking.'

'You're talking. I'm waiting for you to finish so I can go and watch the news.'

I felt as if I were dreaming: you know, one of those quiet nightmares; no blood and guts, no being chased or beheaded, but the kind where at first everything is quite normal and then slowly your world begins to shift and change until friends have turned into enemies, your dog bites and the plants on your kitchen windowsill have all withered and died.

That's when I started to cry and the pathetic thing was that I still expected him to come over to me and put his arms round me. But he just sat there looking bored, glancing sideways at the newspaper next to him on the sofa. By now I knew I was getting hysterical; I was crying so hard I couldn't see. Then, at last, I heard him get up. I covered my face with my hands, embarrassed by what I knew I must be looking like, all puffy and snotty, with make-up running down my cheeks. Some women manage to cry prettily but I was never one of them. I waited for his touch on my shoulders, his voice saying something kind but there was nothing. He'd got up to fetch the remote. Next I heard the television being switched on for the ten o'clock news.

That was too much for me. I ran up to him, screaming I don't know what, until my throat hurt. And he just sat there looking bored and then turned the sound up. If you had looked in from outside you would have thought you'd caught us in different time zones. There I was, crying, yelling, waving my arms around. And there he was, reclining on the sofa watching the news.

I felt like a wasp in a jar.

'Get out, do you hear?' I screamed. 'Go. Leave.'

He stood up in this really leisurely way and switched off the TV.

'Fine,' he said. 'I shall.'

I followed him up to the bedroom and, when he pulled his duffel bag down from the top of the wardrobe, I started to beg. I said I was sorry and that I didn't want him to leave. He just got on with his packing, getting out his boxers and socks, things I had picked out for him, things I had washed and put away neatly in his drawers, and then he paused in front of the wardrobe as if pondering which shirts to pack. I stopped begging and crying then. Instead I sat down on the bed, quite calm all of a sudden, thinking, how can I get this runaway train to stop? No more games, I told myself. This is deadly serious.

'You can't go,' I said finally, as he zipped up his bag, the sound like the very fabric of my life ripping.

'Yes, I can.' He picked up the bag, slinging it over his shoulders like a boy off on an adventure.

'Wait.'

He paused in the doorway.

'Yes?'

'What about the children? What shall I tell them?'

He thought for a moment before saying, 'Tell them I've had to go away for a few days. That'll do until we've had a chance to work out the arrangements.'

'What do you mean *arrangements*?' I followed him down the stairs and into the hallway, pushing past him and barring his way to the front door. 'Why are you doing this?'

'You told me to.'

I couldn't help it but I raised my voice again.

'You never bloody do what I tell you so why do you have to now?'

He put his bag down and I closed my eyes with relief.

'I've been wanting out for some time.'

I snapped my eyes open.

'What did you say?'

He sighed.

'I said I've been wanting out for some time.' He glanced at his watch.

'My God, you're bored.' And I sank down on the floor.

How had this happened? The man who had once stood with me in front of the altar – in a morning suit that was slightly too large as if his mother had got it for him to grow into – swearing eternal love, the man who had looked at me as if I were a Ferrari gift-wrapped in a *Playboy* magazine was now watching me as I whimpered at his feet and he was *bored*.

'I've met someone,' he said. Then he smiled, *smiled*. 'I'm in love.'

I laboured to my feet like an old woman with arthritic knees.

'You've met someone? You're in love?'

'Mandy is fun.' He said her name as if it tasted of honey.

'Mandy.' To me it tasted of charcoal.

He looked down at me and his smile was almost kind.

'Do you remember fun, Leonora?'

'I remember fun.' I grabbed hold of his lapels. 'I thought we were having fun.'

He looked down at my hands still holding on to his jacket and his gaze held a hint of distaste.

I dropped my hands.

'I thought *we* had fun,' I repeated, but my voice barely carried.

'It might have been fun for you, Leonora, but not for me. In fact, it hasn't been fun for a long time. Mandy' – there was that faint pause again while he tasted each letter of her name – 'she's interested in everything. She's interested in *me*. Think about it, Leonora, when was the last time you actually asked me about me?' His voice had assumed a whiney note. 'With you it's either the kids or the hot-water tank or your mother or the bloody cats.'

I looked up.

'The kids? Of course I talk about the kids. They're ours. They're the most important thing we have. Don't you like talking about them? Don't you like coming home and being filled in on all the stuff that's been happening in their lives?'

'Of course I do. But not to the exclusion of everything else. When we first met you were a really interesting person to talk to. You were full of plans and enthusiasm for life, life outside our own tiny little world. But these days – God forbid I should suggest we go off on holiday, just the two of us. Even when I try to do something really nice, like for your fortieth, you manage to turn everything into a problem. You would have thought that a safari in Tanzania would be considered quite a treat but not for you, oh no. For weeks before we left you talked, not about what we might do and see on our trip but whether or not your mother really was capable of judging whether the twins were actually unwell or just faking it before double maths. And were we being mean not taking them, especially as Andrew was so keen on animals. God, you never bloody stopped.' He arranged his face in a look I think he felt was mine and made his voice all mimsy: ' "Maybe we should have booked separate flights? I mean if there's an accident they've lost us both." "Do you think Mother will remember to double-lock at night? What if we have an accident out there? What if we need a blood transfusion? We could get infected." Jesus, Leonora, what happened to you?'

Suddenly I felt angry and as I got angry I grew calmer.

'What happened? Well, let me see. We decided to have children. We had Andrew and two years later we had the twins. *You* suggested I give up work as we were paying the nanny almost half our combined earnings. And I, silly trusting fool that I was, agreed although I was actually further on in my career than you were. I pushed prams and put plasters on scraped knees. I sewed in nametapes and grew increasingly proficient at maths as I helped them with their homework. I cooked and I cleaned and I cheered on the sidelines and put ribbons in glossy ponytails. I wrapped parcels and booked magicians, I walked in the park. I listened and I admonished and I praised. Yes, that's what happened: I gave birth to your children and I looked after them.'

Never confront a man with the truth; it makes him run for cover.

'I don't need to listen to this,' he said, picking up his bag and pushing past me to the door. 'I'll come round at the weekend to get some more stuff.'

My husband walked out on me and on the way he trampled our past underfoot. I stood there wondering how I could have got it so wrong. All those years I had believed that we were pulling in the same direction: building a home, creating a family. Of course we had had our bad patches, what married couples don't? But mostly it had been good, had it not? And fun. But the fun he was talking about was not the same. He meant free-and-easy fun. Nappy-free fun. The kind of fun you can have when you don't have to express milk every time you go out together for more than two hours, the kind that does not involve being back in time to take the babysitter home. The kind when you can get pissed on Saturday night and lie in on Sunday and then make hangover love. The kind of fun you had when you did not give a damn about anyone or anything but yourselves.

How could he? How could he ignore the happy times? The twins' first day of school, the two of them in their uniforms. They were so filled with the importance of the occasion they might have been taking mass. Christmas morning being woken by excited voices shout-whispering, telling each other to be quiet. Teaching them all to ski. Taking them to dinner in a proper restaurant for the first time. Had that not been fun? The greatest fun. Apparently not, not for him.

That was six months ago, just after I saw Bridget and prattled on about how happy I was. He's still with Mandy. She's pregnant and, I'm told, about to go on maternity leave. I almost feel sorry for her now. She has yet to learn that this is what men do: they fall in love with a carefree girl with killer heels and red lipstick, a girl who loves fun and change and adventure. They marry her and tell her they like her best when she's in her jeans and her face is scrubbed clean of make-up. They make her pregnant. And then, when this woman, a little frayed now at the edges with her not quite flat stomach and her bare face marked by too many sleepless nights, has been forced to grow up and be a good mother, they leave her for another carefree girl.

Rebecca

I WAS STILL TRYING to finish my novel but by now I was finding it impossible to work. Every sentence of love and hope became punctuated by the memory of Nick Fuller's bitter resignation or Leonora's hands twisting and untwisting a sodden hanky. When I tried to bring about the happy ending Dominic appeared before me, scowling, shouting, turning virtue into sin, upending his dreams and mine. My mind was filled, not with sweet dreams, but with accusations and counter-accusations, betrayal and wounded, bewildered children.

'To think that it takes my husband leaving me for us to get back in touch,' Leonora had said as we had dinner out together a couple of days after my visit.

There was no need for me to add anything; we both knew it was a poor swap.

I told the new therapist. Charlotte Jessop had left suddenly with just a letter saying she had got engaged: 'All very sudden, I know' (three coy dots and an implied giggle) 'But as my new fiancé's work is in Australia I have agreed to move there to be with him. Dr Angie Bliss will be taking over my practice and I have no doubt that she will be more than able to fill my shoes.'

In fact, I had taken an instant dislike to Charlotte Jessop's replacement, mainly because she was younger than I, beautiful and supremely confident. Yet by the time she had complimented me on my jacket, which was new and rather pretty, told me she could not believe I was forty-two and that she had read every one of my books and could not for the life of her understand why the reviewers had not picked up on the Brontësque sensibilities and the Austinesque wit of the last one my opinion of her was considerably higher.

We had just been discussing my recent contribution to a radio debate with a vicar, a rabbi, an imam and a newspaper columnist known for her forthright views on life in general and the ills of modern society in particular. The subject we were discussing was the disintegration of the family. The vicar, the rabbi and the imam had all agreed that society's fixation with sex and Hollywood-style romance, coupled with the emphasis on the individual's right to fulfilment at whatever cost, was part of the problem. The columnist had nodded, adding that, although she was of course a great supporter of her own sex, feminism had a lot to answer for, telling women it was acceptable to be promiscuous, have affairs, break up families and generally behave like men.

The vicar, the rabbi and the imam added that in their view the solution was a return to the adherence of the founding principles of the great religions.

No surprises there then.

At that point they had all turned to look at me, the purveyor of false expectations. Keen on the principle that if you have nothing new to say you should say it with conviction, I had replied that the sooner people realised that they were not put on this earth to be happy the better off we'd all be. The columnist had agreed and the vicar, the rabbi and the imam said that, although that was indeed so, true happiness *was* attainable through selflessness and helping others.

I began to ask them if that meant that, in their view, we *were* actually put on this earth to be happy and it was just that we had to achieve this aim in a certain prescribed way, which seemed to involve thinking only of other people's happiness, in which case the ensuing selfless acts could be deemed self-serving as they were the sure-fire way to achieve personal happiness. At which point my microphone was turned off.

'I thought you were the one person speaking sense,' Angie Bliss said.

'Thank you,' I said.

'To love others you must first love yourself.'

I nodded.

'Although people wrapped up in themselves make very small parcels.'

I nodded again.

'The world needs happy people. Life is a terminal condition that can be managed but not cured.'

'That's very true,' I said. And I wished life really could be that simple. Looking at Angie Bliss's candy-coloured tweed suit, I thought I could understand how she could afford Chanel. Certainties these days were in short supply and high demand; no wonder the price was astronomical.

Coco took the opportunity to point out that I could most probably get twenty clowns for the price of one therapist.

I asked him who in their right mind would want twenty clowns.

'While we postpone, life hurries by,' the therapist said, raising her voice as if she had noticed my attention was elsewhere.

'Isn't that Seneca?'

The therapist shrugged.

'Might be; he does say an awful lot.' She leant forward in her chair and looked deep into my eyes. 'Are you paying attention?'

'I'm sorry. It's this clown thing. It's in my notes.'

'Don't apologise. You're paying me, remember. It's part of the problem, I think, you being so nice.'

'I'm not really nice,' I said.

'No, of course you're not. You know that and I know that. I should have said you appearing to be so nice.'

'What?'

'We both know that you're nothing like as nice as you pretend to be, even to yourself.'

'Right,' I said. 'I'd better work on that.'

'Just work on your lovely books.'

'But that's why I'm here. Because I don't seem to be able to any more. Charlotte was particularly interested in working with creative people, which is why I went to see her in the first place. I hoped she would help me back to writing.'

'And I'm just like her,' Angie Bliss said, her voice soft and low. 'I shall help you reclaim your creative flame. You just have to trust me.'

I looked at her and it seemed as if her eyes were changing colour. As I stared I realised that she might be right and that maybe she would be able to help.

I dabbed at my own everyday eyes.

'I'm sorry, it's all been a bit of a strain. I don't know what I'd do if I thought I had lost the ability to write for good.' I fished a tissue from my handbag and blew my nose. 'However, I'm beginning to accept that I won't be writing any more love stories.'

'Why?' The therapist's voice was sharp.

'I've changed. I don't believe in those things any more.'

'Those things? You don't believe in love? How can you say such a thing?'

'Of course I believe in love. But romantic love . . . Yes, it is delicious, a delicious madness that cannot, indeed should not, last. Yet people enter into lifelong commitments like marriage and co-parenting on the basis of it, which is about as sensible as buying a house because you liked the pretty flowers in the hall. I've come to the conclusion that my books begin with a misconception and end in an impossibility. So what's the point?'

The therapist had listened with her lips pursed and her arms folded across her chest.

Now she said, 'The point, *Ms* Finch, is that in order to have a dream come true you have to have a dream.'

I thought that was quite profound then I remembered it was from a song in *South Pacific*.

I said, 'Well, I stand by what I'm saying. I tell you, that little bastard Cupid and his arrows of mass-destruction have a lot to answer for.'

'Eros, his name is Eros. Cupid is a vulgar Roman invention.'

I was a little taken aback by how seriously she took her classics.

'Right,' I said, 'Eros it is.'

'And he's not that bad: lazy, yes, sloppy in his work, yes, and come to think of it a bastard, yes, but he's a good boy really.'

'Right,' I said again.

'Are you worried about your age? Is that what this is all about?'

'No. I mean obviously I don't particularly like getting older, who does? And there are times when I ask myself if I might one day regret not having had children. Forty-two is hardly ancient, of course, it's not impossible for me to have them, but to find a man I care for enough, and in time, well, it seems rather less likely.'

While I spoke, Angie Bliss had been reading a file on her lap. When someone you're addressing obviously isn't paying attention you have two options, as far as I can see. One is to stop talking and the other is to go on in an increasingly loud voice until they do pay attention. When I was younger and full of pride and confidence I had favoured the latter. Now I just shut up.

Five minutes later the therapist looked up.

'What was that?'

'If I recall,' I said pointedly, 'I was saying that forty-two is hardly ancient.'

'Getting there,' she said. 'There's certainly no time for complacency. Cosmetic surgery and Botox can get you so far but it can't restore that youthful bloom. The bloom is important.'

'I thought therapy was about making one feel good about oneself.'

'Did you?'

There followed another silence. This time the therapist wasn't even reading but was simply staring in front of her. I began to shift in my chair. I felt uncomfortable, as if I had committed some social faux pas, which was obviously ridiculous because, as Angie Bliss herself had pointed out a little earlier, she was paid a great deal to be bored. It was the same at dinner parties, not the paying, obviously: the table would fall silent and I would feel compelled to speak, to say anything, however inconsequential, to break that silence.

'Why do I always feel as if the world might tumble from its axis if I'm not there to prop it up?' I asked.

If I've told you once I've told you a thousand times . . . Coco replied. *It's because you're self-obsessed and neurotic.*

I wasn't asking you.

Angie Bliss said, 'Because you think of yourself as the centre of everything.'

I felt depressed. If my therapist was in agreement with my inner demons, what hope was there?

'But you're not alone in that.' Angie Bliss gave me a kindly look. 'Most humans feel the same, one way or the other. No doubt because it's too cruel to live fully in the knowledge of your total insignificance.'

'Are you as sure about everything as you seem to be?'

'While I feel what I feel I'm sure I'm feeling that way,' she said. 'But it happens that I sometimes change my mind. Anyway, as I said to you before, loving *oneself* is essential.' She stretched and did a little wiggle in her chair. 'I love myself.'

'I'm not sure if I love myself very much or, in fact, if I even like myself. I'm aware though that those thoughts are self-centred, whereas your matter-of-fact acceptance and love of yourself must mean that you're not plagued by time-consuming insecurities. So, does that mean that someone who loves herself and is therefore really pleased with herself is actually less self-centred than someone who doesn't like herself very much at all?'

'Very possibly,' Angie Bliss said. 'Then again, maybe not. Now I trust that by the time of our next appointment you will be telling me that you're working again.' Her face brightened. 'I have just thought of something that might help you to unblock your block. Where are you in the novel?'

'Stuck where the heroine is about to realise that she's in love with the hero. All I want to say is don't bother, which won't really get me very far in a romantic novel.'

'Unless she gets over such cynical and fruitless doubts.'

'Well, she won't.' I had spoken more sharply than I'd intended but I just didn't think that Angie Bliss was that helpful when it came to writing.

'So, start another book. Start afresh, that was my idea. Show us a woman who is going through a divorce. Don't spare us the details about how wrong and disastrous divorces are. Vent all your bitterness and spleen, then – and this is where the genius of my suggestion comes in – let her fall in love with her divorce lawyer; you can vent some more spleen when you describe his work and then you can get down to describing the touching and deep love that develops between the two, yes?'

'I'm sorry, but it doesn't work like that.'

'What doesn't work like what?'

'I do need to finish this novel, I can't afford to pay back the advance, but not if it becomes some kind of cynical money-making exercise.'

'There you go making that common mistake of thinking that your intentions matter. They don't, only the result does. If the result is good who cares, eh?'

'I would.'

'I thought we were going to work on you not being so self-centred?'

'You turn everything upside down. Anyway, the result wouldn't be good: my readers would see right through it.'

The therapist got to her feet, indicating that our time was up.

'Well, if you're going to be negative,' she said, holding the door open for me.

'Your hair looks fabulous!' I said to Maggie Jacobs.

'Thank you, I had it done this morning.'

One of the reasons I liked Maggie was that she inspired hope for the future. Maggie was older than I, somewhere in her mid-fifties, yet a woman obviously in her prime: radiant with HRT, shiny-haired, plump-skinned and supple of movement. We had first met when she was a student on a writer's course that I was teaching. She wanted to write a book on style. Having achieved what she had set out to achieve with the publication of *If Fifty Is the New Forty and Forty Is the New Thirty Does That Mean I'm Twenty?*, she had not written another word – apart from thank-you letters (Maggie was punctilious about those) and 'To Do' lists for her housekeeper. When asked if she was ever tempted to write another book – *If Fifty Is the New Forty* had been a success, selling over three hundred thousand copies in paperback – she answered with a simple no. And when her friends and her publishers suggested she could have developed her writing into a career she had been equally perplexed. What would she want with a career?

I conceded that she had a point. If you took away the notions of ambition, work ethic and self-fulfilment, none of which seemed to concern Maggie, you were left with the prime motivation of earning a living, but seeing as her devoted and much older husband, Archie, had died leaving her a comfortable fortune – as Maggie herself put it, 'Not enough to make the Rich List but enough to fly business class' – money did not come into it either.

'It's so wonderful that we can all have lunch together – you're usually too busy working,' Maggie said as we walked towards the restaurant.

Without warning, and to both of our embarrassment, I burst into tears. As a rule, in daytime, people did not walk down the King's Road weeping. At night, yes. At night – when the pert and pretty young shoppers and the yummy mummies and the *Big Issue* sellers and the chuggers had been replaced by girls in low-slung jeans and shrunken jackets, squaring up like Capulets to the spaced-out, hazy-eyed Montague boys – weeping, loud, eyelash-drenching, mascara-smudging weeping, was commonplace, but not at one o'clock on a sunny winter afternoon. So people looked.

Matilda was waiting at the restaurant. She got up to give us both a kiss hello, then took a step back and looked at me.

'You've been crying.'

I tried to smile.

'I'm sorry, this is really silly.'

'What's happened?'

Maggie replied in my place.

'It's something to do with us having lunch.'

'You only needed to say if it wasn't convenient.'

I blew my nose with a clean but crumpled tissue I had found at the bottom of my bag.

'That's not it at all. The thing is, I don't go out to lunch when I'm working because getting dressed properly and putting on make-up and actually leaving the house completely disrupts my day.'

The others looked puzzled. Maggie reached across and patted my shoulder.

'You don't have to beat yourself up about it. We're seeing each other now, which is the main thing.'

'No, I'm upset because I *can* have lunch with you. And no, I don't mean it isn't a nice thing to do, but it is a symptom of how bad things have got. No, I didn't mean it like that either. Oh, what I'm trying to say is that I'm not working.' I brought out my compact foundation, checking my face in its mirror, wiping away the mascara smudges and reapplying my lipstick.

'Because you're having lunch with us.' Maggie nodded. 'By the way, after lunch I'll take you to Boots and get you Max Factor's Lipfinity. It's the only long-lasting lipstick that actually does what it says and stays on, and *without* drying the lips.'

Told you, Coco winked at me from an adjacent table.

I made a mental note to ask Angie Bliss if the fact that my imaginary friend knew more about make-up than I did was in any way significant.

'I'm not *not* working because I'm having lunch with you both,' I said. 'And yesterday I had a facial and my toes done. It took *three* hours.'

'And very nice you look too,' Maggie said.

I was still feeling awakward about having cried in front of them. If you were very young and very beautiful, like Angel-face, then the occasional burst of tears could be touching, becoming even. But if you were forty-two and wearing black eyeliner and several coats of mascara that smudged into the faint, but nonetheless visible, lines around the eyes it was merely pathetic.

I said, 'I'm not working *right* now because I'm here with you, obviously, but what's upsetting me so much is that I'm not working full stop, not any time, anywhere; and I feel lost and wretched, pointless, rudderless, aimless . . .'

'I think we get the drift,' Matilda said. 'If you forgive the pun.'

'And then there's the mortgage. If I don't earn I can't pay, obviously. It worries the hell out of me.'

Maggie looked as sympathetic as a woman who had named her bank account Saehrimnir possibly could, Saehrimnir being the roast pig in Valhalla who, having being consumed at one feast, renewed himself in time for the next.

Matilda said, 'You mustn't give up. And not just because of the mortgage. Think of the pleasure you give to literally thousands, even millions, of women.'

'The kind of pleasure you get from stuffing yourself with saturated fat and sugar,' I said. 'And about as healthy.'

'That's a really silly thing to say.'

'My therapist wants me to write about a divorce. She seems to think it would . . . well, kind of unblock me.'

'Maybe she's right. It's worth a try, isn't it?'

'Perhaps. Oh I don't know. I'm tired.'

'Have a complete break over Christmas,' Matilda said, 'Are you seeing your mother?' I nodded. 'Then get back to work in the new year.'

I asked Maggie what she was doing.

'Cobbler's Cove.'

'Nice.'

'The main thing is that you don't give up,' Matilda said again. 'I would give anything to have your success, well, Chris and my in-laws and that bloody house, not my Paddington, though, and probably not the children, but pretty well . . .'

'What's so special about the bear?'

'Bag. Paddington *bag*, not Bear. Anyway, you can't just throw away everything you've achieved, like so much ballast from your hot-air balloon.'

'You know that's where writers should be,' I said, drinking deep from my glass of wine. 'Not in an ivory tower but in a hot-air balloon. Anyway, I don't think I have any talent, not real talent. Real talent writes real things about real lives. Not saccharine-flavoured opium.'

'I wanted a Paddington,' Maggie said. 'A while back, obviously, the pale-blue one. So they told me there was a waiting list. How long? I wanted to know. They told me a minimum of six months. Six months! For a hip replacement I might wait six months, I said, but not for a handbag.'

'Isn't the wait more like two years?' I said.

'Not any more. It's not a classic like the Birkin.'

'I meant for a hip replacement.'

'You don't need a hip replacement, do you?' Matilda asked Maggie.

'A hip replacement? Of course not. I might be older than you both, but no, certainly not.'

'It's just stupid,' I said. 'This being on first-name terms with small leather goods. I have problems enough remembering the names of people's children without having to worry about their handbags.'

Matilda said, 'Do you want to know what I think?'

I shook my head.

'I think it's quite wrong not to respect your own talent.'

'I don't know that I have talent for any other kind of writing. But I do know that I can't write about love any more. You can fake an orgasm but you can't fake a heart.'

'When you do that,' Maggie said, 'fake an orgasm, do you stay quite quiet and just twitch a bit or . . .'

'I'm talking about the writing.'

'Of course. You always are.'

'I'm sorry. I'm being a self-obsessed bore.'

'That's all right,' Matilda said. 'We're used to it.'

'Sure, you go ahead,' Maggie agreed.

'I'm thinking maybe crime, I might try crime.'

'So you think crime is more worthwhile than romance?' Matilda asked.

'At least crime is real.'

'Sure, but look around you right now. What do you see most of?'

'On the King's Road in the middle of the afternoon: romance. But that's like saying you should take McDonald's seriously because there are more of them than there are Gordon Ramsays.'

'Only just,' Maggie said.

'It's quite a good analogy.' I held my glass out for the waiter to refill it. 'Romantic love is about as nourishing as fast food.'

'And crime is as satisfactory as a gourmet restaurant,' Matilda said. 'Good thinking.'

'All right, so the analogy only takes us so far.'

'There's been romantic love for as long as there have been people,' Maggie said.

'I'm not sure that's true,' I said. 'I think romantic love is just another attempt by us to separate ourselves from the other animals by elevating our mating to something less basic and instinctive, to a realm of the divine or spiritual. Christianity with its belief in love as a holy union, the Romantic movement with its theory that emotions are the better guide to living than reason – it's all symptomatic of the sense of uniqueness with which we endow ourselves.'

'I think you're wrong,' Maggie said. 'Just as you can have sex without love so you can have romantic love without sex. Of course, the two often go together or the lines get blurred, but the two emotions stem from different parts of our brains, I'm convinced of it.'

'And what about that quotation you love so much?' Matilda asked. 'I was so touched by it I memorised it.' She closed her eyes: '"In the beginning men and women were round like the sun . . ." no, moon and the sun, oh bother.'

I might have been getting tipsy but I still had excellent recall:

'"In the beginning men and women were round like the moon and the sun; they were both male and female and had two sets of sexual organs . . . they were proud, self-sufficient beings. They defied the Olympian gods, who punished them by splitting them in half. This is the mutilation mankind suffered. So that generation after generation we seek the missing half. Longing to be whole again . . . to be human was to be severed, mutilated. Man is incomplete. Zeus is a tyrant. Mount Olympus is tyranny. The work of humankind in its severed state is to seek the missing half."'

'Well there,' Matilda said. 'Is that not truly a manifesto for what you have been doing in your writing?'

'You don't know how the quote ends, though, do you? Neither did I until recently: "And after so many generations your true companion is simply not to be found. Eros is a compensation granted by Zeus. The sexual embrace gives temporary relief but the painful knowledge of mutilation is permanent." That's Plato-speak for give up, you fools.'

'Since when did you have to believe every word Plato said?' Maggie asked.

'I'm not saying you have to believe every word. But you have to take a philosophy as a whole. I despise the kind of thinking that says we can mix and match belief systems as we please: heaven but no hell, fame without achievement, gain without pain . . . as if it's all just one big pick 'n' mix.'

'With three young boys there isn't much time for philosophy,' Matilda said. 'Anyway, whatever you say now, there are still countless people, me included, who would give their eye teeth to be able to earn a living, an extremely good living in your case, by writing.'

'You will one day. Remember you did before you had the children. You're very good. You just have to finish something.'

Matilda rolled her eyes.

'I know, I know, but between the school-run and football training and the music lessons and doing umpteen loads of washing a day there isn't exactly a surfeit of time.'

'Maybe you could do a couple of hours, or one hour even, once they've gone to school?' I suggested.

Matilda shook her head, sucking air between her teeth like a plumber inspecting another plumber's work.

'That's when I have to get the washing on and do the shopping and phone my mother and Chris's mother and . . .'

'How about once they're in bed?'

'I'm hopeless in the evening,' Matilda said. 'It's all I can do to stay awake for the ten o'clock news.'

'How about before they get up? When I used to have Laura staying I would do a couple of hours before she woke. It's amazing how much you can get done. And no one phones or delivers parcels and whatever.'

'Oh, for heaven's sake, we all know you are a complete workaholic.'

'Sorry. I suppose all I'm trying to say is that if writing is important to you then you need to create some time in which to do it, even if it is difficult. And it doesn't have to be very much.' Getting carried away with my unasked-for advice once more, I went on, 'Anthony Trollope wrote his novels at the crack of dawn before going off and inventing the pillar-box, and Jane Austen . . .'

'I know, I know, she sat by a creaking door writing on a scrap of paper so that she could put her writing away if she heard someone approach, bla bla bla . . . But maybe I need a bit more than snatched moments. You write all day, every day.'

'I didn't to begin with. I couldn't. I was working full-time until the second book was published.'

Maggie had been listening to the exchange, leaning back in her chair, smoking.

Now she said, 'I'm not a morning or a night person, more of a 12.30 p.m. to 3 p.m. with a quick energy-burst between 8 p.m. and 10 p.m. kind of woman, but when I wrote *If Fifty Is the New Forty* Archie was ill and I spent all day and most of the evening at the hospital. I had no option but to write at night.'

I put my hand on hers.

'I didn't know you had all that to cope with. You never really said. I'm sorry. I would have . . .' I stopped myself and thought, enough of the meaningless phrases.

Coco, who tended to go quiet after a couple of glasses of wine, perked up.

So we won't hear much from you for a while then? he smirked.

'Who are you pulling a face at?' Matilda asked. 'Someone we know?'

'Was I pulling a face?'

'You were saying?' Maggie looked at me.

'I was about to say something to the effect that, had I known just what you were going through at that time I would have offered to do something, but then I realised that all I would actually have done is to call you a little more frequently and offer to do things we both knew I had no intention of doing.'

'You did your bit with Laura,' Matilda said.

'I never offer to do things for people unless I really I mean it,' Maggie said. 'Which is why I hardly ever offer.'

'Which is also why you're such relaxing company,' I said. 'One always knows where one stands with you.'

As lunch drew to an end I looked deep into Matilda's eyes, which made her accuse me of being drunk.

'Are you and Chris happy?' I asked her. 'I'm sorry if that's too personal but I really, really have to know. Are you happily married?'

'Yes, I think I am,' Matilda said, before suggesting we split the bill three ways.

On the way home Maggie led me into Ann Summers and bought me a Rampant Rabbit. I really had had far too much to drink because a few minutes later I walked into Vodaphone and handed them the Rabbit.

'Try as I might,' I said, 'I simply can't get a ring tone.'

It had seemed funny at the time.

John

WORK HAD BEEN PARTICULARLY busy this past week. He'd done close to seventy chargeable hours and, although he prided himself on almost limitless stamina, he was tired. So when his mother called he made the mistake, he quite often did, of telling her how busy he'd been. His mother had responded, as he should have known she would, by anxious preaching on stress, high blood pressure, heart attacks and doctors' appointments. Melanie used to ask him why he told his mother he was tired or working too hard when the inevitable result was the fussing that he professed to hate. He didn't explain, but in truth he did it from a weakness for being told he was a clever boy, a good boy. To get approval and because sometimes he was so exhausted, not so much by work but by the need to be always strong and capable and broad-shouldered, that he longed to let go, be fussed and worried over for a bit. Of course after two minutes he had had enough, but by then it would be too late: the fluffy Duracell bunny that was his mother's mind would be off and running along its well-worn track. This time the only way to stop her was to promise to come down to visit that Sunday so she could see for herself that he was whole and hale and not, he said, 'a heart attack waiting to happen'.

'John, don't joke about such things,' she had squealed at the other end of the line, but she had been comforted by the promised visit.

Of course having stayed overnight it took for ever to extricate himself the next morning.

'One slice of toast: that's not breakfast. You should have porridge or an egg at least. They say that actually eggs are very good for you and do not have an adverse effect on the cholesterol levels. When am I seeing you again? And how is Melanie? She's moved out? Why didn't you tell me? Well, I can't say that I'm sorry. I never cared for her. You're still friends? Why? When it's over it's over and nothing good comes from dragging things out.'

'I'm going to miss my train,' he said.

Her voice trailed behind him as he disappeared out of the gate and into the waiting taxi.

'Don't forget it's your cousin's birthday next week. The post to New Zealand takes for ever, as you know. And . . .'

He was running for the train when, on the periphery of his vision, he glimpsed a small child, a baby really, winding her unsteady way along the platform. He took avoiding action but the small girl changed direction and lurched right into his path, bouncing off his shins and landing on her bottom, where she sat, a look of utter surprise in her round eyes before she opened her little mouth into an O and screamed. The father picked her up while yelling invective at John.

'God, I'm so sorry. Is she OK?'

The father replied with another stream of obscenities. John's train was about to leave. The child had stopped screaming, glaring instead from the safety of her father's arms.

' "God, I'm so sorry. Is she OK?" ' The man was mimicking John's voice, exaggerating his RP vowels before reverting to his usual manner of speech. 'If she is, it's no thanks to you, you fucking lunatic. I mean, who the fuck do you think you are? Why don't you fucking look where . . .' On and on he went.

John looked at the child, who had just stuck her tongue out at him. He looked at her father's bullet head and working mouth. He looked at the train about to depart and thought of his client, who depended on him, then he turned on his heels and ran for the train, catching it just as it was about to pull out from the platform.

He arrived in London in time to change and get into court. He presented his arguments, heard the judge sum up in his favour and returned to Chambers where he worked solidly for three hours, preparing for the following day, barely looking up from his desk. When, finally, he took a short break, making a cup of coffee in the Chambers kitchen, his mind flooded with terrifying images: the little girl on life support following undiagnosed bleeding in the brain. Her spleen ruptured from when her little stomach made contact with his knee. Her mother weeping, inconsolable, at her only child's bedside. The fact that the child had landed on her bottom, the fact that she had looked unhurt, made no difference now. He should have suggested a check-up at the nearest casualty department, just in case. He should, at least, have remained at the station until the father had calmed down and was able to assess the situation rationally.

He sat down at his desk, leant back in his chair and closed his eyes, trying and failing to reason his way out of the onslaught. When a colleague put his head round the door and asked him how it had gone in court, John's expression as he replied that it had gone very well indeed, thank you for asking, was of such despair that the colleague thought he had misheard and asked him again.

In the end John could resist no longer and, letting go of reason, he picked up the phone and dialled the number of the transport police. He asked if there had been any reported accidents at Winchester station. The WPC on the other end of the phone asked why there should be. He began his explanation.

'So you're saying that the child was with her father and that she seemed shaken up but unhurt?'

'Yes, but I didn't stop for long.'

'But you stopped and checked?'

'Yes, yes, I did, but as I mentioned, the father wasn't making much sense. He was angry, which is understandable.'

'He was abusive?'

'Yes, he was. But as I said, that's understandable under the circumstances.'

'So let me get this straight, *sir*. You were running for the train when the child ran out in front of you. She was knocked to the ground but landed on her bottom. Her father was there. You stopped to enquire as to the child's condition and you were told that the child was unhurt.'

'I think so, yes. It was hard to hear what he was saying, but yes, that's what I think he said. The thing is that internal injuries or concussion do not always show up until later, sometimes when it's too late. If the father wasn't aware of that risk . . .'. He paused.

'But the child, who was with her father, had stopped crying and appeared unhurt?'

He imagined her rolling her eyes at a colleague. But mixed with the shame of knowing he was coming across as a complete idiot on the end of a phone was the relief of having his fears brought out into the open and hopefully demolished, or, failing that, simply laughed away.

'She stuck her tongue out at me, so yes, I thought she was OK.'

'So the child by now appeared unhurt and was in the care of her father, who, although irate, confirmed that the child was indeed all right. You then left to catch your train.'

'That's about it, yes.'

'So what would you like me to do, *sir*?'

'As I said I was simply phoning to make sure that there had been no reports of –'

'Have you been drinking, *sir*?'

'No, no, of course not.'

'What's your name, *sir*?'

John hung up.

At the therapist's later that afternoon, he said, 'I made an absolute fool of myself as well as wasting time. I can't afford to waste time. And I knew the child was all right. The real me, the logical, sane me, knew that perfectly well, but as usual that didn't matter. I was just sucked into . . .' He paused as Angie Bliss, gazing into space, her eyes opaque, poured herself a glass of mineral water. 'I'm sorry if I'm boring you,' he said. 'OCD is very boring. In fact, it's as tedious as hell, repetitive and pretty ridiculous, so why can't I stop?'

'Some would say it's all a matter of self-discipline, or rather lack of it,' Angie Bliss said. Catching the look on John's face she quickly added, 'But that, as we all know, is not the case.' She glanced sideways at some papers on her lap. 'In fact, extensive research in biochemistry, pharmacology, radiology and genetics has now demonstrated beyond a doubt that OCD results directly from an abnormality in the brain's chemistry, a malfunction that leads to faulty firing of the brain's neurons. As succinctly put by Yale Medical School Professor Richard Peschel, "Recent neuroscience research proves that obsessive-compulsive disorder is a physical, neurobiological disease of the brain."' She looked up with a dazzling smile. 'So how could you bore me? You're *very ill*!'

'No. No, I'm not. I have a condition which, thanks to the increasing understanding of the medical profession, is now eminently treatable.' John too had read the textbooks.

'Excellent.' Angie Bliss sat back, satisfied, in her chair. 'Isn't that good? Now, tell me about your relationship with Melanie Ingram.'

'Aren't we supposed to deal with the order mania? It's got worse again.' Even to himself John sounded like a child whose scraped knee was not getting enough attention.

'One thing at a time,' Angie said. 'Oh, and I spoke to Rupert last night. He is very pleased with our progress.' As John obviously did not look convinced enough she added, 'He thinks the new approach is completely appropriate.' Warming to her theme she went on, 'Freud's theory that obsessions and compulsions arise from unconscious conflicts between the sex drive and . . . well, the bit that controls . . . these things . . . is really helpful.'

'But as you yourself just said, all that's been completely discounted in favour of the idea of it being an imbalance of –'

'Yes, yes, I know the spiel, I've just given it to you. The

thing is, though, that the most avant-garde teachings on the subject are returning . . . slightly . . . to the earlier theory, which is why' – her voice rose – 'I am asking you about your relationship with Melanie Ingram.'

John looked away for a moment, twisting his fingers, but his voice was matter-of-fact as he said, 'She moved out.'

'Really? Excellent, excellent. About time you got shot of her.'

John frowned.

'I didn't get shot of her.'

'So she had had enough of you? Oh dear, that's not so good.'

'It wasn't like that either.'

John thought back to that evening earlier in the month. He had made an effort to come home on time. On his way he had picked up a bottle of Melanie's favourite Shiraz and he walked through the front door determined that tonight they would have a nice evening, no misunderstandings or fighting but a nice, convivial, companionable evening.

By ten o'clock Melanie was well into the subject of his shortcomings and what could be done to correct them.

He had tried passive resistance, smiling and refusing to get riled, followed by diversionary tactics.

'How is work going?'

Melanie's Ph.D. in sports psychology was not going well and it was mostly John's fault.

'If you could even begin to pull your weight at home,' she said.

He had sighed, he had thought inaudibly, but Melanie had heard. Then, making things worse, much worse, he had suggested, in that even, measured tone which never failed to enrage her, that paying the mortgage might be seen as 'pulling his weight'.

'Trust you to bring that up again. I mean how crass, how completely insensitive can you actually get?' Then she rose to her feet, her knees hit the underside of the tabletop and her wine glass toppled. Without stopping to pick it up, she rushed from the room.

He too got up and fetched the dishcloth from the sink.

He was immersed in his task of dabbing soda water on to the red splatters on the cream chair-covers, concentrating on using just the right amount of liquid to dilute the stain but not so much as to wreck the material, when Melanie returned.

'I'm leaving,' she said, her voice high with drama. 'I'm going to my sister's.'

He straightened up, putting the soda-water bottle down on the table and the dishcloth back on the sink. He turned round and faced her.

'Fine,' he said, 'Let me help you pack.'

'I think we need to examine your past experiences in order to try to shed some light on the present . . . mess.'

'To be absolutely honest, I'd rather we dealt with the OCD.'

Sensing his impatience, the therapist turned her gaze on him, her pupils expanding until they filled the entire iris of her eyes, like night filling a curtainless room.

'So, you're quite happy to continue on your way, making women fall in love with you, thinking you're in love with them. Breaking up, moving on. That sets a wonderful example for your young daughter, not to mention giving her a stable home environment. *Not.* What I'm saying is that our job here, yours and mine, is to equip you better for the future.' John was about to speak but she put her hand up to stop him. 'Anyway, the . . . it's all connected. Yes. That's what both Dr Daly and I have been trying to tell you; the two are connected, so part of any treatment is of course dealing with your DVD.' Again John opened his mouth to speak and again the therapist stopped him. 'Only jesting. OCD. I meant OCD all along. But first we should look back, try to learn from the past. Would you, for example, care to explain the *chuck fuck*?'

'*What* did you just say?'

The therapist repeated, 'The *chuck fuck*.' She leant forward in her chair. 'Aren't you ashamed of yourself?'

John felt the colour rise in his cheeks but he looked straight at her, holding her gaze.

'No.'

'So?' Angie Bliss's voice was soft, inviting confidence.

'How do you know about . . .?' John hesitated for a moment and the therapist filled in.

'The chuck fuck?'

'Yes.'

'It's in your notes,' Angie Bliss said.

'It can't be.'

'Don't avoid the subject just because it's painful.'

'It's not painful. It's just not something I would talk about. I'm sure I never mentioned it to Dr Daly. Anyway, what's it got to do . . .?'

'Will you stop questioning everything I say?'

John rolled his eyes.

'You look like my son,' Angie Bliss said. 'He's a boy. You are a grown man.'

Despite himself John had to smile.

'OK,' he said finally. 'It's when you . . .'

'Yes?'

'It's when you sleep with someone one last time just to make sure you really do want to break up.'

'Well!' Angie Bliss threw herself back in the chair and spun right round. When she faced him again her eyes were dark and her lips set tight. 'That's the kind of behaviour that spoils it for everyone. How can you bed a woman, make love to her, allow her to give her body to you, knowing you're most probably going to break her heart once you're done?'

John winced.

'I'm not that calculating. *It's* not that calculating. Nor is it something I make a habit of. As I said, I don't know how Rupert could have mentioned it in my notes because I'm pretty damn sure I never told him about it.'

'So you are ashamed, at least?'

'Yes. Yes, I am.'

'At last we're getting somewhere. Now, tell me why you cheated on your wife.'

'I cheated once. We worked through it.'

'You mean *she* worked through it, don't you?'

'It wasn't the reason why our marriage ended.'

'That's what you say.'

'That's what she'd say too.'

'Once a woman has lost her trust, once the innocence has been plucked from her heart and trampled on, she's never the same again. All kinds of behaviour you might think have nothing to do with your infidelity: nagging, complaining, sharpness, all these things will manifest themselves over unrelated issues and you men, because you know little and care even less, do not notice the connection.'

John put his head in his hands.

When he looked up he said, 'You're right, of course.'

'So will you be able to remain faithful in the future?'

He felt as if he were at a job interview.

'I was entirely faithful to Melanie. I still am. We're considering getting back together.'

The therapist shook her head.

'I wouldn't do that if I were you.'

'We're certainly going to stay in touch.'

The therapist tut-tutted.

'Not a good idea.'

'Why not? I don't like losing touch with people.'

'That's because you lost your father so early on. You have to get over it. Hanging on to spent relationships is no better than hoarding possessions. It zaps your energy and wastes time and space.'

John's eyes narrowed but he retained his smile.

'I'm sorry, but I don't agree with that. Anyway, I'm not entirely sure that it is over.'

'Oh yes, it is. It would never have worked between you.'

'I can't see how you could possibly know that. You haven't even met Melanie.'

'Oh haven't I? I mean I haven't, you're right. But, I . . . oh well, if you want to waste further time and energy on a doomed relationship that's fine with me.' She sat back and crossed her arms over her chest.

'Good.' John too leant back in his chair.

'And the fact that not only I but everyone else is telling you the same thing only makes you more determined to persevere, yes?'

John tried, unsuccessfully, not to smile.

'Possibly.'

'Well, that's just childish.'

'I haven't said that we are resuming the relationship, only that we are still in touch and have not written off the possibility of resuming it. God, I'm sounding like a *Hello!* interview.'

'No, you're not. In *Hello!* they are together at the time of the interview. It's only following it that they break up. Anyway, to change the subject: I've got a small favour to ask you. I have a client, a writer, whose new book features a divorce lawyer. Although she is herself divorced, unattached therefore, she has no experience or real knowledge of the work you do, so I told her I could help. I was sure you wouldn't mind meeting up and telling her all about your fascinating life. May I pass on your email address then?'

In his mind John went over his diary for the next couple of weeks. There was not a lot of slack time.

'If she doesn't mind it would have to be in the evening.'

'Evening? No, I'm sure that will suit her perfectly.'

'I assume you haven't told her I'm a patient of yours?' John was frowning now.

The therapist looked uncertain for a moment then she said, a little too quickly, 'Of course not.'

'Good.' John stood up to leave. 'But you've told me about her.'

'Oh well . . . she said I could. She's very open, very real, very genuine.'

John rolled his eyes.

'I told you not to do that,' the therapist snapped.

'Right,' John said. 'I'll see you next week.'

Rebecca

I FELT I HAD been bulldozed into the meeting with John Sterling and I told Angie Bliss as much.

'Of course I appreciate you getting so involved and if I were to go ahead with the storyline you suggested then I would indeed need to research the lawyer angle, but as I said at the time, interesting as your suggestion is, I don't think it's right for me.'

Angie Bliss looked up with a slight start as if I had interrupted her in some reverie.

'What's not right for you?' she asked.

I sighed inaudibly.

'Your storyline suggestion. And of course it was very kind of John Sterling to offer to help, but I feel that, at the moment, all I would do is waste his time.'

'You never know what might get the creative juices flowing,' Angie Bliss said, using an expression I did not like. She leant towards me, fixing me with an azure-blue gaze. 'Humour me,' she said. She lowered her voice. 'Between you and me, I think he could do with the diversion.' She sat back again. 'And that's all I'm going to say on the matter. Patient confidentiality, you know.'

I did know and I thought she was already in danger of having breached it.

'You don't speak about me to your other clients, do you?' I gave a little laugh to make it sound less of an accusation.

'Of course not. I only mentioned this about John Sterling because it isn't part of his treatment.'

I wanted to ask, what is? But our time was up.

I met up with John Sterling in a wine bar in Primrose Hill. I had insisted on coming to his part of town; it was the polite thing to do, I thought, seeing as he was giving up his evening to advise me.

I was already seated at a small table by the window when a tall, fair-haired man appeared. He looked round until his gaze fell on me.

'Are you, by any chance, Rebecca Finch?'

There was something familiar about John Sterling and as we ordered drinks and he began to tell me about his work, it came to me where I had seen him.

'Have you by any chance been in the papers recently? I mean it's probably not you, but you do look familiar. Something about record settlements for abandoned wives?'

'We've had some very satisfactory outcomes, yes.'

I made a mental note of the rather formal, somewhat pedantic manner in which he expressed himself. His work required absolute precision in speech and thought and he carried that over with him into his private life.

'I have to be honest and tell you that I don't know how much of this research I will actually use,' I explained to him. 'I hope I won't end up having wasted your time.'

He was a friendly, helpful man, I thought, as he immediately protested that he was always happy for an excuse to talk about 'life at the Bar.'

I made another mental note to make my barrister, if indeed I created one, use pompous little expressions like that. This together with the general earnestness of his conversation made an interesting contrast, I thought, to his looks and comparative youth. Angie Bliss had told me that I would recognise him because he would be easily 'the best-looking creature in the room'.

He asked me about my work. I was hesitant at first; men in particular seemed to ask out of politeness rather than because they genuinely wanted to know, but John Sterling was so focused in his listening and looked at me with such warmth and interest as I spoke that I soon found myself telling him about the difficulties I was having, not just with the latest book, but with the whole concept of romantic love.

'What frightens me, more than anything, is that I might never be able to write again.' I began to smile. 'I'm not used to being listened to in that way,' I explained, 'so intently. It's very seductive.' I looked sideways at him, amused in case he might think I was flirting. 'I mean seductive in the sense of making me happy to carry on talking.'

He gave me a quick smile back.

'I know exactly what you mean. But I really am interested in hearing about your world. I don't get much time to read – outside work, that is.'

Normally that statement annoyed me, being, I always suspected, a euphemism for, 'I have better things to do with my time than waste it on stories.' As John Sterling immediately brought out a slim notebook and a pen from his jacket pocket and asked which of my novels he should start with, I decided he might be different.

'I'm not sure they're really your thing,' I said. 'They're love stories.'

'And what makes you think they aren't my thing?'

'You're right, I shouldn't assume that just because you're a man. Not even if you're a man who spends his life wading through the debris of other people's broken marriages. Actually, I don't know how you do it – the wading, I mean. I've had a couple of days of it and I found it very bad indeed for morale.' I told him about my idea of collecting happy marriages for Angel-face and how, so far, it had turned out to be a disaster. 'Are you married?' I asked him. It would make sense if he were, and happily so. He would have seen all the unhappy marriages and learnt what not to do.

'Divorced,' he said.

'Oh. Me too.'

He had a way, just before he smiled, of opening his eyes wide, which was most appealing. Angie Bliss had been right, he was very attractive. And he was divorced and possibly unattached, with a sense of humour and a supple mind. Maybe we would see each other again and maybe we would fall in love. It was perfectly possible, or rather it might once have been perfectly possible, but not any more. I thought of a story I'd read about a man who could see right through people, not in the sense of recognising their character but right through to their bones, so that when he looked at his beloved he could no longer see her lovely fresh face, just a grinning death skull with empty sockets where her bright eyes should be.

I knew now what the poor man must have felt like, because when I looked at the perfect romantic hero seated opposite me at the wine-smeared table all I could see was what lay behind: boredom, disappointment, betrayal, regret and pain, and my heart, which once had fluttered at the slightest excuse, stayed as still as a frozen pond.

John Sterling shot me a quizzical look.

I felt myself blush.

'Mind wandering,' I said. 'Not because our conversation wasn't interesting; well, yours was anyway.' I heard myself babbling and changed the subject. 'So what do you think about our therapist?'

John Sterling sat back and crossed his legs.

'I don't actually know,' he said. 'There will be at least one occasion during each session when I think she's completely barking. I resolve not to waste any more time on her and then she'll say something that makes perfect sense and before I know it I've committed myself to another appointment. She's got a very persuasive personality.'

I laughed.

'Is that man-speak for she's really fit?'

'No, well, yes, she is attractive. Not my type, though.'

'Did she tell you about my clown?'

'No. All she said was that you were a writer and that you needed to talk to a barrister as part of your research. Did she tell you about my OCD?'

I shook my head.

'How did you come to see her, I mean as opposed to some other therapist?'

'Happenstance. I was actually seeing someone else, a guy called Rupert Daly. But he upped and left the practice rather suddenly and he recommended Angie Bliss.'

'That's exactly what happened to me. My woman upped and left; she met a man, got married and moved to Australia all in the space of about five minutes. Angie took over part of her client list.' I pulled a face. 'Maybe she murdered them for the work.'

'Possible,' John Sterling said, 'but not very likely. Good plot for a book, though.'

'I was thinking earlier that someone in your line of work might have the perfect marriage because you would have learnt all about the pitfalls, but I suppose it could be the opposite.'

'I think perhaps the latter, yes,' John Sterling said. 'You know sometimes when I listen to a client's story it's as if I can actually hear it: the sound of dreams shattering.'

'When I was little I thought I knew what a broken heart smelt like.'

'And what was that?'

'Cigarette smoke, wool and Old Spice aftershave.' I stopped and asked him, 'Sorry, have I got lipstick on my teeth?'

'Yes, you have, as a matter of fact, but actually I was thinking that you have an unusually expressive face. You would make either a very good witness or a very bad one, depending obviously on what one was trying to achieve.'

I smiled.

'Thank you, I think.'

He smiled back at me.

'Sorry, I interrupted you.'

'That's all right, I'm sure it wasn't anything important.'

'Broken hearts?'

'Oh yes. No, I was just thinking of Zoe again, my god-daughter.'

John nodded.

'I wanted to be able to console her but I just couldn't. I couldn't sit there and tell her that I truly believed that the two of them, she and her fiancé, would end up living happily ever after. Because the truth is that most couples don't. Obviously if you marry enough times till death us do part becomes increasingly attainable, but for twenty-somethings the first time around? No.'

'Different partners for different stages of one's life,' John Sterling said. 'It's being talked about. But there will always be victims of that way of doing it, children in particular. But if the uncouplings were conducted in an amicable manner and communications were left open, we could have not a splintering of families but an expanding circle, where each new partnership means another person being brought into the family rather than one leaving.' He reached for his wine glass. 'But of course life doesn't work that way.'

I sighed.

'No, it doesn't. I don't think I'd ever contemplate getting married, or even moving in with anyone again. If I met someone, I would insist we each have our own home at least. Men and women simply aren't made to exist together in close proximity for any length of time.'

John Sterling was about to reply when he was tapped on the shoulder. I looked up at a pretty blonde woman in her mid-thirties. She gave me a friendly nod and then, still standing behind him, she bent down and pecked John Sterling on the cheek.

'Hi, darling. I took a chance I'd find you here.' She slipped into the chair next to him. 'Hi,' she said again, to me this time, 'I'm Melanie.'

John looked surprised at seeing her but pleased too.

'This is Rebecca Finch. Rebecca is a novelist,' he explained.

'A writer!' she squealed. 'That's so amazing.'

I smiled, trying to look modest.

'Not really.'

'Oh but it is. I love reading. I don't know why I haven't read you. Oh I tell you what, you wouldn't consider coming to speak at my reading group, would you?'

I wrote down my name and details on the back of a napkin and gave it to her.

'I'd love to,' I said. 'Now I must go.'

Melanie turned to John.

'Why don't we give Rebecca a lift back? You've only had one glass, haven't you? Then that's fine. We can go on to my place afterwards. I wanted you to take a look at this file I got from Derek Flint . . .'

Shutting my front door behind me was like pulling up a drawbridge and blocking out a messy world full of emotion and turmoil. It was good to be on my own, safely at a distance.

What do you mean on your own? Coco popped his head round the kitchen door. *I'm here.*

No, you're not, I said and kicked off my shoes, leaving them right in the middle of the hallway, where anyone could have stumbled over them, if anyone had been there.

Mount Olympus

MOTHER IS FUMING.

'Why didn't you stop her?' she demands.

'Stop who?'

'The Melanie creature.'

'You didn't tell me to. You told me to stand back and watch.'

'And if I told you to stand back and watch me cross the road and a bus bore down on me, would you still just stand there or would you actually think and push me out of harm's way?'

'You're immortal,' I remind her. 'There would be no need.'

'You see, this is what I can't stand: your flippancy, your complete inability to act in a responsible and proactive manner. You know perfectly well what I'm saying. The moment this woman appeared you should have –'

'– Pushed him out of harm's way.'

Mother's eyes are dark-green and her lovely lips are set tight.

'You are either very stupid or very cheeky. Either way I despair. Yes, Eros, I despair.'

I go up to her and try to give her a hug but she steps away.

'No, Eros, I'm serious.'

So was I. I'm fed up with trying to please her, with trying to make her love me. Because she never will, it's as simple as that. There are times when she likes me well enough, she's probably quite fond of me when she remembers to be, but I know what real motherly love is like, I've watched it on the screen. She loved Adonis, though.

'You could have gone down there yourself,' I mutter.

'What was that?'

'Nothing. You told me not to shoot, anyway. You told me it would be too soon, that they weren't fully prepared yet.'

'Yes, Eros, I did tell you that but then circumstances changed and we had an *emergency* on our hands.'

I shrug.

'Sorry.'

Rebecca

ALL I WANTED TO do was find some uplifting examples of everlasting love for Angel-face. A reasonable enough task, I had thought. But I had been wrong. Instead, I opened the newspaper to find a headline shouting, 'A quarter of us regret marriage.' Apparently one in four married people wished they hadn't 'bothered' and one in seven had doubts when walking up the aisle. I thought, OK, that's not so bad: three in four married people did *not* wish they hadn't bothered. Surely it was not beyond me to find just a handful of them? Though I had said I wouldn't use her, I decided to phone Matilda. Time was ticking by, and according to Bridget, Angel-face's doubts were growing each day.

'Hi, Rebecca. How's it going?'

'Hi. Fine. I know I've asked you this before, but you and Chris are happy together, aren't you? Please tell me you are.'

'Chris and I are happy together.'

'I'm serious.'

'Where is this coming from?'

'It's Angel-face's book. So far all I've got are my maternal grandparents.'

'I'm not going to tell you all the intimate details about my marriage just so that you can tell the world.'

'Not the world, just Angel-face.'

'I know you writers.'

'No, I mean it. And I won't say it's you. I'll call you something else.'

'Can I be Nicolette?'

'Nicolette? Sure.'

'No, Theo, I want to be Theo. I've always liked those androgynous names.'

'Whatever you like as long as you tell me you and Chris are happy.'

'We are. We're perfectly happy. He should be Scott.'

'Scott it is, but I don't want perfectly happy, I want completely and utterly happy.'

'Did your mother not tell you beggars can't be choosers? No, no, I don't suppose Vanessa would have done. But they can't. And *perfectly happy* is my best offer. And after twelve years together it's pretty damn good.'

'You and I have been together for thirty-seven years,' I said fondly. 'It's a heart-warming thought. Of course we never had sex. If we had, we probably wouldn't even be talking now.'

Theo's Story

Was the secret of happiness low expectations? Hearing Theo's story you might well think that:

I suppose you could say ours was a marriage of convenience, but now I'm beginning to think that Scott and I are the only happy couple around.

We'd always known each other, through our parents initially. Of course at university he was chasing after you. He used to come to my room late at night, drunk, going on and on about how much he fancied you and how you were his ideal woman but you didn't even know he existed. And you and I used to joke about him. We even took the piss out of his ears. What I never told you was that I rather liked him; I mean admitting that would have been like admitting one liked Val Doonican.

Of course, as we know, Scott never got his dream girl. There's no need to look embarrassed. He still thinks you're great, but love has to feed on something. After university, he and I kept in touch, as you know, bumping into each other at mutual friends,' meeting for a drink or a quick dinner now and then, calling each other up when we had a spare ticket to a concert or the theatre. Neither of us were very lucky in love. It seemed that in life's sitcom we were the eternal sidekicks. In my own case I put it down to my ankles. That probably sounds silly but I really believe that to be a leading lady you need ankles. Scott, of course, is one of those men who narrowly escapes being handsome. If his ears were just a little smaller and his nose a little less beaky . . .

The years went by. I got promoted to features editor and Scott was climbing the corporate ladder very nicely. We both owned our own homes. Mine was a little basement flat in Earl's Court, remember? And he had a rather grown-up place in Pimlico. We should by rights, we told each other, have been the bee's knees and the cat's pyjamas – in spite of the ankles and the ears. Why hadn't we been snapped up? We spent our thirtieth birthdays together (you were away somewhere, researching a book). I had just been dumped by Rob Herbert and Scott was on yet another Arthurian quest for some unobtainable maiden.

He did find a girl, Fiona King, who briefly loved him back, but in the end, of course, she broke his heart; he has the kind of heart, open and trusting, that's easily damaged. For a while there I was worried that he'd never bounce back.

For me there was the old ticking biological clock. I had never been one of those women who dream of motherhood, cooing over every passing pram. In fact you could say I was one of the least cooing amongst our circle of friends, other than you, obviously. But even you were married. Then, as I approached my mid-thirties, I began to find it increasingly difficult to imagine a life without a family. Maybe it's no more profound than wanting curly hair when one's own is straight, or straight when it's curly, but what I had, what I was, single, successful, high-earning, high-spending, home-owning, triple-holiday-taking, didn't make me fulfilled. Instead I peered into prams and lurked by Mothercare windows. I smiled at the crocodiles of four- and five-year-olds in their school uniforms crossing the street on their way to the park and I envied the mothers double-parking in front of the school, some perky, others exhausted, some shiny-haired and some a mess, but all of them purposeful, needed, at the centre of a family and of life.

Friends with children told me how they envied *me*. How humdrum and plain exhausting their lives were, how unfair it was that the brain is the only body part that shrinks when not exercised. They pointed to my Betty Jackson jacket and my Gucci handbag and told me that the last time they'd been on a holiday that did not involve sand-castles and tonsils was so far back in time that they'd forgotten what it felt like to visit an art museum or read a book in the sun. And yet, behind all the tales of woe, lay a basic fulfilment they could not hide. That fulfilment was at the core of them. What was at the core of me? More chic suits and must-have handbags and holidays in the sun with my dwindling group of single, childless friends.

Another lonely Sunday dragged on and I phoned Scott and asked him if he felt like going to the cinema. We ended up watching some art-house film that had received prizes and rave reviews. It was dreadful so we left halfway through, squeezing our way out, apologetic and giggling. With anyone else, I thought, I would have felt the need to stay watching until the last credit had rolled and the camera faded out of another rainy urban street.

We had dinner round the corner and he took my hand as we walked back down the King's Road to get a taxi. As one pulled up, he gave my address and jumped in after me. We didn't speak for the entire journey. He got out first, paid and walked me in through my own front door. It was a new side of him, this decisive, silent man.

He put his hand over mine as I reached for the light switch.

'Leave it,' he said.

That night we ended up in bed together. And it was good.

We woke in the morning and there were no dramas or questions. He got up, whistling, comfortably naked, leaving me to admire his legs that were straight and strong. He went to the bathroom and appeared again, still whistling, a towel around his waist, and went downstairs to the kitchen.

On his way he said, 'You like tea in the morning, don't you?'

He brought breakfast and the papers back to bed and we remained there side by side, reading and sipping our tea, the morning sun shining through the windows.

After a while he said, 'We should treasure this: once the kids start arriving we won't have any mornings like these for a long while.'

Rebecca

`I HAVE WONDERFUL NEWS.´ It was Dorothy, my editor. 'You are on the shortlist for the Great Romantic Read of the Year!'

Coco immediately began to practise his acceptance speech.

Judges, sponsors, Ladies and Gentlemen, losers, I stand before you the winner of this prestigious award. Obviously, less prestige and more money would have worked just as well, if not better, but . . .

Shut up, Coco.

I phoned Maggie Jacobs to ask, 'What should I wear?'

'Not black.'

'Really? I want to feel comfortable, and anyway I don't want to look like a cliché romantic novelist.'

'Nor would you want to look like a romantic novelist trying hard not to look like a cliché romantic novelist.'

Antonia Lavender would not have had this problem, I thought, being a six foot three rugby player whose real name was Reg.

My agent phoned to congratulate me.

'This should spur you on to finish the new novel,' Gemma said. 'How is it going, anyway?'

'Not well.'

'That'll change now, you'll see.'

And for a few days it seemed that she had been right. The monochrome winter that had ruled my soul for months gave way to colourful spring. I woke in the morning smiling before I had even worked out I had something to smile about. I sang as I made my breakfast. I sat at my desk for hours. I even played the piano, Liszt; it went with high spirits.

On the fifth day I read through the pages that I'd written. They were terrible. On the sixth day I reread my collection of books on writing, not for tips or instruction, as most of them were aimed at beginners, but because they were the nearest thing to a chat around the office water cooler that a person, stuck alone in a room for three hundred and thirty-two days a year, could get.

Right now the talk around the cooler went like this:

Rebecca: Hemingway shot himself when he could no longer write.

Writing book: If I were to give you only one piece of advice it would be to keep writing. That's the difference between a real writer and an amateur: a real writer writes.

Rebecca: What if you have nothing to say any more?

Coco: *It never stopped you before.*

Writing book: Ignore the clown. Just keep exercising that writing muscle and something will take shape.

I had turned the gas fire on earlier as the evening had felt raw but now the room was airless and far too hot. Instead of rising from my chair, turning the fire off and opening a window, I stayed where I was, getting some kind of sick pleasure from the throbbing of my head and my dry throat. It was a relief to have my body finally catch up with the discomfort of my mind.

I looked at the blank screen and then I told myself that I could either kill myself like Hemingway or I could write. Coco wanted to know if he would live on when I was gone.

Don't be ridiculous, I told him. *I mean how could you? You're just a figment of my imagination.*

He appeared above the desk, floating on a white feather. *The soul goes on*, he said.

Very possibly, but only if there's a soul in the first place; so trust me, if I go, you go.

Coco gave me a reproachful look as he dropped to the floor.

I leafed through my notebooks, one for each of the novels I'd written, searching for inspiration. If I had done it six times then surely I could do it again. Maybe if I revisited the embryonic characters, the quotes and research, the suggestions for plot lines. I would unearth an idea. Maybe I would find something I hadn't noticed before amidst the scribbles I had produced at night, those thoughts that appeared in that halfway-house between wakefulness and sleep, masquerading as the musings of a genius.

But the notebooks seemed to belong to someone altogether different, someone who wilfully and illogically still believed in happy endings, someone most definitely not me.

I had to leave that person behind and, by two in the morning, by persevering, sticking with it, just NOT GIV-ING UP, I had the first page of a new novel:

The Stream
I shop. After work. On Saturday mornings. And when Sunday comes I parcel up my two small children,

although they come with no receipt and cannot be returned. We brave summer heat and autumn storm and winter snow and we forgo the healing touch of spring sunshine to worship at our temple. Our temple is a drive away. As you approach, burger fat and deep-fried chips beckon you like incense. We evacuate our vehicle, having parked and paid and displayed our law-abiding compliance with a small, white, black-printed square left on the window.

A human tide, rootless, faith-divided, streams along the dirt-stamped walkways, past altars heavy with gaudy sacrifice.

I follow, a true pilgrim, with my little ones at my side, closing my mind's eye to pictures of pleasures past: swings and skipping ropes, sandcastles and hide-and-seek and air and sun and rain. These were answers then to different questions asked. We burrow deeper into a hive of colourful necessities, for the home, our haven, the things we cannot go another day without: a slow-cook pot for busy days, six tall glasses for lazy afternoons, a tower of colourful boxes to store the things I thought, just yesterday, that I could not get through another day without. And on the refrigerator, adhering magnetically, are lists of further wishes reminding you that however much you have you will always need more, more to silence the cacophony of questions: Why? What for? What then?

Exhausted yet exhilarated, I went to open a bottle of wine. I brought a glass back with me to the study and read my new pages. Perched on my shoulder, like Long John Silver's parrot, Coco laughed and then he cried and then he paused to ask which response I thought was most becoming.

Sad happy, happy sad, sad happy . . . puke?

You're right, I said, and pressed the delete key.

Like a spurned lover gazing at the object of her affections, I stared at my laptop with longing and resentment and an ache for how things used to be.

Rebecca

`THIS YEAR´S WINNER OF the Great Romantic Read is no stranger to accolades,' the chairman of the judges said. 'Take this from a recent review, I quote: "A writer seemingly able to mainline into the hearts of her readers, who allows us to believe in the power and mystery of romantic love and that out there is someone for everyone; all we need to do is believe."

'Praise indeed and typical of the kind of response our winner will have got accustomed to by now. And from our winner herself this impassioned defence of the genre in an article in the *Guardian*: "Whereas crime and science fiction have attained a certain literary credibility, romantic fiction remains the genre that dare not speak its name, at least not at smart dinner parties. Why is this? Could it be because the main readership for this kind of fiction is female and that stereotypically female concerns such as love and relationships are somehow seen as trivial, fluffy and downright *pink*? How can that be, when the three basic needs of any human being – no, in fact, any sentient being – are food, shelter *and* love? The words 'woman', 'writer' and 'romantic' do not usually make the literary pundits reach for their superlatives. Instead it seems that those three little words add up to one big embarrassment. The literary editors and the festival organisers, the judges and the critics ask themselves, what are we to do with a genre that *will* go on selling . . . and selling . . . and selling to a public who evidently doesn't know any better?"'

'Gosh, it's you!' Gemma nudged me in the ribs. She turned to Dorothy. 'It's Rebecca.' And back to me. 'It's you? You've won!'

I nodded.

'I know.'

'So why are you smiling like a woman being serenaded by a restaurant violinist?'

'I don't know,' I whispered back.

'Come on, this is wonderful.'

The chairman said, 'It gives me enormous pleasure to announce this year's Great Romantic Read – in case you hadn't already guessed – *Suburbs of the Heart* by Rebecca Finch.'

I stepped down from the podium clutching a cheque for twenty thousand pounds and an inscribed silver fountain pen, the kind that was perfectly balanced in your hand and made a muted click, like the door of a small safe, when you put the top back on. I had thanked the judges and sponsors and, of course, my agent and my editor. People were clapping and smiling, none harder than the four other shortlisted authors, and I looked left and right and smiled and nodded in return.

Jessica, my publicist, diverted me from my route back to the table.

'*Good Evening, Britain* wants to speak to you. We've got a car waiting to take you to the studio.'

I watched the interview on disc in Gemma's office:

Tina Fuller, presenter of the programme (smiles to the camera, then turns to RF): Welcome to the programme.

(Rebecca Finch acknowledges welcome with a return smile and small nod)

TF: You must be delighted?

RF: I'm thrilled, of course. It's a great honour.

TF: Despite all the doom and gloom from the publishing industry it seems reading is actually on the increase. In fact, more books are published in this country than ever before (turns to co-presenter Hugh Williams).

HW: You're absolutely right. Reading has become sexy, hasn't it? It's happened with knitting too, hasn't it? It used to be reserved for little old ladies and now look who's at it: Catherine Zeta-Jones, Keira Knightley, Angelina Jolie. All the big stars are at it, knitting away . . .

TF (frowns then smiles brightly to the camera): There is real affection for you from your readers that seems to go beyond the fact that they like your books. We've been having a little read on Amazon. This review . . . we've printed a few off . . . (picks up a small pile of papers) . . . from Corinne Sanderson of Oxford is typical. Corinne writes of your award-winning novel (*holds up a copy*), 'This is Finch at her wonderful best. Like all her books – yes, I have read every single one – this one will be my friend and companion through the good days and bad. Finch writes intelligently and sensitively about love, allowing us, her readers, to escape into a happier place.' (looks up with a smile and a nod) Great enthusiasm there.

HW: And Georgie Brookes from Eastbourne writes, 'Rebecca Finch seems to know things about me I didn't know myself. Reading her books I feel I'm not alone and that somewhere out there there is someone for me too.' You must feel very touched by those kinds of reactions?

RF (shifts in her chair, looking increasingly uneasy): Indeed. And unworthy.

HW: Surely not (crosses one long slim leg over the other). Although there is, it has to be said, a certain snobbism about romantic fiction. You yourself have not been spared. In fact, one reviewer described your work as 'escapist trivia and skunk for the masses' (turns to camera). Skunk of course being a particularly potent and addictive form of marijuana (turns back to RF). Harsh words indeed. What have you got to say to those critics?

RF: For a start I would like to ask, what's so wrong with escapism? We all of us spend most of our time trying to escape. We try to escape the fact that we are all born to die, that, in the end, all our endeavours will have proven to be futile, that mostly we are irrelevant and that the world can get on very well without us (stops abruptly).

TF (nods, her expression sympathetic): Yes, indeed.

RF (suddenly animated): Critics, publishers and book-sellers are all far too hung up on the idea of categories, when there are actually only two, or at least there should be only two, good books and bad books. For writing to be good it has to be truthful, and truth and romantic fiction are not usually compatible (leans

223

forward in her seat). You see, the great artists always knew the truth about love. Romeo and Juliet had to die so young and so soon after falling in love because, if they had been allowed to live, instead of the greatest love story of all times we would have had 'Romeo, Romeo, wherefore do you have to leave your dirty clothes in a heap on the floor?' and 'Lady, by yonder blessed moon I've had enough of your nagging; I'm going out with the lads.' Shakespeare knew that what was so touching, so intensely moving, was that un-shakeable and utterly misguided belief in love, which only youth and innocence can, or should, harbour.

Shakespeare again is spot on when, in *A Midsummer Night's Dream*, he has Duke Theseus speak of 'the lunatic, the lover and the poet . . .' all in the same breath. I'm not saying that romantic love is irrelevant but I *am* saying that we are profoundly misguided when we allow it to be the cornerstone of our existence. We are in danger of turning the means into the end and biological imperatives into a religion, a religion on whose altar some of us sacrifice everything: family, the happiness of our children, duty, work, friends, sense, brain. So what I am saying is that it's time we put Cupid in his rightful place.

HW: Which is where?'

RF (looks straight at the camera): The periphery, of course.

TF: But some of our greatest writers wrote romantic fiction. The Brontës, Jane Austen . . .

RF: They wrote about romantic love, yes. And they are frequently used to give the stamp of literary legitimacy to romantic fiction. But Jane Austen is no romantic, not really. She wrote about people falling in love and we know, with delicious anticipation, that the book will have what we think of as a happy ending: a wedding. But most of her alliances are formed out of good sense as much as sensibility. Back then, romance knew its place: as a passing diversion from the important issues like a home, raising a family, working, handing something down. Romantic love is the icing. The trouble comes when you eat the icing and throw away the cake. It seems to me that being in love has been added to our ever-growing list of 'rights'. Going back to Jane Austen . . . look at how she portrays the actual marriages. These are not filled with romance but, in the best cases, with friendship and mutual interests, a feeling of pulling in the same direction, though more frequently the couples in question view each other with bemused, sometimes irritable, tolerance. If you want the truth about love, look for it in the works of Shakespeare and Tolstoy, Strindberg, Ibsen and Flaubert . . .

HW (raises two quizzical eyebrows): So where does all this leave your own books?

RF: I have begun to wonder if they should carry a safety warning: 'Handle with care or this book may seriously damage your chances of leading a sensible life.'

TF: You are advising our viewers not to buy your books.

RF (catches eye of publicist, who is smiling in the manner of a hostess who has forgotten to turn on the oven): No, I wouldn't go as far as that. But these kinds of books, my books, are simplistic fairy tales. There's no real truth or depth to them.

TF (turns to the camera): So there you have it, from the horse's mouth. Unfortunately we are running out of time, but thank you to award-winning novelist Rebecca Finch for this . . . this candid exchange. Next week on the programme . . .

Gemma switched off the DVD player and turned to me.

'I think we can safely say that with that little effort you will have managed to alienate just about every one of your readers.'

Coco clapped his white-gloved hands.

I told you it had gone well.

'That was never my intention.'

'So what was your intention?'

'To be truthful.'

'Does the name Gerald Ratner mean anything to you?'

'The guy who said his shops sold crap?'

'That's the one.'

'Ah.'

'Have you spoken to Dorothy?'

'She's not pleased, is she?'

'Not terribly, no.'

'Maybe not that many people saw the interview.'

'I think the average viewing-figures for the programme are five million and then of course there are the newspapers, in case anyone did manage to miss the actual interview.' Gemma picked up a pile of clippings from her desk. ' "Love a cosmic yoke, says award-winning romantic novelist Rebecca Finch." That's a good one. And this one, oh yes, "Hell has no fury as a middle-aged woman scorned as real life turns sour for award-winning romantic writer."'

'That's outrageous,' I said. 'I was *not* scorned. I was the *scorner* and anyway no one thinks of forty-two as middle-aged these days.'

'I don't think your reaction shows any real awareness of your situation right now,' Gemma said.

I covered my face with my hands.

'Oh shit! I've screwed up, haven't I?'

The fall-out continued. There was a suggestion that I hand back the award, although in the end the organisers decided that would be inappropriate as the prize was for the novel, not the author. I was hit by an egg at the Woking Way with Words festival and faced hostile questions following a talk at Cheltenham. Questions like this one, from a middle-aged woman with a fixed smile and yesterday's eyes: 'What right have you got to achieve fame and fortune through your readers' hopes and dreams, tears and disappointments only to turn round and ridicule it all?'

Letters arrived, and messages on my website: 'Your books meant something to me. They were my friends. Each new publication was an event for me and I would read and reread your books. I thought you understood what it was like being me. I thought you had a heart. How wrong I was. Instead it appears that to you it has been nothing more than a money-spinner. I expect you've had a good laugh at the expense of your poor, silly, deluded readers.'

The postman arrived with a parcel and an accompanying note: 'These are returned to you with the contempt that you have shown us, your faithful readers.' I picked up the copies of

my novels, staring at one dog-eared, well-thumbed, marma-
lade-stained, coffee-splashed, once-loved paperback after the
other and I wept with shame. How could I have done it,
offended and hurt all these kind, loyal people?

You were just being yourself, Coco said.

I'm a good person.

Coco looked stricken.

Whoever told you that?

Gemma suggested I write an apology on my website.

'Tell them you were ill,' she said. 'Blame your mother or
your cat or me; I don't care as long as you retract.'

I tried to do as she had asked but I met with the same
difficulties as when I had tried to respond to Angel-face's
questions – the only way I could was if I lied. I could of course
write that I was deeply sorry to have caused offence to my
readers, readers who had supported me, literally, through the
years, who had given me an identity, allowed me to turn
doing what I loved into a career . . .

*And given you the financial independence to ditch every man
in your life without any thought to the financial implications*,
Coco joined in.

Yes, I could write all those things, well almost all, but what
I could not do was take back what I had said in that interview,
so what kind of apology would that make? 'Sorry I upset you
but I meant every word I said.'

Coco suggested that I try it.

I turned on him.

This is all your fault. Everything was fine until you reappeared.

*Didn't your therapist tell you that you had to stop referring to
me as a separate entity?* Coco reminded me.

Yes, and she also suggested that you had served your purpose and I'm sure she said something about not getting into conversations with my inner demons.

Coco, in turn, pointed out that a ban on inner demons did not, to his way of thinking, cover inner clowns.

I put my hands over my ears and clamped my eyes shut.

Oh very grown-up.

A little later I decided to call Bridget. I hadn't heard from her or Angel-face since the TV interview. I hoped they hadn't seen it or the newspapers.

'Nice of you to call.' Bridget's voice was tight. 'Zoe saw you on *Good Evening, Britain*.'

'Oh no.'

'Oh yes. She's told Zac that she needs time out to think. She's in New York, staying with her other godmother.'

You see, Coco said when I had put the phone down and resumed what was an almost habitual pose these days, head in hands. *You* are *responsible for everything and everything* is *your fault*.

Mount Olympus

MOTHER´S BIG DAY. SHE´S dressed up for the occasion: fancy frock, killer heels, rocks – the works. Ares says maybe he should dress up in full armour every time they report on the war in Iraq and everybody thinks he's like so hilarious. Mother ignores him. She's sitting right in front of the screen, her lunch on her lap. The others are at the table; they're watching too, but pretending not to. I grab a plate and pull up a stool next to Mother, avoiding that cow Hera's gimlet eye.

'How's it going?' I nod at the screen. It's important to show interest, solidarity, especially with the rest of the guys being there.

'Hush.' Mother frowns.

I can feel Hera sniggering and my cheeks go red. (People go on about eternal youth but they don't think about all the stuff that goes with it, like going red when the look you're aiming for is cool and dignified, or the never-ending zits . . . and don't get me started on the involuntary erections.)

On the screen all these mortals are having their meal too, seated around little tables in a large room. The lighting is bad. No wonder Mother looks smug. The lighting up here's always just so, soft golden dawn.

Anyway, this old guy walks up to the lectern and starts spouting. I look around for something to drink but Hera has the jug right by her elbow and she's not going to share, not with me.

Down amongst the mortals, the old guy drones on but Mother seems to like it. She even claps once or twice. Athene arrives late and sits down at the table pretending not to notice what's on the screen.

Mother claps again; the sound is kind of muffled on account of her wearing those gloves.

Rebecca Finch gets her award . . . she's not looking her best, though, I have to say; the clothes are all right, not black for once, but she has a funny glassy-eyed look, like she's running a temperature, and her cheeks are a bright pink, which actually clashes with the pink of her suit. She goes to sit down but instead she's dragged off to do some TV interview.

Mother zaps until she finds the studio.

'Oh it's *Good Evening, Britain*,' she says. 'That's wonderful PR.'

I'm not really concentrating on the screen when I sense Mother stiffening beside me. I start to listen.

It's Rebecca.

'Shakespeare again is spot on when in *A Midsummer Night's Dream*,' she's saying, 'he has Duke Theseus speak of "the lunatic, the lover and the poet . . ." all in the same breath.'

Up here everyone's looking at Mother, who has not moved; she's sitting stiff-backed, her wondrous eyes fixed on the screen. Then Ate titters and Hera puts her finger to her lips as if to shut Ate up when actually she's loving it. I want to do something, turn the screen off, whack Ate across her smirking face.

'Being in love has been added to our ever-growing list of "rights",' Rebecca Finch continues.

'If you want the truth about love . . .'

Mother grabs the remote and zaps into another channel: it's Martha Stewart, Hera's favourite.

But she can't help herself, saying to Mother, 'Why, dear, don't switch over on my account. We were all enjoying your little show, really we were.'

'Yeah,' Ate says. 'Some homage.'

Athene says, 'Rebecca Finch speaks well. What she says is true.'

'Rebecca Finch speaks well. What she says is true.' Who does she think she is, the bloody oracle?

'We have tried to tell you,' Hera says. 'Haven't we, Zeus dear? Aphrodite's cult is not what it was.'

'That's rubbish,' I tell them.

Hera glares at me.

'I'm sorry, we've all been pussy-footing around for far too long but the truth is that nothing good can come from a cult presided over by someone like her.' She points at Mother and I think how much I'd like a raven or an eagle or something to swoop down and snap her finger off. 'A feckless single mother of . . . well, I've lost count of how many. One of them a complete delinquent.' She shoots me another look. 'No, I'm afraid we've all seen this coming, haven't we, Zeus dear?'

Mother rises from her seat. Her dress is crumpled and her tiara has slipped down over one eye.

'I don't know what everyone's talking about: my cult is flourishing. They're falling in love all over the place,' she says, but in a voice that hardly carries.

People turn from Mother to Zeus and back again but it's Hera who pipes up again.

'Any fool can get them to *fall in love*,' she says, turning towards me. 'Even him.' Someone should tell her it's rude to point. I narrow my eyes at her but she doesn't care. 'Don't ask me why, but more was expected of you, Aphrodite. You have a seat up here. With such privilege comes responsibilities.'

I try to catch Hephaestus's eye; maybe *he'll* stick up for Mother, he's her husband after all, but no, he's no help whatsoever, avoiding my gaze and Mother's, making a big thing of checking on a crack in one of the table legs instead.

Mother just stands there taking it all, the preaching, the ticking-off, the tittering, until I can't deal with it any longer.

'Just cool it, you guys,' I say. 'She's doing the best she can.'

All right, for a comeback that was kind of pathetic, especially as my voice did this hike up half an octave. But I had to say *something*.

'Anyway, if someone's fucked up on the love front it's me.'

Well, they all seem to agree on that, at least.

Now Zeus speaks.

'So, my child.' He looks at Mother and I can see her shrink beneath his awesome gaze. 'You are being mocked.' That is all he says. It is all he needs to say.

Without a word she exits the left portal in the direction of her chamber. Usually she kind of just glides by, head held high, eyes glowing, a small smile on her lips, followed by the gaze of every guy present as if she had their eyeballs on a leash. But not now, now she more like *scurries*. That really freaks me.

I have been loitering by her half-open door when she spots me and says, 'Oh, it's you.' It would have been nice if she'd said it more perkily, like it was a really good thing it was me, rather than a disappointment, but there we are.

'How are you doing?' I step inside.

'How am I doing?' She stops before me, eyes flashing teal. 'How do you think I'm doing? I've been made a laughing stock. I've been humiliated in front of the entire family. Have you any idea what that feels like?'

'Er, yes.'

'Rebecca was favoured, that's what hurts so much. You know the way I've been praising her in front of the others, how I've held her up as an example for how one should be worshipped and one's cult promoted. And now she goes and does this: turns on me, betrays me in the most public way possible.'

'I don't suppose she knew you were saying those things about her.'

'Well, of course she didn't.'

'So how could she know she was meant to be grateful, I mean?'

'Just go away if you're going to be difficult.' She sinks down on to a couch. 'She was favoured, Eros, favoured.'

Mother hangs her lovely head and I take a step towards her. I put out my hand but then I don't know what to do with it so I pull back, trying instead to think of something helpful to say.

'So we have to really get that thing going with John Sterling.'

'Thank you for pointing that out, Eros.'

I hate it when she's sarcastic.

'Having said that, I don't know that the little minx deserves happiness after the way she's behaved. Yes, why should she have her appalling behaviour rewarded with a relationship with . . .' She pauses and her eyes go a soft heavenly blue. 'A quite beautiful young man.'

Her eyes never go that colour when she looks at *me*.

'Not that young,' I mutter.

'No, I'm beginning to think John Sterling deserves better, the best even.'

And we all know what she means by the best. I turn round and face her straight on.

'No!'

Mother loses the dreamy smile in favour of a frown.

'What do you mean no?'

I see all my hopes for the future going down the toilet. No seat upstairs for me, possible demotion and eternal shame for Mother, and Athene and that cow Hera triumphant, all for the sake of a pretty face: John Sterling's.

'I mean you can't drop that amazing plan you had to win the bet with Athene and emerge triumphant as the foremost goddess on Mount Olympus.'

'You might be right, Eros.' She reaches out a slender arm and strokes my cheek with the soft back of her hand.

'Might I?'

'Yes, you clever boy.' Although her gaze isn't heavenly blue it's a pretty neat shade of turquoise.

'Me, oh right.' Inside I'm calling out hurrah.

'Then again it is a very pretty face,' Mother says, each word lingering on her lips.

Damn!

'Only kidding.' She throws an apple at me from the bowl at her side. 'Catch.'

I grin at her and throw it back.

'Catch.'

Rebecca

BURIED BENEATH THE ANGRY missives on my website, I found the message from Lance Cooper: 'Guess who? Long time no see! I had to get in touch and congratulate you on winning such a prestigious award. (It was my mother – you remember Margaret? – who alerted me to the announcement in the paper; she's a great fan of yours.) I'm not surprised that you've had a glittering career: there was always something special about you.'

Really, I thought, just not as special as Julie Fitzgerald's DD breasts.

He went on to say that he had returned to London after having lived in Edinburgh all these years and could we meet up.

I wrote back and said I'd love to.

'What would you think of a man who had an affair while his wife lay dying?' Lance Cooper's large brown eyes searched mine for an answer.

We were sitting eating dinner at an Italian restaurant just off the Kings Road. We had spent drinks and the first course catching up and filling in: No I haven't seen Amy for years, not since she moved. Leonora, yes, poor girl. Yes, the usual . . .

Your sister died? God, I am sorry. Here, take mine, it's clean. Yes, Lily and I married.

That's great. We all thought you would . . .

So you're divorced . . . ten years ago . . . Anything since then? Oh an arsehole. Bad luck . . .

Lily died! That's awful. Poor Lily. God, how terrible for you. Five years? Is that all you had . . .

No, no children . . .

Me neither . . .

Yes, I did find someone else; we got married actually, but it didn't work out, we divorced a while back . . .

Rebound?

Afraid so. I just couldn't bear being on my own.

In Sickness and in Health – or Not

Lily and I had a textbook university romance, but it didn't end there, we married the summer after she graduated. Pretty much everyone told us we were too young but they were wrong. We were utterly, ridiculously happy. God, she was lovely: dark hair and creamy complexion, rosebud lips, great body, the lot. Very cool. Very laid-back. Smoking these tiny cigars. She graduated with a first, although her friends claimed that no one had actually seen her do any work. I think most people were a little in awe of her. And I continued being in awe of her even after we were married. She worked in an art gallery. Just the kind of job you would have expected her to fall into. And she was good at it. The artists loved her, of course. We wanted children but we weren't trying very hard. Things were pretty damn perfect as they were, really.

When she got ill we refused to take it seriously. Illness did not happen in our world and, if it did, you got well again. Only she didn't. She died, bit by bit over the course of two years. In the beginning I handed over a lot of work to my partner so that I could go with her to every appointment, every chemo session. I remember so clearly sitting with her in the hospital canteen as a hot summer's day slowly turned into a balmy evening. Lily had had the operation and finished her first round of chemotherapy and we were going to get the results of her latest tests.

She had been gazing out of the window at the street but then she reached across the table and placed her hand in mine. It weighed nothing, as if the substance was already being leached from her body.

'I just wanted to see if I could do it,' she said.

'Do what?'

'I wanted to make sure I could touch you.'

I asked her what she meant. Of course she could touch me.

'Because you are well and I am dying. Don't you feel how far apart that puts us?'

'What are you talking about?' I said. 'You're not dying.'

But when we did get called in to see the specialist the news was bad. The treatment wasn't working. She could embark on another course but quite frankly, he said, if it were him he would go home and try to enjoy what was left of life.

In the car she was calm, no tears, no why me.

But she did object to one small thing.

'Dr Phillips said if I were you . . . as if we were talking about which train to catch or what book to read.'

'He does have experience of . . . of this whole thing.'

'Of dying young?'

'No, no, of course not. But sadly he will have seen it happen.'

'Ah,' she said, 'but there's the rub – when it comes to dying it's all about personal experience.'

She went to a local cancer-support group twice a week. More and more it was as if she were leaving our house to go home. When I picked her up in the car I would usually find her at the centre of a group and I would watch her for a moment before letting her know that I was there, because in that room with these other people, sick people, she was more alive then I had seen her since the cancer struck. They were all ages, both sexes, some bald, some wigged, some looking quite healthy. I learnt that the healthy-looking ones were usually the ones who'd given up on treatment. Like Lily.

You know when we were kids hanging out and someone's parent would appear? You remember how we used to go kind of stiff and formal and pissed off all at the same time, exchanging glances and speaking of nothing in a stilted way? That's how it was when I approached Lily and her group after those meetings. I felt like one of our parents and I understood how annoying it must have been for them, as if they actually gave a damn what we were talking about. One woman in particular really annoyed me. She was in her fifties, clumsy-looking, big-boned. She had lost all her hair but she never covered up. I half expected her to be wearing a badge with 'Proud to have cancer' on it. She was always talking and when I or anyone else appeared, anyone who wasn't part of the group, she'd lower her voice and draw the others in; it was this kind of *us against the world* trip.

I said something about it to Lily as we drove back home

one night and she turned on me with a look that said I was the enemy.

'Come on,' I said, 'it's me. We're on the same side, remember?' I took my hand off the steering wheel and put it on her knee, giving it a pat. She drew away from my touch.

Then there were the times when she just wanted me to hold her and never let go.

'If we stay here,' she said as we lay in bed, just hugging each other, 'maybe nothing, not even death, can find us.'

She would ask me, over and over again, if I loved her and I told her I did, more than ever. Then she wanted to know if I still fancied her.

That broke my heart because the truth was, I didn't. Obviously I never told her that. I loved her so much it ached, but that love grew more and more like the love for a child or an ailing parent. Just the thought of sex with her made me feel like some kind of pervert. Maybe she sensed it because she let me off the hook, telling me she just wanted to be held. I could do that.

Then there were the jokes. She and her cancer friends all made brave little jokes about their illness, the way it made them look, the treatment, all of it. And I had to laugh although I didn't find it funny. Friends would look at me with sympathy and say, 'Of course you don't find it funny: you're losing her.' But actually, the main reason I didn't find it funny was because all their jokes had been done before, in the columns and blogs of all the other poor devils with cancer: 'I never thought the day would come when I was named Slimmer of the Year.' Or, 'At least I will be saving on the waxing.' I couldn't do it, laugh and admire their guts.

We lived in Cancerland and I had to get out.

It was the usual sordid little fling. At a conference, to compound the cliché. She wasn't even that pretty, but she was healthy. Everything about her, her wide hips and full breasts, her strong teeth and smooth skin and thick, glossy hair, exuded health. She prattled on about her plans for the future. She got pissed. Her jokes were not particularly funny but at least they weren't brave. So I fucked her.

Lily died four weeks later. I didn't tell her what had happened at that damn conference but I think she knew anyway.

The thing is, I'm not a bad guy. And I loved her. I really loved her. And that's what haunts me as much as anything: is that all I'm capable of, the best I have to give? I loved her, she was dying and I betrayed her. I haven't told many people, it's not the kind of thing you advertise, after all, but those I have confided in tell me not to be so hard on myself. That it was just a physical outlet. That it had nothing to do with my feelings for Lily. But it did. It had everything to do with her. So now I never tell a woman that I love her. How can I?

Lance and I had stayed at the restaurant until every table but ours had been cleared and laid for lunch and the waiters had taken to checking their watches each time they caught our eyes.

'We should go,' I said. 'They probably have a really early start.'

'Relax, it's their job,' Lance said, but he agreed to leave.

He put me in a cab and watched and waved as it drove off.

Back home I went straight to my desk and switched on the computer. I had to work. Lily Cooper had died young. If I were to die tomorrow, did I want to leave behind unfulfilled wishes to wilt and die like flowers on my grave?

Who cares? Coco said. *You'll be dead.*

I decided now was the time to try my hand at the crime novel I had been thinking about for some time:

Mr Zimmerman's Holiday

The last thing he was heard saying before he disappeared was, 'It's good to be alive.' Spring had arrived overnight and on the early-morning streets people blinked against the unaccustomed sunlight as they peeled off their winter layers, everyone but Morris Zimmerman, that is. Mr Zimmerman in his white shirt, discreet tie and heavy wool three-piece suit stepped out of his immaculate front garden at nine o'clock precisely and turned left towards his studio on a nearby street, the same as he did every weekday morning. No one had ever seen Morris Zimmerman out and about in anything other than a woollen three-piece suit, and if you knocked on his door, at any time at all, he always answered the door dressed in that same way. If you visited his studio there he'd be in front of his easel, brush and palette in hand, still in his three-piece suit, so when you thought about it, it seemed nothing short of a miracle that there was never the merest speck of paint on the dark cloth. Neighbours speculated that he even wore his suit to bed but as Mrs Zimmerman had died over twenty years ago there was no decent way of finding out if this was true. That was why, at first, none of his friends and neighbours put two and two together when the news came that a body had been found wearing Bermuda shorts and a Hawaiian shirt.

*   *   *

I must have fallen asleep because the next thing I knew sunlight was flooding my desk and my phone was ringing.

It was John Sterling.

'How's the book going?'

'The book? Oh the *book*.' Inwardly I was cursing Angie Bliss. 'Still very much at the ideas stage, I'm afraid. There's been so much going on lately. I don't know if you've seen but I've caused a bit of an upset lately.'

'The – my books are rubbish – statement.' He chuckled.

I sighed.

'I didn't actually say that; the newspaper made it up. Then again, I did say something very similar.' He seemed to be waiting for me to continue speaking so I asked how he was.

'Very well, thank you.'

'And how is Melanie?'

'Melanie? I'm sure she's fine.' Which was an odd way to speak about one's partner, I thought. 'I feel our meeting was cut short the other week,' he said finally. 'I thought I'd check to see if you needed some more information, but if you've dropped the idea . . .'

'That's really kind. And I might well pick it up again. In which case I would love to take you up on your offer.'

'Great,' John Sterling said. 'I look forward to it.'

'Bye.'

'Bye.'

John

`BREAK THE CYCLE, THAT´S the trick.'` Angie Bliss handed
John an ordinary rubber band. 'Put it on your left wrist,' she
ordered. 'No, I'm serious, put it on.' As he did what he was
told she leant over his arm and said, 'You're lucky you're not
hairy.'

'Am I? Right. Now what do I do?'

'It's simple. Every time an obsessive thought enters your
mind you snap the band.'

'I snap the band?'

She leant forward again and took his wrist.

'You snap the band – like this.' She inserted her finger
between his skin and the band, pulled it out and let go. 'Snap,'
she said, her voice husky.

John looked at the red band.

'I'll give it a go,' he said. 'I just need this whole thing sorted
out. I've wasted enough time. I've got my daughter staying
this week. I want to be able to focus on enjoying my time with
her.'

'Lovely. And how about Rebecca Finch? Have you seen her
lately?'

'I spoke to her on the telephone – last night, as it happens. I
told her that I would be happy to help should she require any
further information.'

'She's a very attractive woman, don't you think?'

'I suppose she is.'

'What do you mean you suppose she is?'

John frowned.

'I haven't really thought about it. I'm helping her with her research, not asking her for a date. You really think this rubber-band business is going to help?'

'You'll have to work at it,' the therapist said. 'As I'm sure Rupert would have told you, this is a long process. Now, I know I've asked you this before, but there's no harm in a little reiteration, is there? What would you say your ideal woman was like?'

'Ideal woman? I don't know that I have one.'

'Try. There is a point to all this, I assure you. You do want to get on top of this OCD thing?'

'Of course I do. But I don't see what that has to do with my ideal woman.'

'I don't know if Rupert ever explained this to you, but for therapy to work there has to be trust. So trust me. Tell me, what is she like, your ideal mate?'

John raised his hands in resignation and sat back in his chair.

'Lively,' he said.

'Good.'

'Energetic, interested.'

'Excellent.' The therapist nodded in approval and John began to feel as if he were answering a quiz rather than giving his opinion.

'And pretty would be nice,' he said.

'Personally I've always had a weakness for freckles.'

'Freckles?'

'Freckles. Not all over, perhaps, but a becoming sprinkle across the nose and maybe some on the forearms and a tiny little bit on the décolletage. As for age, I don't know about you but I always think it's so much more impressive to see a successful man with a woman his own age at his side, an interesting-looking woman as opposed to some pretty-pretty bimbo.'

'I can't see why she can't be interesting-looking *and* pretty.' John realised he sounded as if he were negotiating.

'Well, yes, yes, it's not impossible. Depending of course what you define as pretty. Now what about noses? The most attractive woman I've seen for many a day has what I'd call a proper nose. Not one of those cosmetic-surgery teensy-weensy things.'

'A big nose?'

'I did not say *big*. I said *proper*. How about hair?'

'Hair is good.'

'We won't get anywhere if you won't take this seriously. Hair?'

'Blonde, I suppose.'

A small frown appeared on the therapist's alabaster brow. 'Are you sure? You don't think light-brown, for example?'

'Brown hair can obviously be . . .'

'I didn't say brown' – the therapist's tone was sharp – 'I said light-brown.'

'The hair colour really doesn't matter that much,' John said.

Angie Bliss relaxed and continued.

'Long?'

John nodded.

'Long's all right. Short's all right too.'

'Thick, shiny and wavy?'

'Obviously all of that would be very nice.'

'Of course it would be. And we don't like small button noses?'

'Don't we?'

'No. We like noses with character. And eyebrows. Proper eyebrows.'

John looked at the therapist's nose and wondered if perfection came under the heading of character.

He said, 'She should be independent.'

'Career woman?'

'I think so. Someone with her own life, her own interests, although not a lawyer, preferably.'

'Absolutely,' the therapist said. 'Opposites, that's what one wants.'

'Yes, complementary but different. And I'd like her to have children of her own. One of the problems with Melanie was that she didn't understand that Susannah was a priority. So definitely someone who has children.'

'Or someone who has lots of experience with children, many godchildren, for example. Yes, that would be the best of all worlds. She will have the experience and temperament to deal with your daughter, she will understand your child's needs but she won't be preoccupied with her own offspring. Perfect.'

'I suppose that could work. If there really is someone like that.'

'Trust me, there is. So, you want someone who's maternal yet career-minded, sharp and independent yet kind and feminine with pretty, light-brown hair and a sprinkling of freckles. Self-reliant but affectionate, and you said energetic. Personally I think someone who's happy in their own company, doing nothing, just being, is very attractive.'

'I suppose so,' John said again. 'But I still don't see what this exercise has to do with OCD.'

'You wouldn't. That's why I'm the therapist and you're not. And please remember why you sought help from professionals in the first place.'

'Because my ex-girlfriend told me to.'

'What are you, a man or a hen-pecked wimp?' She paused for a moment and then, as if she had had a sudden inspiration, her brow cleared and she told him, 'Anyway, quite apart from all of this, the latest research shows that a supportive spouse is key to conquering OCD.' She leant across and patted him on the knee. 'But we'll get there, don't you worry.'

In preparation for Susannah's visit John went to Hamley's to get the latest Barbie doll. Last time his daughter had stayed the night he had incurred his ex-wife's wrath by getting the Barbie Floral Vanity Unit. It had been unpacked and assembled ready for Susanna's arrival when Lydia, marching ahead to her daughter's room, had taken one look at the toy and hissed, 'Could I have a word?' While their daughter rushed over to the pink plastic furniture, Lydia told John that he was out of order, spoiling the child, trying to buy her affection, attempting to outdo Lydia and Adrian . . . The accusations had got shriller and Susannah, roused from her play of dabbing imaginary blusher on her peach cheeks and mascara on her dark silky lashes, had turned round. Seeing the looks on her parents' faces, she had burst into tears.

Lydia, unable to hide a glint of triumph in her eyes, had knelt down in front of the child and explained in a sorrowful voice that Daddy had made a mistake and that the vanity unit would have to go back to the shop.

'Maybe Santa . . .'

'Father Christmas,' John muttered.

Lydia had glared at him, shaking her head before continuing with exaggerated enunciation, 'Maybe *Father Christmas* will bring you one for Christmas.'

John had looked from his weeping daughter to his ex-wife, who was still squatting in front of the child. He remembered the time, not so long ago, when Susannah was born. He had stood by, unable to do anything much other than be in the way, as his wife went through the pain of labour. As the hours wore on he had wished fervently for a dragon or two to appear so that he could prove to his wife his love and gratitude. Yet now, barely six years on, if a dragon knocked on the door he would keep hold of Susannah and then stand back, politely offering him Lydia.

'Be my guest, dear fellow, and enjoy.'

This time, determined to get the visit off to a good start by pleasing Susannah without enraging his ex-wife, he had stood before the rows of California Surfer Barbies, Fairytopia Elina Barbies and Barbies On the Go at a loss to know which one to chose. A young woman shopper with a toddler in a pushchair smiled conspiratorially at him. A female sales assistant with an air of motherly competence asked him if she could help. He said he was unsure which one his six-year-old daughter would like the best. The sales assistant said that California Surfer Barbie was very popular at the moment.

The young mother interceded with, 'My eldest is completely in love with her Fairytopia.'

She and the sales assistant exchanged amused glances as John picked up one of the dolls, looking at it with complete bafflement.

The assistant said, 'Why don't you go for Fairytopia Elina? As this lady says, all the little girls adore her.'

John nodded.

'Yes. Yes, I think I shall. Thank you both very much.'

As he wandered off towards the cash point the assistant shook her head and smiled at the young mother.

'Bless.'

Now he was pacing the sitting room of his Primrose Hill house, pausing every minute or so in front of the window to look for the silver Mercedes Estate. He had checked Susannah's bedroom twice already, making sure it was aired and that her toys were arranged just the way she liked them. Then he had worried, the way he often did, that Susannah's desire for order and straight lines might be the beginnings of obsessive-compulsive behaviour.

A couple of weeks back, when he and Lydia had been having a particularly vicious row, Lydia had turned on him, her dark eyes sparkling with malice, and said, 'Maybe it's best Susannah doesn't spend too much time with you; I mean what with your problems.' She had rolled the word 'problems' around her mouth as if it were a chocolate, melting deliciously on her tongue.

He had felt doubly betrayed; she knew about his OCD only because he had confided in her during a recent truce, telling her to watch out for signs of related behaviour in their daughter.

'There is a slight genetic component to the whole thing,' he had explained.

And at the time, Lydia had smiled and thanked him for being so frank. She was an expert, his ex-wife, in drawing out a confidence, storing it up and throwing it back in your face.

He went into Susannah's bedroom one more time and having studied the row of soft toys lined up on the bed he picked up Pooh and moved him away from Mr Woofy, sitting him next to Polly Pig instead: a small break in the order would be healthy. He took a step back, studying his handi-work. Then again, maybe it wasn't right separating the two friends. Maybe instead of gently discouraging any obsessive-compulsive tendencies in his daughter, it would simply upset her to see her possessions rearranged. So what about if he moved *both* Pooh and Mr Woofy away from their spot just below the picture of the funfair and placed them further down towards the foot-end of the bed? Yes, that was better, enough of a disruption of what could be developing into an obsessive arranging of her toys by his daughter but not so much as to unsettle her.

Back in the sitting room he was half expecting the phone to ring and to hear Lydia's voice, faux-commiserating, inform-ing him that Susannah would not be coming after all. These conversations would always begin with, 'It's not about *us*, it's about a little girl.' He, so accustomed to dealing with other people's imploded lives, other people's messes, was power-less. 'Susannah has been invited to a sleepover and I really don't think we should be selfish about these things.' Or, 'Susannah didn't want to tell you herself, you know how kind she is, but she was getting quite agitated and it turns out that she really wanted her Aunt Jenny to come over and look after her.'

A large framed school photograph of their daughter stood in the window alcove. Rosy-cheeked, a little plump, with her auburn hair brushed glossy and tied back with a regulation red ribbon into what she had informed him was 'a half-ponytail', she smiled out at him with her best gappy smile. He smiled back. He did this every time his gaze fell on her picture.

He could not remember when this latest tic had begun (he called them tics, the compulsions, as if using such a harmless little word would make them less disruptive). He would feel the dead-weight of fear in his stomach as he thought how just such photographs like that one of Susannah were plastered across the front pages of the newspapers with heartbreaking regularity because the child in question, the shiny-haired, trusting little girl, or the grinning, self-conscious boy, had been lost to some terrible calamity or brutal crime. His thoughts would circle the pain of the parents, tiptoe up to the moment when someone is told that the worst that life could do to them had been done, the moment when the light goes out of their lives never to return other than as a pale reflection. Then he would make it doubly worse by asking himself if all these thoughts, heavy with negativity and doom, could somehow invite the very disasters he so feared. In order to disable such dark thoughts he had to smile and smile again at his daughter's photograph.

What was he doing, a man of forty-three, a successful, well-respected professional, pacing up and down grinning like a monkey at a photograph? It had to stop. It could not be allowed to go on. He looked down at his left wrist. When Angie Bliss had suggested it, he had thought the idea of wearing some rubber band round his wrist, twanging it at every marauding thought, faintly ridiculous, but not, he decided, as ridiculous as his behaviour right now. What he aimed to give his daughter, what mostly he managed to give her, was a calm and collected father, a robust and fatherly father, and if twanging a red elastic band round his wrist would help him to continue to achieve that aim, then twang it he would.

Finally, and almost half an hour late, the silver Mercedes estate drove up outside. He hurried to the door, pausing for a moment in front of the hall mirror to smooth his hair. He flung open the door, bent down and picked his child up in his arms, lifting her high before hugging her.

'Daddeee.' Susannah squirmed in his arms, pulling at her skirt that had ridden up at the back.

He put her down and met his ex-wife's eyes. She gave a little shake of her head, managing to look pitying and reproachful both at once.

'Daddy, guess what?'

'What?' He smiled at the excited child.

'I've got a puppy and you're going to help me look after him while Mummy and Adrian are away.'

'A puppy?' John looked at Lydia.

'It was a surprise. I told Adrian it wasn't the best timing.' She smiled indulgently. 'But he was so excited.'

'Was he? How sweet.'

She narrowed her eyes at him.

'Don't be childish.'

'Well, I just think it would be nice to be consulted once in a while, especially if I'm supposed to pick up the pieces.'

'What pieces? You're looking after a puppy, for Christ's sake. You want to be consulted? You should have thought about that before playing away from home.'

They looked at each other: High Noon.

'Can we do this later,' he said, directing a meaningful look at Susannah and praying that Lydia's maternal side would win over her ball-breaking side so that, for once, their daughter could be handed from one parent to another without feeling she was passing through a war zone. Lydia said nothing, confining her animosity to another glare, so he turned to Susannah, saying in what he hoped was a light and jolly manner, 'A puppy, eh? I hope it's house-trained.'

Lydia rolled her eyes.

'Do you have to be such a stick-in-the-mud?'

John took a deep breath and counted slowly to ten before saying, 'OK, let's meet it.'

'Him,' Susannah said. 'He's a him and he's called Albie.' From the tone of her voice to her stance, head to one side, hands on hips, she seemed suddenly very much like her mother.

'OK, let's go and meet Albie.'

A small sticky hand was placed in his, pulling him over to his ex-wife's car.

Susannah was asleep. The lamp on the white-painted chest of drawers was left on, rotating gently, throwing its patterns of moons and stars on to the ceiling. His daughter lay tucked up in a nest lined with soft toys with the puppy curled up by her feet.

There had been a tricky half-hour after John had placed the tiny Border terrier in his basket on the floor by the bed.

'But he won't like it.'

'What won't he like?'

'He won't like sleeping on the floor when all the toys are on the bed.'

'He's not on the floor, darling, he's in his own comfortable bed. Anyway, dogs don't think like that.'

'How do you know?'

'OK, I don't know, not for sure, I'm extrapolating, but even if I were wrong and he had similar thought processes to us, he would probably be thinking how lucky he was to have his own cosy bed and not have to share.'

Susannah thought about this for a moment then she sat bolt upright and said, 'No, he gets really jealous.' And with that she made a sweeping movement with her arms, pushing most of the toys on to the floor, picking the remaining ones up by a leg or an ear and chucking them over the side to join the others. 'There,' she said, arms crossed against her round belly.

John looked at his small daughter, at the defiance mixed with a little bit of worry at maybe having gone too far, and tried not to smile.

'Goodnight then, darling.' He bent down and kissed the downy cheek.

He got no further than the kitchen when a small voice called out, 'Daddy?'

'Yes?' he said from her doorway.

'Daddy, I can't sleep without my toys.'

He picked his way across a floor that looked like an illustration of massacre in Toy Town.

'Well, let's put them back on your bed then.'

'But Albie will be upset.'

What he felt like saying was, 'Albie can piss off, as can the little prick whose bright idea it was to get him in the first place.' But what he actually said was, 'Dogs really shouldn't be in the bed with you. He's happy in his basket – just look at him.'

Susannah leant over the side of the bed, peering down at the puppy.

'I think he looks sad.' At this she herself began to cry.

He picked her up in his arms, where she lay limp against his shoulder, weeping.

'Darling, Albie is fine, I promise you. Happy as a sandboy.'

Hiccuping and sniffing, Susannah wailed, 'It's not him that's sad, it's me. I miss my mummee.'

John stroked her slippery hair thinking, why does she not use her little fist to punch me in the heart while she's at it?

'And I'm sure Mummy misses you, but it's nice for Daddy to see you. I miss you lots too, when you're not here.'

Susannah wiped her nose on his shoulder and struggled out of his embrace, sliding back down under her duvet.

'Mummy said you should have thought about that before you went off with the trollop.'

He winced.

'Sarah. Her name was Sarah. And I didn't go off with her. I . . . I spent time with her, which was very wrong of me because married people should not spend that kind of time . . .'

'What kind of time?'

'The kind of time you should only spend with the person you're married to.'

'What *kind* of time?'

'*Bed* time. I spent bed time with Sarah and that was very wrong and Mummy was quite within her rights to be very angry. But I didn't go off with her.'

'So why are you and Mummy not together?'

'Because sometimes, although you think you've repaired the damage you caused, you haven't actually done such a good job. There's still a tiny crack and, if you're unlucky, that crack just gets wider and wider until all the nice feelings fall into it and disappear.' He glanced at Susannah, who was looking worried again, and he added, 'Although they are still there; just . . . well, further down.'

'Mummy spends bed time with Adrian, so are you angry?'

'No. No, I'm not angry because Mummy and I aren't married any more so Mummy can spend as much bed time as she likes with Adrian.'

'I'm not married.'

John laughed.

'No, you're not.'

'So I *can* spend bed time with Albie.'

Rebecca

`I KNOW YOU DON´T want to write the divorce-lawyer book but you have been thinking about crime so it can't hurt to meet up with John Sterling again. You never know, it might inspire you in other ways too.'

I watched the young women passing by the café where Matilda and I were sitting.

'Look at them.'

'I know. Why they can't make the top of their trousers and the bottom of their tops meet I do not know.'

'That's not what I meant. They think they look great. They crimp and primp and shop and diet. They polish and wax and flirt. They dance before us on the high streets of Britain for a brief while and then, then they end up like us.'

'Looking at this lot' – Matilda gesticulated towards the pavement – 'I think they'd be so lucky. Anyway, you need to cheer up. Get back out there.'

'I don't want a relationship, if that's what you mean. Just the thought of it makes me shiver.'

'I'm not talking about a relationship. Have a fling. Have a fling with John Sterling. He sounds nice and you said he was good-looking.'

'And he's in a relationship, I think. Anyway, I'm not the fling type, you know that.'

'You've changed. Maybe you've changed in that way too?'

'I'd rather work. I suppose it was talking to him about legal stuff, but I have had an idea. It's for a play, a courtroom drama called *Eros on Trial*.'

'Ah you've got a title already; always good to have the title sorted.'

'Exactly. It's half the work done, isn't it? Anyway, Eros is literally on trial, for crimes against humanity. The play would be made up of witness statements, mostly for the prosecution. I thought I'd use the uplifting stories of happy marriages I was collecting for Angel-face. As you might recall they weren't so uplifting after all, apart from yours, of course. My agent actually quite likes the idea. She said, and I'm quoting, "It would at least be a different audience, one that doesn't feel utterly let down and betrayed."'

Matilda considered.

'Could work, I suppose. What does your legal adviser think?'

'You mean John Sterling? I haven't asked him.'

I read every book I could find on play-writing. I started to write down my witness statements. Were people allowed to stand up in court and give such lengthy statements? I decided to email John Sterling and ask.

Later on that evening I was about to sit down to supper when the phone rang.

'Hi, it's Melanie. We met the other day, with John.'

'Absolutely. And what a coincidence. I've just emailed him. I need to pick his brain.'

'Oh he'll love that. He likes nothing better than talking about his work. Anyway, I've read your book. I loved it, I really did. I tried to get John to read it as well, but you know men.'

Not all of them, to be fair, Coco pointed out.

Leave me alone, I'm on the phone.

'Hello, are you still there?'

'Sorry, yes. I know he's very busy.'

'He's a complete workaholic. He defines himself entirely through his career.'

'Easy mistake to make.'

'Big mistake too. I mean he's successful, but how long will that last? There'll soon be someone else coming on to the scene, someone younger and hungrier.'

I laughed.

'You make him sound like a supermodel.'

'Honestly, though, it goes on in all professions; yours too, I'm sure. I mean there's always someone younger, a fresh new voice waiting to take your place.'

'I try not to think about that,' I said.

'Well, I was really calling about my reading group. I told you about it when we met. As I said then, I would love it if you could come and talk to us. On the other hand, before you say yes I should check with them. They can be a bit snooty about their book choices – you know how it is.'

'Yes.'

'Anyway . . .' Her voice was hesitant before regaining its confidence. 'So many people would really benefit from reading your stuff. John, for one. I was really surprised when he agreed to me moving out. He's always done the running in our relationship. Towards me, not away, if you see what I mean?'

'Absolutely.'

'You wouldn't think so from the way he looks; I mean he's gorgeous, even if he could do with a few more hours in the gym, but he's really naïve when it comes to women.'

'I would have thought his work would have cured him of any naivety,' I said.

'Oh that's different, isn't it? You should see his exes,' she snorted. 'No wonder he thinks I'm completely gorgeous.'

'Two gorgeous people,' I said. 'How perfect is that.'

'You would have thought so, but actually, it's not. He's quite mixed up.'

I knew I should end the conversation there. A person of style and integrity would not listen to this kind of puerile gossip about someone who had been both kind and helpful to them.

'Is he really? In what way?'

'I just don't think he knows who he is. He plays parts. Behind all that professional bravado there's this frightened little boy.'

Another one, I thought to myself.

'Most women wouldn't have seen that side. If I did one good thing, and I think I did quite a few, actually, it was getting him to see a therapist. I think it's really helping him. Then again he's good at dissembling. He's quite obsessive. Life is a series of goals to him. When he and I met, he was totally focused on finding the perfect woman to settle down with, someone attractive and independent, so I knew he wouldn't let me go that easily once he'd found me. As I said, I was quite surprised he didn't try to stop me from moving out; male pride, I suppose. It was really quite touching how pleased he was to hear from me when I phoned him up. Anyway, I just wanted to tell you how much I *loved* your book. We must get together. Just the girls, I mean. It would be fun.'

I almost never drink whisky but somehow, having finished the call with Melanie Ingram, I felt the need for a glass of the stuff.

Mine's a double, Coco said, throwing himself down in the armchair and putting his large feet up on the coffee table.

I put on some music, Dolly Parton. I adore Dolly Parton. I don't care what anyone says: the woman is a marvel.

I topped up my glass. Dolly sang, *I'll always love you.*

This time I had to take issue with her.

'You know, you just think you will, but really you won't. You might, however, end up singing things like this: *I'd be devastated if I lost him, but it would mean I could redecorate the house and get rid of that ghastly old winged chair.* Or, *I wouldn't say we're happy exactly, but then life's not about that, is it?* Alternatively, you could just cut to the chase and tell him to bugger off.'

Dolly obviously wasn't listening, begging instead for Jolene not to take her man away.

My grandfather on my mother's side used to bring my grandmother breakfast in bed each morning: a tiny pot of tea, some butter and jam, a rack of toast and always a single orchid, whatever the time of year. He adored her. When they married he was twenty-five and she was thirty-eight. He loved her so much that he wouldn't let her grow old.

He killed her? Coco asked.

No, of course not. You know he didn't.

He just didn't allow her to grow old. Wherever he went, she went. He travelled to Paris or Rome, so did she, even when she could no longer walk or see. He hired the services of a nurse, who was also trained in dressing hair, so that every morning my grandmother would be looking her best, not for him, because to him her beauty was undisputable, but for my grandmother herself, who had indeed been a renowned beauty and vain with it.

'But she can't see,' my mother had protested.

'She knows,' he had replied, 'she knows just by putting her hand to touch her hair if it's right or not.'

Towards the end, my grandmother confided to my mother that she would very much like just to lie back and rest; no travel, no trips to the opera, no visitors, just quietly rest, with her hair going grey and the bald spot left for all the world to see.

'So tell him,' my mother said.

'Oh no,' my grandmother replied, 'it would break his heart.'

She died aged ninety-eight, while watching *La Bohème* from their box at the opera.

Was it love that my grandfather had felt for my grandmother, or was it obsession?

Let's call it obsession, Coco said. *It'll make you feel better.*

I had asked my mother, not so long ago, if it had been wonderful growing up in a home with such happily married parents. She told me that it wasn't especially because she, their child, was just the pale fruit on the tree that was their love.

I had no doting husband and no fruit of my love, pale or otherwise. Instead, I was destined for a life in which weekends were my least favourite time, summer holidays were spent insisting to my friends that I had always preferred travelling on my own, and Christmas meant weighing up the pros and cons of decorating a tree just for me. When I woke up with a start, jaw aching with silent screams, from the dream where my sister lies helpless on the floor and I can't reach her to ease her back into her chair because my feet are welded to the floor and my arms weighted with irons, there would be no one to reassure me. No longer could I turn towards the comforting shape of a lover, touch his sleep-crumpled face and feel the warmth of his breath as I snuggled close enough for our legs to touch but not so close so as to wake him.

Then again, Coco said, *you can always have lots of casual sex – at least until the time comes when you need your pubic hair dyed.*

Why do you have to be so vulgar?

That's exactly what I was about to ask.

Mount Olympus

'I KNOW REVENGE IS a dish best served cold,' Athene says to Mother, 'but surely yours must be frozen by now?'

'You're so pleased with yourself, aren't you?' Mother hisses at her.

Athene just smiles.

'Hera and I have been discussing the matter and we thought that perhaps you should consider retraining.'

I'm thinking that if I couldn't be a god I'd quite like to be a wolf.

But then Athene continues, 'Of course, it's one thing for Eros to spend his time facilitating mortal coupling – after all he's only getting younger – but you, Aphrodite, should you not think about doing something a little more suited to your talents? For example . . . well . . . I'm sure we'll be able to think of something. Free your mortals from the shackles of romance and they'll flourish. Their families will benefit because without the thwarted passion, the jealousy, the impossible expectations each parent will be free to cooperate with the other parent to act in the best interest of their offspring. And their politicians will be able to do what comes naturally without the need for resignations and upheaval, because their life partner, if they have one, will be no more troubled than a sister or brother by something which would not even be termed unfaithfulness any more. So you see, Aphrodite, there really is no downside.'

Mother stands there, looking like she'd been struck by Zeus: her arms hanging limply, her mouth open, her eyes blank.

Athene sensing victory goes on, 'And Rebecca Finch would be free to write something useful.'

'Like a computer manual,' I say.

'Exactly.'

Mother totally stuns me by saying, all meek, 'Maybe you're right.' And with that she walks out of the room leaving Athene and I looking at each other, baffled.

'I didn't expect it to be that easy,' Athene says. 'Still, who's complaining.'

None of us sees Mother for a bit after that but then she's back in her room reclining on her couch.

When she sees me she pats the seat next to her.

'Sit down, Eros.' Then she says in this slow, thoughtful voice, 'They do need us, you know. I have thought long and hard about it, and those wretched mortals need us.'

I'm thinking that she's looking like her old self again.

'Of course they do.'

'So you agree.'

'Sure. With what?'

'Eros, pull yourself together. I am saying that the mortals need us even more than we need them. You see, I haven't just been moping while I've been away, I've been researching.' Mothers points at a pile of papers on the floor. 'Their scientists confirm what you and I already know: romantic love really is an integral part of what it is to be human, and not just a cover for the sexual urge. The brain is shown clearly to differentiate between the two. Different parts of the brain are stimulated by romantic and sexual urges. And guess which is the more powerful? Guess which is the winner?'

To be honest it's all getting a bit technical for me.

'Dunno.'

'Romance!'

'So the bet is back on?'

'It was never off,' Mother says.

Rebecca

LANCE PHONED ME TO ask if I'd like to go with him to see the play at the Royal Court.

'We could have a bite to eat first,' he said.

I was glad he had called. As a single woman it was important to have male, as well as female, friends. It was, like everything, a matter of balance.

Then Angie Bliss contacted me to say that, due to 'unforeseen circumstances', she needed to rearrange our session for that week. Could I make it for Friday afternoon at five instead of our usual slot at ten on a Tuesday morning? I explained that I couldn't and why.

'It's vital that we keep up our weekly meetings,' she said. 'I feel we're close to a breakthrough, close to finding the answer to the reappearance of the clown and the subsequent loss of creativity. I have come across some very interesting research into what's termed Adult Imaginary Friend syndrome.'

'You're kidding?'

'I never "kid", as you call it. The theatre doesn't start until seven-thirty, yes? That gives you plenty of time to eat beforehand *and* come here.'

'You really think it would be detrimental to my treatment to skip just one session?'

'Oh yes. Then again I don't know how serious you are about getting back to full mental health and back to work.'

'Deadly serious, you know that.'

'Well then, I'll see you Friday.'

When I told Lance he insisted on picking me at Angie Bliss's rooms.

'I'll have the car,' he said. 'That way we'll be able to take our time over dinner.'

I told Angie Bliss about my idea for the play.

'I can't say that I'm very taken with it,' she said. 'All those angry, bitter people sounding off and blaming their mistakes on poor Eros.' The therapist seemed to be taking it all literally.

'As I said, Eros being simply a device, a personification of the idea of romantic love.'

'Well, opinion is divided on that one,' she said. 'Anyway, all this resentment is bad for mental hygiene.'

'It's not resentment that has made me see clowns,' I protested. 'It's false hopes and impossible dreams.'

'In that appearance of yours on television you spoke of Shakespeare.'

I nodded.

'Well, I'm asking you, where would he have been without love? We would have had a whole load of politics and propaganda but no *Romeo and Juliet*. At the end of that play the warring families make peace. Now, if Romeo and Juliet had died in some other way, fighting like Tybalt or poor little Mercutio, then their families would have slipped further and further down the spiral of hatred and revenge. As it was, Romeo and Juliet lost their lives for love and so

269

their families saw the dreadful error of their ways. Love showed them.'

'I hadn't thought about it like that.'

'Well, you should. And while you're at it, count the great works of art, poetry, literature and music that have been directly inspired by romantic love then see where you'd all be without them.'

'That's art, not life,' I said.

'Since when did you get to be so dismissive about art?'

'I'm not being dismissive, I never would be. But however important art is, it's still just an aspect of life. As is romantic love. The problem is that romantic love doesn't know its place; it's fast become the new opium for the people.'

'And what's wrong with opium?'

'Ha ha.'

'Absolutely. Only jesting.'

'The thing is that romantic love is all part of this great myth we entertain that says that we have a right to be happy. That we have a right to be happy and fulfilled and successful and loved and that if we're not then something's gone terribly wrong.'

'And you're saying that humans should not be happy, fulfilled and loved?' Angie Bliss tut-tutted.

'No, yes, I mean it's obviously wonderful if we are, but it's not to be expected. Believing that it's the norm is what makes us even more unhappy than we need to be.'

'So romance gives you hope and dreams. The scoundrel, the villain. Off with his head.'

I gave her a pale smile and shrugged.

'Oh I don't know. Maybe I'm being overly negative. Maybe I've got bitter. But I still feel I need to warn people, not encourage them in their delusions; people like my god-daughter, people who still have a virgin heart.'

'And quite right too,' Angie Bliss said. 'Never take a chance. If you can't have a guarantee of a happy ending never embark on the journey. How inspirational, how courageous and how very productive. As the chances of any mortal achieving a happy ending to their life are . . . how shall I put this . . . well, nil, you should all, by your logic, run screaming back into your mother's womb the moment you're born. I mean what's the point of doing anything else?'

'Good question,' I said. 'No, I do believe there is a point to life, there has to be. We have to make sure there is.'

'How? By never taking a risk? By never loving?'

'I don't mean that.'

'So what do you mean?'

'I can't explain. I just know what I know.'

Angie Bliss leant forward in her chair.

'Congratulations.' She took my hand, shaking it vigorously. 'It's better than knowing what you don't know. Now, answer me this: the happiest people are those who love and are loved, true or false?'

'True, I suppose. But the unhappiest ones are those who have been disappointed and betrayed in love.'

'You're wrong. The unhappiest are the ones who have never known love at all.'

'Tell that to the couples trailing around Homebase arguing about which tiles to use for the utility room. I'm sure most of them started off being in love. And that's my god-daughter's concern; she's not naïve, she doesn't expect the intensity of emotions experienced at the start of a relationship to last for ever. Like most sane people she knows that it wouldn't even be desirable. For a start you would never get anything done, your career would go down the drain and you would lose all your friends, she knows that. What she is asking for is that the something that makes two people not just friends, joint mortgage-holders and parents but also lovers remains.' Angie Bliss folded her arms across her chest and leant back in her chair. I knew she was annoyed. 'You know Plato?' I asked.

She frowned.

'Plato?' Her brow cleared. 'Oh yes, Plato. I wouldn't say that I knew him as such; we might have met once.'

I laughed politely before saying, 'Well, there is that bit about mankind being severed, the bit that goes, "They defied the Olympian gods, who punished them by splitting them in half. This is the mutilation mankind suffered. So that generation after generation we seek the missing half. Longing to be whole again . . . to be human was to be severed, mutilated. Man is incomplete. Zeus is a tyrant . . ." Are you all right?'

'Yes, yes, I'm fine, I just don't like this carping about Zeus. Personally, I would never . . .' She paused and looked around her as if there might be someone else present in the room. 'I would never,' she said again, 'say that he was a tyrant. Firm, yes, decisive, yes but a tyrant, no, not at all. Apart from that I think Plato makes perfect sense. In fact, I couldn't have put it better myself.'

I looked hard at her. Was this another of her attempts at a joke?

'I'm sure he'd be delighted to hear you say that.'

'Don't be silly, he's dead.'

'Yes. Yes, he is. But the thing is there's more: "And after so many generations your true companion is simply not to be found. Eros is a compensation granted by Zeus. The sexual embrace gives temporary relief but the painful knowledge of mutilation is permanent."'

'I'm sorry, but here I have to disagree with him. Eros, in spite of his name, is not just about sex.'

'But even so, isn't Plato actually telling us that mankind is condemned to yearn but never be satisfied, to search but never to find? It's cruel and I don't understand it.'

As I spoke Angie Bliss's expression softened and, although she was probably a good ten years younger than I, there was something motherly in the way she looked at me, as if she wanted to give me a hug or at the very least explain but had decided that the explanation was beyond me.

'But don't you see,' she said, 'that it's the yearning and the searching, the hoping and the dreaming that distinguishes you from all the other creatures on this earth. If it wasn't for that, you would be running round naked in the fields and woods with the other animals.'

'Why do you say you and not we?' I asked her.

'Did I?'

'Yes. You do it quite often. As if you are something other.'

We both laughed at the thought.

My hour was up and as I walked out into the waiting room Lance walked in through the front door. Out of the corner of my eye I glimpsed a young boy peering out from behind the potted palm. Lance waved. He opened his mouth to speak but said nothing, clasping his hand to his chest instead. At that moment Angie Bliss came tearing out of her room and placed herself in front of me, full square, as if she were protecting me from someone.

'Is everything all right?' I asked her.

'Your umbrella,' she said. 'Did you leave your umbrella?'

It was a beautiful sunny afternoon.

'I didn't bring one,' I told her. 'But thank you anyway.' I turned to Lance. 'And are *you* all right?'

'Yes, fine.' But he was looking at me in an odd way. I would have said a loving way, if it hadn't been so unlikely.

He was rubbing his chest so I asked again.

'Are you sure you're all right?'

'Absolutely! Never felt better, in fact.'

Just then the front door opened once more. It was John Sterling.

'John, hi. How are you? I thought you saw Angie at her other rooms.'

'I do usually,' he said, pausing to shake hands with Lance, who had been standing very close to me, his arms crossed.

'Oh I'm sorry. Lance, this is John, John, Lance. So how come you're here?'

'There was a flood or a leak or something in the other place so I was told to come here. Oh, hello, Dr Bliss.'

'Time is ticking on,' said Lance.

'Oh yes, sorry, John, we're off to the theatre.'

'We're having dinner first,' added Lance.

John smiled at him.

'I won't keep you then. Have a wonderful evening.' He turned back to me. 'Well, you know where I am if you need to do some more research.'

'Yes I do, thank you.'

I waved goodbye as Lance put his hand on my back and ushered me out on to the street.

Mount Olympus

I WAS TRYING TO help!

Mother had phoned John up herself to say that Angie Bliss's City consulting rooms were flooded and could he come to the Knightsbridge rooms for his next session. This pissed him off somewhat as it was like half an hour on the bus or subway or something but he agreed. Him being so anal could be helpful at times because once something was in his diary that was it, it had to happen.

Next she had called Rebecca Finch to ask if she could re-schedule her appointment. So far so pretty good.

Then according to the plan, Rebecca Finch, primed for the last time by Mother as to what kind of man she could not live without, would walk out of the door only to run straight into the arms of an equally primed John Sterling, and zing-zap, I'd shoot and we'd have a result (a result that, because of all the priming and so on, might actually be a lasting one, or at least one lasting the five years of the bet). Cue Rebecca Finch swooning over her newfound love, regretting her cynical behaviour and ready to write her soppy books once again. Mother wins the bet. *She's* pleased. I get invited upstairs on a permanent basis. *I'm* pleased. *Everyone's* pleased. Apart from Athene, obviously. How was I to know that this other bloke would step right in front of me? I got him through the heart and was aiming the next shot at Rebecca when Mother comes flying out of the room, blocking her. So then she, Mother, that is, gets the arrow instead, just as John Sterling comes through the door. Talk about crap timing!

So now Athene's floating around being gracious in victory. Hera really hurt me by saying that this just goes to show that the Romans got it right turning me into this gross, baby-type guy with like *no* dignity because look how I can't be trusted and if I think I'm going to get a permanent seat at the table I'm seriously mistaken because after this I'm lucky if I'm allowed up at all, even as a casual visitor.

And Mother . . . she's blanking me. I can cope with her being angry, but when she's like this, not looking *at* me but through me, talking about me as if I'm not even there, that really freaks me.

'It's not fair,' I tell her. 'How was I to know that other guy would turn up?' I don't even bother to point out that she had in fact completely forgotten to prime Rebecca because they had been too busy wittering on about Plato. There was no point, she wasn't going to listen.

Hera gives Mother this chummy look and rolls her eyes in my direction – I tell you, I wish they would just go on rolling one day, out of her ugly mug and along the marble floors and *squish*.

'You would have thought even *he* would have considered bringing a photograph,' she smirks.

'They don't look entirely dissimilar,' Harmony says, trying to help.

I send her a grateful smile.

'Yeah, and the light wasn't very good.'

But Mother isn't having any of it.

'And what about me, eh? Of course I am mightier than your wretched arrows but it's still going to be an effort, keeping away from John Sterling.'

I have an idea.

'So why don't I just get her, Rebecca, when she's next with the other bloke. As long as she's in love again we've got a result, no?'

'No. Have you not listened to a world I've said?' She starts speaking really slowly and with emphasis like I was retarded or something. 'This time it *has to last*. Lance Cooper is entirely *wrong for her*. They're wrong for *each other*.' She shoots me a mean glance. 'Only an idiot would fail to see that. He's weak and she's strong. He'd end up resenting her and she'd despise him. And that would be just the start of it. No, Eros, I just think we have to face up to the fact that you're not yet ready for a permanent place up here.'

I try not to show them how upset I am. I have to blink really hard and open my eyes wide.

'And don't give me that insolent look,' Mother says. She turns to Harmonia. 'No, you can make all the excuse you like but the problem is he just doesn't care, not about anything.'

What's the point? I really want to know what *is the point*? I never get a break. Mother like actually *hates* me right now. I suppose I can't blame her. I did cock up big time – again.

Rebecca

OVER DINNER LANCE KEPT looking at me in that loving, yet puzzled, manner that he had displayed ever since he picked me up at Angie Bliss's rooms. And I remembered the girl who, a little over twenty years ago, had got ready for an evening with the boy she thought she loved. I smiled to myself as I thought of how I had bleached my hair just because someone had told me Lance preferred blondes. I remembered it all: my hand trembling with delicious anticipation as I applied mascara, the feeling that life was beginning right then and that everything that had gone before had been a rehearsal. And I found myself wondering what our lives might have been like if we had got together that New Year's Eve. Would we have married? Perhaps.

And by now you'd be divorced, Coco said, *which is a comforting thought as it shows that, when it comes to love, whichever path you choose you end up in the same place.*

Lance smiled across the table.

'We didn't even know each other that well when we were kids, but it's been so easy just picking up where we left off.'

'Not knowing each other that well, you mean?'

It was meant as a joke but Lance flinched.

'I meant the opposite, actually. I meant that it feels as if we . . .'

I put my hand on his.

'I know what you meant and I'm sorry, I was being facetious.'

He looked up at me, holding my gaze with his, and I quickly withdrew my hand.

'Time is as vulnerable to inflation as money,' I said. 'We didn't just get a whole bag of gobstoppers for our penny pocket money when we were kids but a serious chunk of living in the space of a few weeks as well. I suppose it means that when it comes to childhood friendships you just get more bang for your buck.'

'I would hardly say we were children,' Lance said.

'No, perhaps not,' I said, my attention wandering.

'Penny for your thoughts,' Lance said.

'Work.'

'You're busy on a new book?'

'No. That's why I'm preoccupied. I've got an idea for a play but at the moment it's not much more than that. I miss writing novels; without a book at the end of it all my days pass like so much waste floating by on its way down some universal plughole. It's like recycling, I suppose: I need to recycle life into fiction and now I can't and I'm all clogged up. And instead of trying to improve my miserable little mind in order for it to be able to create something other than love stories, instead of rereading the classics or taking a philosophy course, I watch soaps and shop for things I don't need, like another handbag. This in turn makes me suspect that I lack depth.'

To my surprise I realised that Lance was actually listening, his gaze fixed on me as intently as if he were attempting to catch each word with his eyeballs. When I paused he refilled our glasses. It was a warm evening and I downed the chilled white wine to quench my thirst.

'I don't see why handbags and philosophy should be mutually exclusive,' Lance said.

It was a nice thought. I tried it out.

'Epicurus and handbags,' I said. 'OK, so the desire for another new handbag is natural but the bag is not necessary, although it seems that way to the woman in question. The ability of a certain handbag to offer us happiness does not lie in the handbag itself but in the circumstances we find ourselves in and the attitudes we have when we desire it. Thus, in the right circumstances and with a different attitude, a bag from Accessorize could bring as much pleasure as a bag from Prada, which means that the objects of our desire carry no intrinsic value but are simply a reflection of our state of mind.'

Instead of looking bored, which he had every reason to do, Lance looked at me proudly as if I were his very own pet performing an especially clever trick.

Still, I changed the subject.

'What is your passion?'

'I'm like you, I suppose, in that work is my main interest, that and sport. It's always been rugby and cricket, but lately I've got more and more into motor sports.' He paused for the briefest of moments. 'And of course I really enjoy reading.'

'Oh, what writers do you enjoy?'

'Gosh, I'm hopeless with names but I do like a good thriller.'

'Have you read Henning Mankell? Though I suppose he's more crime than thriller.'

'Well, I am definitely more of a thriller man.'

I really didn't mind that the conversation seemed to be going nowhere. In fact, I didn't really care that much what Lance thought of me. He was good-looking and sweet and it was perfectly pleasant spending time with him. Yet not so long ago I would have seen him the way I used to see practically every man between the ages of thirty and seventy and in possession of their own teeth: as a potential love interest. Not any more. I was free. Free to be myself.

Free to be both boring and bored, Coco said. *That's what I call progress.*

'You're smiling,' Lance said. He had a pleased, expectant look on his face.

'I was thinking how nice it is just to sit here having dinner together, two old friends, nothing more, nothing less.'

'Nothing more, nothing less: are you sure about that?' He reached for my hand.

I checked my watch and got to my feet.

'Goodness, is that the time? We'd better find our seats.'

Lance was hungry again so I asked him up to the flat. I made an omelette and put out cheese, biscuits and a bowl of grapes.

'How many grapes count as one of your five a day?' I asked him.

'Probably about ten,' he said.

I poured us some more wine. Lance ate his omelette and then some cheese and biscuits, finishing off with a small bunch of grapes.

'Have to get my five a day,' he said.

He walked around to my chair and pulled me to my feet and I realised he was about to kiss me.

As we reached my bedroom, arms around each other's waists, I thought that this was the difference between youth and middle-aged lust: middle-aged finished its supper first.

* * *

He phoned me from work the next day.

'And how are you this morning?' His voice was conspiratorial and congratulatory both at once.

'Very well, thank you.'

'Last night was wonderful.' He had lowered his voice and I could hear his breath against the receiver.

I moved it a fraction from my ear. Then I realised that he was waiting for a reply. Thinking that an 'It was fine' most probably wasn't the reply he was after, I settled for an indistinct mumble that could be thought of as agreement.

'Are you free this evening?'

'I'm not, actually.' There were at least three TV programmes on that I wanted to watch.

'How about Sunday lunch? We could drive out of London. There's this great little pub I know just this side of Oxford.'

The forecast was good. I wouldn't have to cook.

'That would be lovely,' I told him.

In the weeks that followed it was tempting to play along with the spring sunshine and the chirruping birds and act like a woman in love. We made a nice couple. We walked hand in hand, some of the time. We laughed at each other's jokes. We enjoyed some of the same films and we liked a lot of the same kind of food. So what about the irritation that sat at the base of my chest? It threatened to spill over when he didn't wring out the dishcloth and left it sopping wet in the sink, or when he made a joke with a waiter and then went on trying to explain even though the man clearly didn't understand him. And today it had made me smack his hand away when he reached round from behind and pulled me close as I was standing by the kitchen table reading the paper.

'What's wrong with you?' he complained. 'You're always grumpy these days. I thought we were having a good thing here.'

I turned round and smiled and apologised.

'I'm just worried about work, that's all.'

'You're always worried about work.'

'I know. I'm sorry. Let's go out and eat.'

'You're not regretting us, are you?'

'Of course not. It's really good being relaxed in a relationship for once. To be two independent adults who enjoy spending time together without the dramas and the panting and the sighing and the losing weight and sleep. Anyway, shall I call and book a table?'

'Let's go to Paris,' Lance said.

'Paris?'

He laughed and took my hands.

'You know Paris? The city. The capital of France.'

'Maybe not Paris,' I said.

'So what about Rome?'

I thought of jasmine-scented nights and walks along the shady side of the street. I thought of pasta and red wine and late afternoons in bed and drives out to the ruins of Hadrian's Villa. For some reason I wanted to cry.

'Not Rome,' I said.

He looked surprised but he didn't question me.

'New York?'

'Amsterdam,' I said. 'I've never been to Amsterdam.'

'OK. But it's not the most romantic place, you know.'
I did know.

The next morning I woke to a soft caress with a rough finger on my cheek. I opened my eyes and saw Lance smiling down at me, a tray with coffee and croissants balanced on his other hand.

'Good morning, darling,' he said as I sat up, blinking and wondering what on earth I looked like in the unforgiving light. He placed the tray on my knees and perched down next to me. 'I used to love my place but lately I don't want to be there at all.' He ruffled my hair. 'I wonder why that is?'

'But your place is lovely,' I said. 'Really, really lovely.'

'Mmm.' He bent down and kissed me. 'But you're not there.'

I looked at the clock on the bedside table.

'Oh look, it's almost eight. You'll be late for work.'

He checked his watch and got to his feet slowly, as if he were being peeled away.

'I don't want to go,' he said, pouting, reminding me of Dominic. 'And I won't see you tonight either – I've got that work thing.'

I sat up straighter against the pillows.

'I know, such a bore. Still, I'll see you tomorrow.'

Mentally I was mapping out my morning. Breakfast and the papers. A fast half-hour walk to clear my head and then work. Later in the day, and if work had gone well, I might see if Matilda or Maggie was free to go and see a film. I hadn't seen either of them much since I had started meeting Lance and I missed them.

He leant down and kissed me one more time. He was a good kisser.

'I'll get out of the dinner. Yup, that's what I'll do. Wasn't there that Jane Austen film you wanted to see?'

'Yes, but . . .'

He put his finger on my lips.

'No buts, I want to be with you.'

'No.'

Lance had been on his way to the door but now he stopped and turned round.

'I thought you wanted to see it.'

'I do.'

He frowned.

'So what's the problem?'

'I want to see it with Matilda,' I said, sounding, I realised, like a truculent five-year-old.

'Oh.'

'You're going to be really late,' I said.

'I'm fine,' he snapped. 'Why don't you want to see it with me? Aren't we meant to be doing these things together?'

'Of course. Sometimes.'

He walked back to the bed and sat down. He took my hands, which I had made into claws, in his.

'What's the matter?' he asked. 'You seem out of sorts.'

I pulled the claws from his grasp.

'I'm not.'

'Call me a romantic old fool,' he said, smiling now, twinkling, in fact. 'But I enjoy spending time with you. It's what lovers do, remember?'

I thought about it.

'Yes, it is,' I said.

'Good.' Once again he got to his feet and made for the door. 'I'll see you about six then.'

'No.'

'What do you mean?'

'Lance,' I said, 'I don't think we should see each other again.'

I listened to the front door banging shut and with a sigh of relief I lay back against the pillows.

It's nice, being just us, Coco said.

It is, I agreed.

Mount Olympus

MOTHER IS BEING TOTALLY weird. She didn't even mind when Rebecca went to bed with that other bloke. Which suited me in a way because it got me off the hook for a bit. But, and this is a *big* but, I think the reason she's not pissed off is because she's decided to have John Sterling for herself. I know, I know, it's my fault. I'm the one who messed up. But she is Aphrodite. She should be able to rise above it. But no, she's wafting around with this goofy smile last seen when she was hanging out with Adonis and we all know how *that* ended. So it looks like we've well and truly blown it, which really depresses me.

Then just as I think it's all over and that we've lost the bet with Athene I get some good news. Rebecca Finch has dumped the Lance guy. He's pretty sore but he's the type that heals fast so I don't anticipate any real problems there.

So I go and find Mother to try and make her see sense. I mean someone has to be mature around here.

'Rebecca Finch has dumped him. So we're back to plan A, right?'

But she turns misty eyes on me and says, 'Oh Lance will do. I'll make sure they're in the same place one more time and then you get her and everything will be fine.'

'No.' I slam down my bag of arrows on the marble. 'We've been through all this. You said it yourself. The wager is about something else. We were going to get these two specific guys together and it would last and we would show everyone the power of love. That was the deal. I mean *come on*, this is about us getting back some respect.' And about me getting my own seat at the table. But I don't say that because I don't think she really cares about that bit. 'And it's not like you have a future with John Sterling. He's a mortal. You know the rules. I seriously can't believe that you're prepared to throw it all away for a fling. I can't believe you're that irresponsible.'

Mother waves her hand in a dismissive kind of way. She doesn't care. She is in *lurve*.

'And isn't that just typical of this place,' she says instead. 'Gods can love a mortal, no problem at all, but when it's a goddess then it's against the rules, *verboten*. And whose rules are they? *His*, of course.' She gesticulates towards the great hall.

Has she no fear? I look around me but luckily there's no one else there.

'You're meant to turn Rebecca back into a worshipful mortal, remember? Get her back to writing those lame books.'

'Maybe she will now she's in love.'

'But she isn't.'

'Then shoot her when she's with Lance Cooper, I've told you already.'

'No! It's not enough. Not this time. This time it's meant to be different. You're the one who said it. And you were right. They're just not suited. He just pretends to like the same stuff as her.'

'They all do that.'

'Yes, and that's one of the problems we're always facing. And it goes deeper than that. They don't get each other's souls. So it would be short-term, again, and she'll end up even more bitter and twisted than she is now. Just think what that'll do to our credibility.'

'Credibility-senility: it's just a wager.'

'Just a wager!'

I despair, really I do. It's like we've reached the end worse off than when we started. Mother will have zero respect, and me? Well, I'll be on my own. I had set my heart on moving up here. I thought Mother quite liked the idea too. She's never said as much but she's not the demonstrative type, well, not with me anyway. But it seems she really doesn't give a damn. She doesn't give a damn because she's got her sights on John stupid Sterling. I knew it, I knew there'd be trouble the first time I clamped eyes on him.

And guess who has been listening after all, hovering behind a pillar? You've got it, Athene. Now she steps out of the shadow with this sickly smile; it's so sweet I reckon it'll stick to her teeth.

'We should have known, shouldn't we?' she says, her voice all soft. 'We should have known something like this would happen. But we shouldn't blame you, Aphrodite dear. It's in your nature, after all. Just like it's in my nature to be wise.' The smile drops like there's weights attached to the corners of her mouth. 'So there we are. I won.' And she turns and glides off. I swear to you even her behind looks triumphant.

'Bollocks you did,' I yell. 'Mother and I haven't finished yet.'

John

JOHN WAS SHOPPING LATE at his local Sainsbury's, trying to find the various things his daughter liked to eat. Her favourites changed from one visit to another so he had checked with her over the phone before he went off.

'Spinach and ricotta ravioli,' she had told him. 'And pomegranate jelly. And Fizzy Fish.'

As he was searching in vain for pomegranate jelly there was a light tap on his shoulder and he turned round to find Angie Bliss in a floaty white dress, a black beret pushed down on her Titian locks. She was smiling at him.

'Fancy seeing you here,' she said.

'I work just round the corner,' he pointed out. Then he asked her about the jelly and she said she didn't have the faintest idea but wouldn't this do? She pointed at a packet of raspberry jelly. John said probably not, but he got some anyway.

They ended up having a cup of coffee together in a café down the road.

It was hard not to stare at Angie Bliss. Everyone did: men, women and children. Only dogs kept their distance. John had noticed that she was attractive before, of course, but away from the formal setting of her consulting rooms she was more than that, she was beautiful. Beautiful in a curiously old-fashioned way, with her soft curvy body and wide, somewhat flat face.

As he stood at the counter waiting for their second coffees, full milk latte with a caramel shot for her, black for him, he asked himself if it were possible that she was hitting on him. He told himself not to be ridiculous. He, with his life centred round the law and his child, and added to that his OCD, was hardly a catch. He must seem tediously dull to her. Thinking about it, he probably was quite dull. Then again, what was so wrong with that? In the past few months of living on his own with no relationship to speak of and therefore no one to disappoint but himself, being him – a little dull, no doubt, not quite human possibly, obsessive and workaholic undoubtedly – did not seem like such a big problem.

'You're looking happy.' Angie Bliss said as he sat down.

His smile grew wider.

'I was thinking that our sessions must be yielding results. I'm feeling more relaxed than I've felt for years.'

'Well, isn't that marvellous.' Her voice was soft as she leant in towards him. 'I'm so glad that I've been of help. After all, it's what I live for, helping others. It's my mission to make the world a better place.'

John shifted backwards in his chair. Was she actually saying those things? She sounded like a contestant in some third-rate beauty contest. She looked at him as if she was expecting a reply.

'That's . . . that's very laudable,' he tried.

'Laudable,' She giggled, her small white hand touching his sleeve. 'What a sweet word.'

'Is it? Well, that's good.' Is it? Well, that's good. He sounded like a complete idiot.

Angie Bliss did not seem to mind, though, as she gazed at him with eyes that were Irish blue and sparkling.

Surely she wouldn't risk her career by attempting a relationship with a patient? Whatever he might think about her methods it was clear that she was dedicated to her career. He was just misinterpreting her; easy to do seeing as she had such a different approach to . . . well, to everything really. Usually he found women like that interesting. Angie Bliss was more odd than interesting, though. Away from the purposeful exchanges of the consulting room she was quite difficult to talk to. He himself was no good at small talk. He needed a proper topic to warm up with, something specific.

So he asked her about her work: what had made her decide on psychology in the first place? Where had she practised before? Which branch of the subject interested her the most? But she seemed curiously reluctant to answer any of his questions. He started talking about Susannah and how he was concerned that the animosity between Lydia and himself was causing her distress. Angie Bliss began to fidget.

Then she looked at him as if she were trying to drink his eyes with hers.

'We all just need to love one another,' she said.

'Right, well, I don't think there's any chance of Susannah's mother and I ever loving each other again. I would be happy if we could manage to be civil.'

Angie Bliss's eyes flashed green.

'I wasn't talking about you and your ex-wife,' she snapped. She reached out and touched the tip of his nose with the tip of her index finger. 'There I go, getting quite cross with you.' She laughed.

John attempted to steer the conversation towards a subject to which he could contribute.

'There's been a really interesting development in the area of family law,' he began.

Angie Bliss's eyes glazed over, not that he blamed her. The law as it was practised as opposed to how it was portrayed on film and television bored most people, at times even the lawyers themselves, just not him. He remembered a friend saying to him, amused as she had watched a woman come on to him, 'You use your work as a chastity belt. You begin to bore on about it and you know you're safe.'

He tried one more topic of conversation.

'Have you seen the Bauhaus at Tate Modern?'

She shook her head.

'I haven't got time for kitchen equipment,' she said. John waited for her to laugh and when she didn't he thought, good God the woman's dim. 'Speaking for myself, if the right man came along I would give up everything else and just serve him.' She looked up at him under her long lashes.

'You must never do that,' John said, appalled. 'If it goes wrong, what then? No, you must never give up who you are and what you do. It places an impossible burden on the two of you and, as I said, if it goes wrong then what are you left with?'

Angie Bliss pushed her chair back and slammed down her mug on the table.

'Why has no one cleaned this?' she asked, turning round and waving at a uniformed employee. 'Girl, come here. This table needs wiping.'

He gave the waitress an apologetic smile.

Turning to Angie Bliss he said, 'Well, I must be off. This has been great, thank you.'

Her arm shot forward and her hand descended on his.

'Do you believe in destiny, John Sterling?'

He remained seated.

'Only the kind you make yourself,' he said.

'You don't think that certain people are meant to be together?'

He shook his head.

'No. Not really.'

'Really, you really don't?'

He gave a little laugh.

'Well, I have always had this picture in my mind. Most of the time I don't think about it, but then every now and again up it pops. It's of a girl. A young woman with slanted eyes and a pale face and long fair hair rippling down her back. She's wearing a hat, a red woolly hat of all things.' He pulled a face. 'It's probably an image from some film or a book that I read when I was young. Although . . .' He paused. 'Although I thought I recognised her in someone just the other day.'

Rebecca and John

ANGEL-FACE WAS GETTING MARRIED. The day had come. The wedding reception was taking place at her Uncle Alexander's place just outside Oxford, where the garden was big enough for a marquee and a bandstand. The village church with its old graveyard was exactly as Angel-face had described it, 'adorable'. In fact, it had been used on at least three occasions by film crews for wedding scenes.

'I don't really see why being surrounded by dead people should add to the picturesqueness of all it but somehow it does.' Angel-face had made this rather gloomy observation over the phone to me a week ago but other than that she had seemed entirely happy about her forthcoming marriage. Staying in New York with the good godmother, and away from Zac, seemed to have restored her faith in their relationship.

At home in London I checked myself in the mirror one last time. Over my shoulder I spotted Coco. He looked as if he were about to speak but changed his mind, contenting himself with a smile, an approving, brotherly kind of smile, then he was gone. I had not needed Coco to tell me that I looked good this morning. I was wearing a red-and-white checked dress and with it a cropped red jacket that I had found at the back of my wardrobe, but which went perfectly.

I had been in the millinery department in Harrods, about to decide on a black feathery concoction that barely covered the top of the head, when a young man appeared out of nowhere. He was holding a red cloche hat in his hand and insisted that I try it on. I was amused and a little flattered by his interest. He was so young, just a boy really, a beautiful boy at that, with fair curls and a face like Michelangelo's David. I wondered fleetingly if he was taking the mickey. I looked around me for signs of giggling friends but he was on his own, earnest and most anxious that I should consider the red hat.

'How strange,' I said. 'The dress I'll be wearing is exactly this red.'

'I just thought it was your colour,' he said.

I decided he was an embryo fashion designer.

'So, what do you think?' I turned away from the mirror towards him.

He reached up and adjusted the brim.

'There,' he said, and when I checked on my reflection I saw that he was right and that it was perfect.

'You're very good at this,' I said, still gazing at my reflection.

There was no reply and when I turned round the boy had vanished.

As I drove along the Embankment the hat was sitting beside me on the front passenger seat, Coco's seat. But he wasn't there, his appearances having grown less frequent of late.

Outside my car window the river was the nearest thing to blue that I had ever seen it. I decided this was a good omen.

Who could say for sure that Angel-face and Zac would not confound the depressing statistics and live happily ever after?

Experience, Coco suggested.

Don't sit on my hat! Anyway, I thought you were off to haunt someone else.

I come, Coco said, then as he faded into the distance he added, *And I goooo*.

Maybe Angel-face and Zac would not fall out of love and begin to bicker and torment each other. Maybe Zac would not be unfaithful and maybe they would not be found, ten years hence, eating in stony silence in their local restaurant. Maybe after twenty years they would still be excited at the thought of going on holiday together. Maybe they would celebrate their silver wedding anniversary able to say, 'I know exactly why I married him/her and I love him/her just as much, in fact, more.'

Maybe, Coco conceded, *but not likely*.

John Sterling got up from the desk in his study, where he had been working since five that morning, and realised that he was running late. The other week he had received an invitation from an old university friend, now teaching at Oxford. The invitation had said simply 'A Reunion'. John had been surprised, but pleasantly so. He had not seen Douglas Lewis or his wife Fiona since before Susannah was born; they had a son the same age and on the few occasions when he had time to think about these things he had been sorry that they had lost touch.

There had been an address but no phone number so he had simply written back with his acceptance. The invitation was for one o'clock and it was gone eleven now.

Within twenty minutes he was in the car, having showered,

shaved and changed into Chinos and a cream linen jacket. He was about to start the engine when instead he got out of the car and ran inside to his bedroom to grab a tie. He didn't stop to put it on but just folded it in the pocket of his jacket before hurrying back to the car and driving off towards the North Circular.

A choir was singing. The tiny church was scented with flowers and humming with excited voices.

The usher asked me, 'Bride or groom?'

'Bride.'

I had paused for a moment to consider where to sit when Angel-face's grandmother spotted me, beckoning me forward.

I waved back and walked up to her.

'I don't think I should sit this near the front,' I whispered.

'Nonsense,' Bridget's mother said and patted the empty space beside her.

How would Angel-face be feeling right now? Nervous probably. Happy? One hoped so. I also hoped that my god-daughter really had forgotten, for now at least, the doubts and fears of the past few months and was immersing herself instead in the prescribed happiness of a young bride. And darling Bridget would be fussing around, wiping away a tear or two from her cheeks, the bridesmaids would be checking the veil one last time and Angel-face, if she had any sense, would be smiling at her lovely reflection. It would be a happy day, I told myself, and maybe that was good enough for now.

A few minutes later Zac walked up to the altar, the best man at his side, and Bridget slipped into her seat in the front pew. The organ struck up and the church portals opened to reveal the bride on the arm of her father. Her steps were light, her dress was a cloud, her veil a stream of mist – if she didn't cling on to her father's arm, I thought, she might float up to the sky.

The two little flower girls led the way. The four brides-maids followed behind and as Neil handed over his daughter to the young man waiting at the altar a communal sigh of delighted anticipation was heard from the congregation. A big adventure was about to begin. I joined with the others in a prayer. Who knew, this time the prayer might be answered.

John had arrived at Douglas Lewis's house to find no one at home. He rang the bell several times. Then he walked around to the back and peered through the windows: the place was deserted.

Eventually a neighbour appeared.

'Can I help you?'

John explained that he was a friend of the Lewises and that he was there for the party.

'Party? I don't think so.' The woman was looking at him suspiciously. 'They're away.'

'Away? Really?' John went up to the low fence dividing the two gardens and handed the woman his invitation.

She looked it over and her expression grew friendlier.

'That is odd,' she admitted. 'In fact they've been away for the past three weeks and they're not expected back until the end of the summer. A proper break, they told me. They're on a driving holiday around the States. They were very excited setting off, especially little Andrew.' Then she remembered to be suspicious. 'They've got an alarm and we all check on the place.'

John thought that his old friend must have put the wrong month on the invitation. Still, he told himself, it was a nice day and even if it were as a result of a mix-up he was away from his desk and enjoying the sunshine. Now he was here, he might as well look around some bookshops.

By two o'clock he was hungry. The birds were singing, lawns were being mown, and passers-by were wearing shorts. John walked back into one of the bookshops and bought a *Good Pub Guide*.

He sat outside in the gardens of the Oxford Arms, reading the newspapers, taking his time as he finished his coffee. He thought he must get away more often. It felt surprisingly good having no particular place to be, no time to keep, so when, soon after he drove out of the village, John came upon a diversion he was relaxed about it. The signs took him on a ridiculously convoluted route. He was still nowhere near where he wanted to be when, rounding a bend, he came close to running down a woman standing in the middle of the road.

He slammed down on the brakes.

'What the hell do you think . . .' He stopped. It was Rebecca Finch. She looked different. Like someone else, someone half remembered. Maybe it was seeing her out of context, or perhaps it was that ridiculous little red hat pulled down low over one brow.

She was smiling and apologetic both at once, talking loudly at the open car window.

'God, I'm so sorry. I didn't mean to . . . Oh it's you. Goodness. It's me, Rebecca Finch. How are you? I've got a puncture, you see.' She gesticulated behind her and he saw the cream Beetle convertible halfway into a ditch.

John pulled in to the side of the road and got out.

'I'm sure I charged my mobile but I must have forgotten after all because it's dead as a –'

'Dodo,' he filled in.

'I always try to find something a little less obvious,' she said. 'Force of habit. But dodo, absolutely. Not that you're obvious. No, I didn't mean that at all. I mean it's a perfectly good simile, it's just . . . anyway, there hasn't been a car for ages. I expect there's one of those AA or RAC phone boxes somewhere along here but I'm not a member of either. I'm supposed to be covered by a Volkswagen scheme but as I said my mobile seems to have run out.'

He went to the back of his car and brought out a jack.

She was flapping around him.

'You don't need to change the tyre for me. I mean look at you, that cream jacket. And I'm sure you must be on your way somewhere – one usually is. So if I could just borrow your mobile to call a garage that would be great.'

John Sterling removed his jacket and rolled up the sleeves of his pale-blue shirt.

'It won't take a minute. You do have a spare wheel?'

Mount Olympus

'COME ON, GUYS, IT's the wedding!' I try to snatch the remote from Athene but she slaps me on the wrist.

'Don't get too comfortable, young man.' She turns to Mother. 'And you should remember that they might be about to get married but the bet was for them to last at least five years.'

'I'm confident,' Mother purrs. 'We can make it ten if you like.' She's seated next to Zeus in the place of honour and even Hera is treating her with respect. 'She's stopped talking to herself *and* she's working on a new book.'

Athene is messing about with the remote. I'm beginning to think she's trying to make us miss it on purpose.

'It's Italy,' I tell her. 'They're getting married in *Italy*.'

Athene says, 'She might be writing but we don't know what kind of book yet. She was meant to revert to paying homage to you, remember?'

'And she has,' Mother says. 'She's writing *A Biography of a Happy Marriage*. That's the working title. Isn't it charming?'

'Ooh goodie,' Hera says, 'I do like a nice biography. Whose happy marriage is it?'

Mother shifts in her chair and inspects her shell-pink nails.

'She's still researching, but a lovely couple, I'm sure.'

In a corner Ate laughs. But Mother pays no attention, not today.

'And once she has done this book I don't think it will be long before she returns to writing her novels. I've been looking in on John and her this past year and when I tell you that . . .'

I put my hands over my ears.

'Don't want to know, don't want to know – they're *old*.'

'Oh Eros, don't be such a baby. Now that you're going to take your place up here' – she smiles and gives my hand a little squeeze, then tries to look stern – 'you really will have to do some growing up and . . .'

I stare at her. Is she for real? Am I up here for good? Wow. I look around, grinning, and catch Ate's eye. I stick my tongue out at her, really quickly, which is fine as everyone else is busy listening to Mother describing all this lovey-dovey stuff.

'And it's not just that side of things either,' she continues. 'No, there's a real meeting of minds. Truly, if they had been brought together all those years ago when they were meant to be' – here she turns to me but I don't care: she's said I'm moving up – 'I think they would still be together today. She doesn't try to change him. His somewhat serious –'

'Pompous,' I mutter.

'. . . Side is balanced by her lighter personality. He in turn has brought kindness and security to her life and each of them has brought laughter to the other. Oh I remember their first proper date. There was an immediate sexual tension . . .'

I start singing to myself. I wish she could do this without like totally grossing me out.

'. . . But they also talked together with such ease. About diaries, as I recall.'

'Diaries?' Hera asked.

'Yes, appointment diaries, personal organisers, that kind of thing.'

'Wow, hot stuff,' Ate titters. When is someone going to realise that she certainly isn't supposed to be up here?

'Nothing wrong with being organised,' Athene says, surprising everyone by being almost nice.

'Oh it was code, I expect,' Mother says. 'Or perhaps a cover for all the emotion. I can't remember how they came to the topic but she told him how she never stops searching for the perfect *system*, as she called it. "It can't be electronic," she said. "I must have paper. I know a Filofax is really practical and you can transfer data from year to year but there's something about the fact that the pages are on a ring-binder, disposable, that I don't like.'

'He said he completely agreed. He'd been using the really quite small Smythson featherweight diary for several years now and he'd saved them all so that he had a record of what he'd been doing on each day in each year. She got quite excited and asked if he filled in *after* the event. For example, if he'd made an entry in the diary that said, "whatever show and dinner" because at that stage he had not yet decided where he was going to eat, did he go back afterwards and fill in the name of the restaurant?

'He said that sometimes he did but not always. So she told him, with such a sweet smile, that she did it sometimes too but that she felt that maybe that was cheating somehow and he said he knew exactly what she meant and then the conversation moved on to notes and "To Do" pages and if it was best to have them separately at the back or one alongside each . . .'

'Shush,' Harmonia says, 'it's starting.'

*   *   *

As we wait for the bride to arrive I think back to how I did it. I do that quite often. I'm pretty proud of the way I sorted it out in the end although Mother behaves as if it was all thanks to her.

You see, once I knew where Rebecca Finch was going to be that Saturday I arranged for Hermes to drop John Sterling the fake invitation. That way I would have them vaguely in the same place at the same time.

I followed him to the lunch place. The diversions were a doddle: their roads are complete chaos anyway, signs and cones everywhere, especially in the summer when, ironically, they get used the most, so once I knew where he was heading I just moved some signs around.

An arrow through the tread of the front-left tyre of Rebecca Finch's car – and the plan was beginning to come together nicely. I was especially pleased with the symmetry of the whole thing. Them meeting on the road once more. The red hat was a nice touch too, though I say it myself, but it was pure luck that she was stupid enough to run out into the middle of the road – again. After that it was easy, one well-aimed arrow at her as she watched him change the tyre then one for him as he looked up at her: job done.

And now they're getting married.

Here she comes, Rebecca Finch in a red dress and the hat I found for her. John Sterling had especially asked her to wear it again. She's looking good. He is too, although he's put on a bit of weight in the year they've been together. Harmonia says that's a sign of a contented man. Athene pretends not to hear and Hera nods wisely as if she'd been backing this thing all along.

The wedding is on the terrace of a hotel on the Amalfi coast. She walks down towards the celebrant, no father, no bridesmaids, just her in her red dress and hat. When John Sterling turns round and sees her coming towards him, he looks as if he's glimpsed a piece of heaven.

'Ahh,' I hear Mother and Harmony sigh behind me.

I have to say John and Rebecca do look kind of cute, for a couple of old guys, that is.

After the ceremony they all sit down at this long table looking out across the Bay of Naples. They've brought over around twenty friends and relatives. Her mother is there, telling everyone how proud Rebecca's father would have been. His mother is the faded-looking woman in pastel-blue, crying. She hasn't stopped, actually. She must have about a hundred tissues stuffed up those sleeves. Next to her is his cousin Amy; his kid's there too . . . She's all right for a kid, although she seems to think she's the main event.

Then John Sterling gets to his feet.

'My wife and I . . .'

Of course they all whoop and cheer at that.

And he goes on to tell everyone about when they first met (that is, when they *think* they first met).

'What I most remember from that night in the bar in Primrose Hill is how we both agreed that we really enjoyed living on our own. Not for us, not any more, the mistake of putting a love affair at the centre of our existences.' John's grinning as if it's the biggest joke rather than a sensible precaution. 'There were so many important things other than relationships, we said.' He turns and looks down at her and she looks back up at him. He takes her hand in his. 'But I can safely say that in this instance we are so happy to be proven

wrong. As you all know, Rebecca and I have done this before
. . . separately, obviously.'

'Yeah yeah, we get it,' I say as the guests all laugh and now
it's Hera's turn to tell me to shut up.

He takes her hand again and she gets up to stand at his
side, leaning lightly into his shoulder, her face raised to his.

And then he says it.

'But, Rebecca,' he says, 'my darling Rebecca, this time it
will be different.'

So she rubs at her eyes making a mess of her make-up and
says, 'Dearest John, I know it will be.'

The sun sets over the sea. The party is over. The bride and
groom walk hand in hand across the lawn back to their room.

And that's it, *The End*.

Mortals – don't they just crack you up?

ACKNOWLEDGEMENTS

My warmest thanks to Alexandra Pringle, Marian McCarthy, Georgia Garrett and Linda Shaughnessy for their support and editorial advice throughout the writing of this novel. My heartfelt thanks also to Michael Patchett-Joyce, Jeremy and Rachael Cobbold, Harriet Cobbold Hielte and Fabian Hielte for their generous and insightful input and constant support and encouragement. Also again to Michael for all the help with matters of law, and to Harriet also for her brilliant help in getting the final draft in shape.

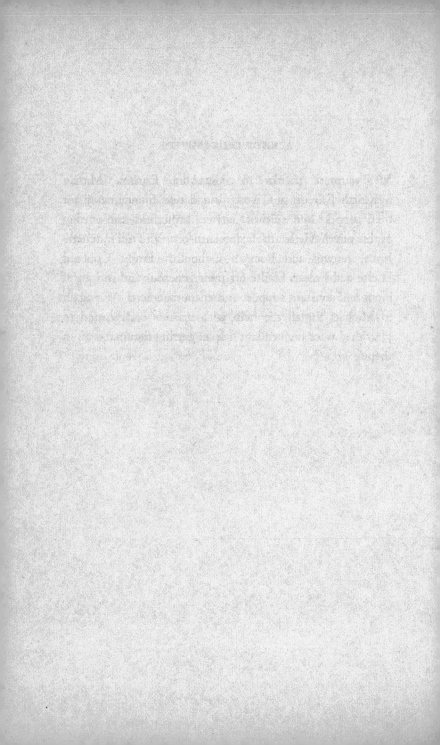

A NOTE ON THE TYPE

The text of this book is set in Adobe Caslon, named after the English punch-cutter and type founder William Caslon I (1692–1766). Caslon's rather old-fashioned types were modeled on seventeenth-century Dutch designs, but found wide acceptance throughout the English-speaking world for much of the eighteenth century until being replaced by newer types toward the end of the century. Used in 1776 to print the Declaration of Independence, they were revived in the nineteenth century, and have been popular ever since. There are several digital versions, of which Carol Twombly's Adobe Caslon is one.

ALSO AVAILABLE BY MARIKA COBBOLD

GUPPIES FOR TEA

Amelia Lindsey is an exceptional young woman. She shares her days between a grandmother whom she loves, a mother whom she tolerates with patient fortitude, and Gerald. Gerald had fallen in love with Amelia two years earlier, when he was in his artistic phase, and had begged her to move in with him. Now (no longer in his artistic phase) he is showing signs of irritation. And suddenly Selma, the talented and much-beloved grandmother, has become old. As life — and Gerald — begins to collapse all round Amelia, she is determined that the one person who will not fade is Selma. Fighting a one-woman battle against Cherryfield retirement home, Gerald's defection and her mother's obsession with germs, Amelia finds herself capable of plots, diversions, and friendships she has never imagined before.

*

'Poignant, funny ... A delightful and enchanting novel to read'
JOANNA TROLLOPE

'Cobbold is the wittiest of writers ... quite glorious'
SPECTATOR

'A nice understated sense of the absurd ...
keeps our sympathy mobile, our laughter on edge'
TIMES LITERARY SUPPLEMENT

*

ISBN 9780747562047 · PAPERBACK · £6.99

BLOOMSBURY

SHOOTING BUTTERFLIES

By the time Grace is eighteen, she has been orphaned, moved countries and lost touch with her only brother. Talented, awkward and a little fierce, she can't help thinking that she's managed to lose anything she's ever loved. So she decides to revisit her past in America, and she's brought her camera — she's going to catch these memories and pin them down to keep. What she isn't expecting that summer in New Hampshire is to meet the love of her life. Some years later, now divorced and flourishing as a controversial photographer, Grace lives alone — she likes the fact that everything will be exactly where she left it. Until Grace finds that she is, quite literally, being haunted by the past…

*

'This gripping and moving story is an honest chronicle of what happens to relationships over time, and a sharp observation of one woman's emotional life'
THE TIMES

'*Shooting Butterflies* is more than just romantic fiction. It is a perceptive and delicately written study of human relations and motivations, painful, funny and fresh'
OBSERVER

'The heroines of her novels are so strong and so independent of their lovers … readers will flock to support her now her secret's out'
GUARDIAN

*

ISBN 9780747568100 · PAPERBACK · £6.99

ORDER YOUR COPY: BY PHONE +44 (0)1256 302 699; BY EMAIL: DIRECT@MACMILLAN.CO.UK
DELIVERY IS USUALLY 3–5 WORKING DAYS. FREE POSTAGE AND PACKAGING FOR ORDERS OVER £20.

ONLINE: WWW.BLOOMSBURY.COM/BOOKSHOP
PRICES AND AVAILABILITY SUBJECT TO CHANGE WITHOUT NOTICE.

WWW.BLOOMSBURY.COM

B L O O M S B U R Y